# V FOR VENDETTA

# V FOR VENDETTA

A NOVELIZATION BY
**STEVE MOORE**

SCREENPLAY BY
**THE WACHOWSKI BROTHERS**

BASED ON THE GRAPHIC NOVEL BY
**ALAN MOORE** AND **DAVID LLOYD**

**POCKET STAR BOOKS**
NEW YORK   LONDON   TORONTO   SYDNEY

An *Original* Publication of POCKET BOOKS

 A Pocket Star Book published by
POCKET BOOKS, a division of Simon & Schuster, Inc.
1230 Avenue of the Americas, New York, NY 10020

ISBN-13: 978-1-4165-1699-6
ISBN-10:  1-4165-1699-9

This Pocket Star Books paperback edition February 2006

10  9  8  7  6  5  4  3  2  1

POCKET STAR BOOKS and colophon are registered trademarks of Simon & Schuster, Inc.

www.vforvendetta.warnerbros.com
www.dccomics.com
Keyword: DC Comics on AOL.

Manufactured in the United States of America

For information regarding special discounts for bulk purchases, please contact Simon & Schuster Special Sales at 1-800-456-6798 or business@simonandschuster.com.

*Remember, remember,*
*The Fifth of November,*
*The Gunpowder Treason and plot.*
*I know of no reason*
*Why the Gunpowder Treason*
*Should ever be forgot.*

# ONE

A strange, shadowy room, somewhere deep beneath the streets of London.

Of old, old London that had seen so much, in two thousand years, of war and terror and despair. Founded by the conquering legions of imperial Rome and, within twenty years, reduced to ash by raging Boadicea, who, in her fury, killed eighty thousand of her own countrymen and hardly touched the Roman lords at all. Abandoned to the Saxons, decimated by the Black Death, erased once more in the Great Fire, shattered yet again by Hermann Göring's Luftwaffe.

Always falling, rising up, then falling still again . . . fallen now once more, and yet to foes more strange than plague, or fire, or war.

For London, now, most famous city in the world, had fallen to its own.

Yet in that strange and shadowy room, a tall and equally shadowy figure moved with a slow and confident step, dressed in a long, Puritan tunic of deep, undecorated black. Almost without thought, he flicked on a television set as he passed, then instantly turned his back. After all, he knew exactly what would be broadcasting at that time, and when the show was called *The Voice of London,* it hardly needed to be watched at all.

But then, anyone looking round the man's home might wonder why he would be interested in such a program anyway.

The room itself was but one of a number of interconnected chambers, their stone walls windowless and each surmounted by a vaulted roof that gave the place an ancient, medieval look, like the crypt of some vast church or cathedral, or perhaps the wine cellar of some Renaissance millionaire. But no hallowed bodies were interred here, no barrels or bottles either. Rather there were treasures of another sort: books, paintings, sculptures, and various other artworks, some specially displayed and picked out by subdued lights that made them glow like gilded icons amidst their dark surroundings, yet did nothing to dispel the air of mysterious and all-pervading gloom. Others were merely stacked to take up as little room as possible, held in storage against a future time when they could be properly exhibited or restored to their original homes. A vast collection of rescued objets d'art, of literary flights of fancy, of histories and anecdotes and thoughts; rescued from oblivion, from destruction, from vandals . . . and, most of all, from the government.

Passing by a bookcase packed with curious political visions, from Thomas More's *Utopia* and Campanella's *City of the Sun* through Karl Marx's *Das Kapital* to Adolf Hitler's *Mein Kampf* (some banned now, and some required reading), the man made his way toward a dressing table, settling himself before a large mirror surrounded with little electric bulbs, brought here from some theater changing room; a relic of the times when theaters still showed plays, not mere burlesques or propagandist farces. And as the canned audience applause track died on *The Voice of London,* the introductions over, he pulled on black, close-fitting leather gloves. Then, as the deep, plummy, oh-so-English voice of Lewis Prothero, the show's host and eponymous "Voice of London" (not because he *was,* but because someone too high up to argue with had said that this was so), bade his audience welcome to the evening's program, those same gloved hands reached out and switched on the makeup mirror's lights.

As the feeble radiance spread out into the shadowed room, it showed a wall behind the dresser, plastered over with ancient movie posters from back before the Second World War; for this underground gallery gathered more than the art that most would call "eternal." Here too were the artifacts and ephemera of popular culture, of television shows long vanished from the screen, of games that none had played for years, of songs no longer sung. And as the light flickered, the power supply being nothing like the way it used to be, the man's eyes lit upon Bela Lugosi in *Son of Frankenstein,* and a faint ironic smile quirked his lips as Prothero started to speak.

"I say," began the Voice of London, "I read today that the formerly 'United' States are so desperate for medical supplies that they've allegedly sent us several containers filled with wheat and tobacco. A gesture, they said, of goodwill . . ."

The light came up a little then, revealing a shoulder-length, black wig upon its own head-shaped stand, and with it a mask. As the gloved hands reached toward the latter, Lewis Prothero asked, "Would you like to know what I think?"

Was that the slightest shake of the head as the mask was raised toward the man's face? Hardly worth asking, perhaps, for once the mask was strapped in place, all trace of its owner's expression, of his thoughts and very feelings, disappeared; and all that remained was that of the mask. For to wear a mask is to give up who we really are and to become, perhaps for just a little while, perhaps for rather longer, that persona that the mask itself appears to represent.

The mask. The masquerade . . .

Almost white this mask, with something of a debonair and Harlequin look, the cheeks a little rouged, the lower lip a little pink, the eyes a little more than slits that seemed to smile at times, at other times to squint, yet always having something of the vulpine. The ebony-painted goatee, the inky-black mustachios forever curling upward at the ends. The smile forever fixed.

Beguiling. Bedeviling.

A Guy Fawkes mask.


"Would you like to know what I think?" Lewis Prothero was asking on another television screen, in a room about as high above the ground as the previous one was far below. A far more poorly decorated room this, the rent alone consuming too much of the occupant's monthly paycheck to allow for fripperies or frills, in a run-down backstreet not far from Paddington Station. Here too a figure sat before a mirror, putting on disguise.

Not a mask this time, but the disguise that women wear, of lipstick, eye shadow, powder, and mascara, that says, "My eyes are dark with mystery, my lips are red with passion, my skin is young and smooth." Not that there was anything about this particular woman that needed such disguise; and frankly there was something about Gordon Deitrich, the prospective target of these wiles, that made Evey Hammond wonder why she was bothering in the first place. But she knew the answer to that question anyway. If she wanted to get on and up that damnable career ladder, this could be the most important date in her life. That was the way things worked these days. So gild the lily, then, and take whatever's offered.

Besides, more money and better career prospects might enable her to get a place in one of those new condominiums they were building, safe behind their own security fences, entrances protected by their own armed guards. Where, even if the food and fuel and other necessities of life were still to be had only with the appropriate ration coupons, at least one could live with a little less fear.

And Evey Hammond so very much wished to live without the fear that haunted all her days . . . and more, and worse, her dreams.

"You're watching my show," the Voice of London

continued, though Evey was really doing this no more
than a certain other of the program's audience, not so
very far away, "so I'll assume you do. I think it's high time
we let the colonies know what we really think of them. I
think it's high time we paid them back for a little 'Tea
Party' they threw for us a few hundred years ago."

With an apparent mastery of the dramatic pause,
Prothero stopped while the technicians cranked up
the canned applause once more.

Her makeup finished, Evey slipped into her best
dress and smoothed it over her hips as she checked
herself in the mirror. Full lips, high forehead, brown
eyes, and straightish golden hair that fell and spread
across her shoulders; a lithe figure that filled out in
just the right places. Yes, she liked the way she looked,
and if Deitrich didn't . . . well, actually, if he didn't,
what did it really matter? Either she'd get in his good
books, which might eventually lead to a promotion, or
she'd just stay where she was and carry on the same as
usual until another opportunity came up.

And if the worse came to the worse, she could always try to find another job. There were plenty around
these days. Or, more to the point, there were far fewer
people around than there used to be to fill the same
number of vacancies. People of a certain type . . .

Actually, she thought, biting her lip nervously, a
promotion would mean quite a lot, for the way the
Party organized things these days, promotions brought
more status as well as money. And that would mean
more food coupons, for a start.

"What I say," Prothero's voice came again, when

the applause had died down, "is that we go down to the docks tonight and dump that colonial crap where *everything* from the Ulcered Sphincter of Asserica belongs!"

A pause, but this time not long enough for the applause to start again.

"Who's with me?"

Then a further silence, until the dramatic tension seemed almost unbearable. Finally, in his best rabble-rousing voice: *"Who's bloody well with me!"*

And only then did the applause crash in, as the entirely fictitious audience went wild with apparently hysterical approbation.

Evey shrugged. She knew the show like the back of her hand after all, with all its tricks, all its prompts. She even knew who wrote Prothero's stuff and wrote his "ad-libs" too. And heaven knows she knew the message it was trying to get across. What she didn't know was why anyone swallowed it.

But they did. They *did,* and they had done so for more than ten years now.

And it looked as if they always would.

Of course, no one was really going to dump wheat and tobacco in the docks. They might make a show of it for the cameras, throwing a few empty boxes into the water, but the wheat and tobacco would simply be spirited away to feed and soothe the Party elite. If there was ever any there at all, that was, and the whole thing wasn't just another propaganda fraud to prop up British notions of superiority.

These days she knew, as an insider working at Jordan Tower, you couldn't believe anything the government said apart from death threats and prohibitions.

The applause storm having died down once again, Lewis Prothero continued in a much calmer, more intimate voice ... a lighter, knowing voice that suggested sharing a joke with his viewers, and a common point of view.

"Did you like that? USA? The Ulcered Sphincter of Asserica? I mean, honestly, what else can you say? There was a country that had everything, and now, twenty years later ... is *what?* The world's biggest leper colony. Why?"

Now the Voice gained in confidence once again, became more emphatic, began to sound hectoring. Demagogic. And loud.

"Godlessness. Let me say that again. *Godlessness.* It wasn't the war they started. It wasn't the plague they created. It was ... *Judgment.*"

More applause, while Evey could only think about how perceptions changed. When she was a little girl, after all, the USA had been regarded as one of the most Christian countries in the world, with right-wing Christian Republicans governing the place for year after year, with American Protestant missionaries taking their unwanted Bibles to all the other parts of the happily unredeemed world; and then there'd been the war. After that, the only things anyone remembered about the old America were its militarism and its conspicuous consumption, and what had been the Promised Land became nothing more than Rome and Babylon. And now no one cared about the state of the American soul, not here in England anyway. Because now it was England that God smiled upon, and nowhere else at all.

By then Prothero was really beginning to get into his stride: "No one escapes their past. No one escapes Judgment. You think *He* is not up there? You think *He* is not watching over this country? How else can you explain it? *He* tested us, but *we* came through!"

Her expression souring by the moment, Evey clipped on her earrings and began brushing out her hair. She knew perfectly well what was coming next, and Prothero delivered exactly what she expected. The building rant, the reddening face that went with the words, the rising blood pressure, and, eventually, the shouting.

"We did what we *had* to do! Islington. Enfield. I was *there*. I saw it *all*. Immigrants. Muslims. Homosexuals. Terrorists. Disease-ridden degenerates. They had to *go!*"

And now the punch line, same as ever: " *'Strength through Unity, Unity through Faith!'* I am a God-fearing *English*man, and I am goddamned *proud* of it!"

"And that's quite enough of that, thank you very much," said Evey, twisting round to turn off the television, just as Prothero began to give the goddamned salute. And then she turned back to the mirror to check her appearance one more time. Yes, she did look good, and she knew it, no matter what that nervy little voice in the back of her head might say.

But perhaps just one last look in the mirror. The

mirror with the photos tucked all round the frame. Her friends. Her workmates. Her parents. And it was that last one that always brought the same old lump to her throat. And on a night like this, perhaps that wasn't one to linger over.

"Listen," she said, though whether to herself or to the photos or the empty air she really didn't know. "He's a very nice man. He makes me laugh. But I'm just going to be honest with him, and if that costs me a job . . . well, that'll suck, but I've dealt with worse, haven't I? A *lot* worse."

And then her eye lit once again on the picture of Mum and Dad, and she had to look away. And as she did so, her glance took in the clock.

It said one minute after eleven o'clock.

"Oh, *shit*," exclaimed Evey with sudden desperation.

With sudden fear.

And with that she grabbed a small piece of paper with an address scribbled on it from the mirror frame and dashed toward the door.

And out into a night more dark than any she had ever known . . .


Underground.

Back in that room of shadows and illusions, of literary dreams and cinematic fantasies, the dark-dressed man had, by now, completed his theatrical attire. The mask strapped on, the wig in place, long and soft black leather boots upon his feet that ran up above his knees, an inky cloak about his shoulders, and on his head, a tall and tapering Jacobean hat, its round brim wide enough to add another layer of mysterious shadow to his already enigmatic, grinning features.

Something of the dandy, something of the scarecrow. Something of the night.

Checking his appearance one last time in the mirror, he turned off the dressing-table lights and turned toward a nearby bust of Shakespeare. Then, striking a pose, he began to declaim, in a rolling, oratorical tone, to his audience of solitary stone.

" 'Nor Mars his sword, nor war's quick fire, shall burn the living record of your memory . . . ' "

A bow, a swirl of the cloak, and then, in a much lighter, more mischievous voice: "Don't wait up for me, Will. I intend to enjoy myself tonight."

And with that he was gone, and the lights were all extinguished.

And all that then remained were galleries of shadow.

# TWO

A ll her nerves jangling like overstretched violin strings being pizzicato-plucked by a demented Paganini, Evey Hammond made her way with desperate haste along the ill-lit streets, heels clicking a percussive accompaniment on the concrete paving slabs. Above her head, a passing swath of heavy cloud had smothered up the moon and stars and settled like a blanket on the eerily quiet streets, adding darkness to darkness, silence to silence. No cars drove here, no omnibuses passed, their cargoes of late-night revelers long since delivered home. Not that anyone reveled much these days anyway, except perhaps the upper echelons of the elite. But who was she to really know anything about what *they* did, whatever she might have been conjecturing earlier about wheat and tobacco? After all, the scandalous stories she heard around the office were probably nothing more than that: stories. The Party was building the New Jerusalem here, not the New Babylon. Though where she was now, heading toward Goodge Street, seemed far from either.

Here there was only silence and empty streets and the clicking of her heels, grown now to almost thunder-cracking loudness in her oversensitive ear.

And the omnipresent surveillance cameras, all labeled FOR YOUR PROTECTION, but to her, at this time of night, the greatest threat of all.

If only she hadn't left it so late.

Hurry on. It wasn't far to Gordon Deitrich's home in Bloomsbury now, and light and music, good company and wine and warmth.

And safety.

Whatever reservations she might have had about seeing him before had completely disappeared. All she wanted was to be there in his house, even in his arms if necessary, so long as she could stay there until the morning light, when everything would be back to normal, and she could pick up the usual course of her life once more.

Because right now, frankly, she was scared out of her wits.

Not far. If only these back roads north of Oxford Street weren't so dank and ill-lit . . . but then she didn't dare use the main streets at this time of night, where her presence would be far too obvious. Hurry on. Through the litter that kept building up because "proper English people" considered it beneath their dignity to clear up these days, and they'd got rid of all the other people. Past the tattered flags and placards left over from one of those Party rallies held a few days before, which only reminded her of the authorities and how they handled breaches of the law. Faster. If only she'd put on her other shoes, she could surely have walked more quickly than in these; but, no, she'd had to dress for looks rather than comfort. And running in these was quite out of the question. Hurry. Hurry.

And stop.

Was that someone there ahead of her, a little farther up the street? Or just a trick of the light, a moving shadow caused by a breeze-blown piece of litter?

But there shouldn't be anyone here. *She* shouldn't be here.

In a sudden panicked fluster, Evey turned aside and made her way into a shadowy cobbled alley. And began to hurry once again. The alley didn't look at all inviting, littered with trash cans and garbage as it was, but if she could just avoid that mystery figure . . . go round and find another alley that would lead her back to the same street beyond the place he lurked. If he was still lurking there.

If he wasn't following her. If he wasn't just about to grab her . . .

Run. Bad shoes and lack of breath or not, just run. And glance back. No one there, but run anyway.

And run smack into something right in front of her, while she was still looking back behind. Something firm but yielding, soft on the outside but hard within.

Her head spinning and her body reeling, her eyes lit on a poster pasted on the alley wall, in the light of a small lamp. One of those posters that were everywhere, saying the same old thing: *Strength through Unity, Unity through Faith,* with a little angel-winged cross beneath it. The slogan that welded the nation together, kept everyone in line, ensured that no one went astray.

And then there were strong arms uniting round her waist, supporting her, stopping her fall. But whether there was anything of faith about the big man in the tweed coat that she'd run into was very much an open question. As for angel wings, definitely not.

"Whoa!" he exclaimed in one of those theatrical, catchphrase voices. "And *excuse me*, miss!"

Regaining her physical equilibrium, though still far too flustered to think straight, Evey stammered out, "I'm sorry, I didn't see you—"

"In a hurry, are we?" the man said in an exaggeratedly calming voice, though his attempt at an avuncular smile somehow kept slipping to a smirk. Evey tried to step back, but his big hands were still there on her waist. And she knew exactly why he wasn't taking them away. Big, powerful hands, to go with a muscular, big-boned body and a hardened, worldly face. A smugly evil glint lit up the man's otherwise cold and brooding eyes. Eyes that said, "My lucky night here. Caught myself a babe . . ."

"I was just—"

The man in the tweed coat interrupted, and now his voice was flat and cold. A statement, not to be argued with: "After curfew, you know."

"My uncle . . ." said Evey, trying desperately to think of some sort of explanation, as the alley seemed to grow darker and more threatening around her with every passing second. "He's very sick. . . ."

"Oh, a sick uncle, is it?" Tweed Coat grinned, almost as if he hadn't heard that one before, releasing her waist now and running a lock of her long blond hair through his calloused fingers as he turned to address a newcomer, emerging from the shadows. "What do you think of that, Willy?"

"Load of bollocks, is what I think," said Willy, coming up behind her. Another powerful man and no more pleasant-looking than his companion. Worse, in fact, for this one had an unpleasant scar across his forehead that even a flopping lock of hair did nothing to disguise.

All the alarms were going off in Evey's head by now. Two bulky, threatening men. A gloomy back alley. No one anywhere nearby to appeal to, or even to hear her screams. Trouble.

Big trouble.

She glanced round, looking for a way out, tried to step back. But she was between the two of them now, and the alley was narrow enough for them to easily block her escape. Slowly she started to slip a hand into her pocket, hoping they wouldn't notice.

"I made a mistake," she said, a little calmer now and determined to try to talk her way out of this if she possibly could, before she had to try something more desperate. "I shouldn't be out after curfew, I know that. But my uncle . . ."

"Well, maybe you could take care of us before getting back to your uncle," said Tweed Coat, grinning wolfishly, all pretense disappearing now. "See, my friend here . . . he's kinda sick." An evil laugh. "Ain't you, Willy?"

"Oh, yeah," sniggered Willy, reaching out to grab her free hand roughly. "*Real* sick. Bad case of the blues, it is. Here, you can feel 'em."

With that he thrust his crotch forward and tried to press her hand between his legs, hardly able to suppress his mirth, but with a sudden panic strength Evey managed to pull away. And with her other hand, she pulled out the canister of pepper spray she'd had concealed in her pocket all this time.

"Don't touch me," she grated, as coldly and as threateningly as she could, brandishing the spray in front of her, backing up against the alley wall.

"Oh, look at that, Willy!" guffawed Tweed Coat, hardly impressed by her show of determination. "Kitty's got claws!"

A gap-toothed smile broke out on Willy's lips as he sidled up beside his companion to face her.

"She just threatened us," he remarked blackheartedly. Somehow, then, he seemed to Evey as evil and villainous a bastard as she'd ever seen. As bad or worse than the ones who'd come in the night . . . that terrible night, so many years ago . . .

"That she did," Tweed Coat smirked back at him. "That she did. That's a Class G offense, ain't it?

"You know what that means?" he asked, turning back toward Evey and suddenly pulling out a badge. "It means that we get to exercise our own judicial discretion."

"And you get to swallow it," concluded Willy, chuckling lewdly.

"Oh, God, you're Fingermen," said Evey, final realization suddenly dawning. The same ones . . .

"She's getting the picture." Tweed Coat winked at Willy.

"Oh, no, please," Evey began desperately, fear making her knees suddenly weak. "I didn't know. I'm sorry—"

"Not yet you're not," Willy told her with a cold laugh and a glint in his eye of pure sadistic lust.

"But you will be," said Tweed Coat casually, even though he seemed suddenly uninterested in making any attempt to restrain her as she started to slide along the wall, hoping to make a last break for the end of the alley. "If you're not the sorriest piece of arse in all of London by the time the sun comes up, you'll certainly be the sorest."

And still he stood there, doing nothing except turning, knowingly, toward Willy as they spread themselves across the alley, blocking off one direction completely. And as they glanced round for another exchange of winks, Evey was off and running the other way, terrified, desperate.

Unseeing once again.

And running straight into a third Fingerman whom the other two had obviously been aware of all the time, coming up behind her; this one even bigger than his companions. Like running into a brick shithouse, as Gordon Deitrich would say in one of his cruder moments; the impact knocked all the breath out of her. And after that it was the work of an instant for the man to twist her arm painfully up behind her back, forcing her to drop the pepper spray. It clattered on the cobbles with a small, tinny clicking noise that, to Evey, seemed somehow to signal the end of the world. Or of hers, anyway.

"Oh, God, *no!*" shrieked Evey, now in a complete panic with her last defense gone and pain shooting through all the joints of her arm, from shoulder through elbow to wrist.

"Please don't do this!" she began to beg desperately, terror making her nauseous. "I'll go home! I won't do it again, I swear! *Please!*"

"Watcha think, fellas?" asked the third Fingerman, forcing her arm farther behind her and bending her forward at the waist.

"Spare the rod, spoil the child," Willy snickered evilly, leering suggestively to his mates and starting to unzip his pants fly with exaggerated, theatrical emphasis. Only one rod in mind there, then.

As the alley filled with coarse, masculine, and thoroughly unpleasant laughter, with jokes about Willy getting his willy out and arguments about who got sloppy seconds, Evey felt a foot against the back of her calves, and she was forced down to her knees. Then, still twisting her arm, the Fingerman behind her grabbed her hair with his free hand and pulled her head up.

*"Help!"* screamed Evey at the top of her voice, cold, hard cobblestones pressing painfully against her kneecaps. "Please! Someone—*help me!*"

She knew it was useless, of course, and so did the Fingermen. What made it somehow worse and more degrading was that it was all happening in this dank, filthy back alley where she was being reduced to nothing more than another piece of garbage, like the garbage all around her. Something to be used and thrown away. Willy stepped toward her, belt undone now as well, and started to drop his pants.

Suddenly, from somewhere in the nearby darkness beyond the light of the poster-illuminating lamp, a voice rang out. A rich, declamatory Shakespearean voice, aptly choosing its words for the situation revealed there before it in the alley, though the quotation quite passed by the major players in the scene.

" 'The multiplying villainies of nature do swarm upon him.' "

"What the hell—?" the third Fingerman shouted, looking up toward the pitch-darkness farther down the alley.

And then, from out of that inky blackness, something began to emerge a few feet above the ground. Something so bone white it seemed to glow, that looked at first like a grinning skull suspended in the deep, oppressive night but, as it slowly approached, transformed before their eyes into a slightly more human face, dead white except for the merest touches of color on lip and cheeks, the blackness of an upturned mustache and goatee, the smile forever frozen.

A mask . . . the forehead shaded by a wide-brim hat.

"We're Fingermen, pal!" Tweed Coat yelled fiercely, though he was well enough aware that he was shouting in the dark, trying to drive off this unnerving specter by the power of words alone.

"Bugger off!" added Willy, eyes fixed on the mask, hands starting to drop toward the pants around his ankles, all thoughts of sexual gratification suddenly wilted in the face of sudden threat. It might be just a passing lunatic . . . God knew, the world being the way it was, there were still enough of them about, in spite of the efforts to have them all locked up or shot . . . or it might be real and present danger. Might be both. Whatever or whoever it was, it needed dealing with right now; the girl could be left until later. But somehow a sudden rush of fear prevented his fingers from getting a proper grip on his clothing.

" 'Disdaining fortune with his brandished steel,' " the voice came once again, the mask now approaching more swiftly, " 'which smoked with bloody execution.' "

A gap appearing suddenly in the cloud, a shaft of moonlight then shone down into the noisome alley, glinted on the damp and greasy granite cobblestones, the rusting garbage cans and tattered boxes, picked out the black-clad, swirl-cloaked figure that wore the mask . . . and flashed alarmingly from the lengthy steel blade he held so firmly in a dark-gloved hand.

"He's got a knife!" shouted the third and biggest Fingerman, suddenly producing a heavy police baton from inside his coat. That cry, at least, freed Willy from his paralysis, but all he could do was trip and fall, the pants still tangled round his ankles. And before he could even get to his knees again, it was all over.

Not quite sure what was happening, Evey could only watch the ensuing destruction in a state of terror that rapidly gave way to astonishment, not entirely sure how any human being could move so fast, unable really to see whether the newcomer was using fist or foot, punches or kicks; though there was no question at all about the long and deadly knife. Everything became a whirlwind blur of violence she could hardly see, and which she understood still less.

With lightning speed, the masked man was there among his opponents, cloak streaming behind him, knife in one hand, the other bunched into a hammer-like fist. That fist seemed to Evey to catch the baton-wielding Fingerman in the gut with enormous power and sent him hurtling backward to crash against the wall, his head snapping back to crack loudly on the brick. The baton slipping from his fingers, he slid slowly down the wall and collapsed into an unconscious heap. Perhaps even terminally unconscious. Somehow, he seemed to be bleeding too, but she'd seen nothing of the cause. Could anyone wield a knife too quickly for the eye to see?

By then Tweed Coat had managed to pull out his pistol and cock it, but before the hammer could fall, a thrown knife flashed swiftly through the moonlight, took him in the shoulder, and sent him spinning away, reeling for balance, as the gun discharged wildly. Before he could get off another shot, he too was lacking consciousness completely, and the knife was snugly back there in the belt sheath from which, mere moments earlier, it had been drawn. Was he still alive? Evey had no idea at all.

And that just left Willy, still struggling with his pants in an animal panic and desperately trying to get to his feet. Not so he could fight. So he could run for his life.

He'd only just managed to get to his knees when a

big black shadow loomed over him, like the finally closing lid of a heavy funeral casket.

"Jesus Christ!" yelled Willy, and if he had any inkling that he was kneeling there before his enemy in much the same position as Evey had done before him a few seconds previously, the irony was completely lost on him. "Mercy—please! *Mercy!*"

" 'We are oft to blame in this,' " the masked and caped figure remarked contemplatively, and only then did Willy notice his companion's long and heavy baton was nestling in the man's black-gloved hand, was slapping threateningly in the other palm. " ' 'Tis too much proved, that with devotion's visage and pious action, we do sugar o'er the devil himself.' "

"Wha . . . wha's *that* mean?" whimpered Willy uncomprehendingly, looking up in wide-eyed terror at the expressionless mask above him. But, no, as he looked again, he realized that the features weren't at all expressionless, unmoving as they were. As the moonlight improved a little more, the smile became more obvious. And plainly, for Willy, it was not a pleasant smile.

"Spare the rod . . . ," the newcomer patiently explained.

And then the baton slapped down with a wet, sickening crunch.

After that, Willy couldn't get up.

All this time, of course, Evey Hammond had sprawled there on the alley floor, watching without understanding anything of this at all. Not knowing how or why someone had suddenly appeared and dealt with three hulking Fingermen who were threatening her with the traditional "fate worse than death" . . . possibly to be followed by death itself. Not knowing how he *could* have dealt with the brutes at all, let alone so swiftly and so violently that she'd hardly had time to take in what he'd done. She'd seen her share of violence, of course . . . everyone had, in times like these . . . but nothing like *that*. And usually it had been handed out *by* the agents of the Finger, not *to* them.

Worse, she had no idea what the newcomer was intending to do next.

As the masked man turned toward her, almost as if he were noticing her for the first time, she hurriedly scrambled across the cobbles, picked up the pepper spray that she'd been forced to drop earlier, and held it up defensively before her as she waited for him to make the next move. Even as she did so, she couldn't help thinking about how useless it had been to her earlier; thought, in turn, that it would probably be even more useless now.

"I assure you that I mean you no harm," he said calmly, almost gently, with just the merest trace of a bow. And if there *seemed* to be a genuine concern for her in his voice, Evey still wasn't quite convinced.

"Who—who are you?" she asked nervously, pepper spray still raised, even though she knew, after what she'd just seen, that he could almost certainly take it away from her as easily as candy from a child.

"Who?" he queried, in an almost puzzled tone. "*Who* is but the form following the function of *what* . . . and *what* I am, is a man in a mask."

"I can see that," Evey responded, though she still felt just as confused as ever.

"Of course you can," he told her patiently. "I'm not questioning your powers of observation. I'm merely remarking upon the paradox of asking a masked man who he is."

"Oh," said Evey hesitantly. "Oh, right."

"But on this most auspicious of nights," he continued, now becoming increasingly grandiloquent, "permit me, then, in lieu of the more commonplace sobriquet, to suggest the *character* of this *dramatis persona.*"

A grand and extravagantly theatrical gesture followed, taking in somehow the whole of himself, from crown of hat to sole of booted foot and, at the same time, also managing to separate out his black-clad form from the darkness of his surroundings. "Voilà!"

The slightest pause, perfectly timed for maximum effect, and then: "In view, a humble vaudevillian veteran, cast vicariously as both victim and villain by the vicissitudes of Fate."

Evey simply stared and forgot to hold the pepper spray quite as high as previously. And, as if taking her silence as willing agreement to his carrying on, he raised one hand to indicate his mask.

"This visage, no mere veneer of vanity, is a vestige of the *vox populi,* now vacant, vanished; a vital voice once venerated, now vilified. However, this valorous visitation of a bygone vexation now stands vivified, and has vowed to vanquish these venal and virulent vermin vanguarding vice and vouchsafing the violent, vicious, and voracious violation of volition."

He paused for effect then, and Evey felt her jaw dropping. But perhaps that was the effect he was after. And anyway, before she could say anything, let alone ask him what the hell he was talking about, he was off again.

"The only verdict is vengeance," he declared. "A vendetta, held as votive, not in vain, for the value and veracity of such shall one day vindicate the vigilant and virtuous. Yet verily, this vichyssoise of verbiage veers most verbose, so let me simply add that it is my very great honor to meet you, and you may call me V."

And with that he made a deep and grandiose bow and extended a hand toward her, intent on helping her to her feet. She stared at the gloved hand before her, rather as if it might be dangerous. Like a snake.

"Are you," she began to murmur hesitantly, "are you, like . . . a crazy person?"

"I'm quite sure they'll say so," he told her, proffering his hand more pointedly than before. "But to whom, might I ask, do I have the pleasure of speaking?"

"I'm . . ." And still she couldn't help hesitating, though finally she dropped the pepper spray back into her pocket and reached out to take his hand. "I'm Evey. Evey Hammond."

"Evey?" he remarked, with just a hint of puzzled surprise, as he began to help her to her feet. "Ee-*Vee*. Yes, of course you are."

"What does that mean?" she asked, starting to dust herself down and straighten her clothes. God, she looked such a mess. But then that was hardly surprising, after everything that had happened.

"It means"—a thoughtful tone now in his voice—"that I, like God, do not play with dice, and do not believe in coincidence.

"Are you hurt?"

"No, I'm fine," she told him, having finally checked herself out and feeling that she could now turn her attention to her rescuer. Not that she could tell much about him, cloaked, masked, and costumed as he was. Had he been on his way to some sort of fancy dress ball? Perhaps better not to ask. "Thanks to you—"

"I only played my part," he told her with another, less formal, but far more self-deprecating bow. And then, after a moment's contemplation: "But tell me, Evey, do you enjoy music?"

"I suppose so," she replied, not entirely sure exactly what sort of music he had in mind. But the question brought back memories of her childhood; after all there was so much more music then. Jazz, reggae, rock 'n' roll, world music . . . all gone now, and nothing left to be heard except the "approved" music they played on the government-controlled radio stations. Mostly militaristic crap. But why on earth should he ask her a question like that, when he'd just pulled her out of a hellhole situation like this?

"You see, I'm a musician of sorts," explained the man who called himself V, "and on my way to give a very special performance."

"What kind of musician?" Evey asked, suddenly nervous again, and not entirely sure she really wanted to know the answer.

"Percussion instruments are my speciality." Somehow the grin upon his mask seemed wider than before. "But tonight I intend to call upon the entire orchestra for this particular event. And . . ." Again, the briefest pause, the slightest bow. "I would be most honored if you could join me."

"Oh, I don't think so," she said hurriedly, suddenly remembering all that had happened in the last few minutes and, being out after curfew as she was, could still happen all over again. "I think I should be getting home."

But while she stood there flustered and uncertain, he stepped closer and took her hand, raising it toward his mask almost as if he were about to kiss it. She looked at him in astonishment, having only seen gestures like that in the historical TV shows, the ones set in the nineteenth century and earlier. The gestures of an old-fashioned English gentleman, a species she'd convinced herself had long ago ceased to exist.

"I promise it will be like nothing you have ever heard or seen," he said, his voice insistent and magnetic. "And that afterwards you will return to your home quite safely."

And somehow, she knew that there was only one thing to say to such a politely phrased assurance.

"Well . . . alright."

After that, of course, the sense of adventure and excitement began to overwhelm Evey's nervousness. How often, after all, did she get the chance to be roaming through the empty streets of London at nearly midnight, accompanied only by a masked and mysterious man-in-black who could take out three of the feared and hulking Fingermen in little more than the blink of an eye? And she felt she owed him something for that, so if he wanted to take her to some sort of musical performance, it would be less than gracious to tell him no.

On the other hand, he wasn't exactly forthcoming about where this concert was going to be staged, or even precisely when. But as he led her along the streets, circling to avoid surveillance cameras and dodging occasionally into shadowed doorways or alley mouths when a passing patrol car cruised by, she began to think such questions mattered less and less and gave herself over entirely to adventuring. Or "venturing," as V would probably prefer to call it, alphabetically obsessive as he was.

As if in response to her lightened mood, the breeze blew the cloud away, and the stars appeared, spattered like diamonds across the velvet cloak of night, and a brilliant silver moon sailed into view, almost at the full, and shone its beams down on old London as it had for the last two thousand years, without fear or favor for any of its inhabitants, regardless of their innocence or guilt.

The nerves did come back though when, after a fairly circuitous route that roughly followed along New Oxford Street and then wove back and forth across and along High Holborn, they arrived at the Farringdon area and, instead of conducting her into some sort of concert hall, he led her up a fire escape and onto the roof of one of the taller buildings in the area. She was quite a long way from her Paddington flat now too, despite his assurances that he'd see her safely home.

But that feeling of nervousness was immediately overwhelmed then by the wonder of the view they could see all round them, silvered in the purest moonlight and sparkling beneath the stars. Ahead of them rose the Old Bailey or, more properly, the Central Criminal Court, a massive pile of stone surmounted by a copper dome, which, in turn, supported the famous bronze statue of Justice, a blindfolded woman with her arms extended straight out to either side, the scales of justice suspended from her left hand, the fearsome judicial sword rising from the right. A little to the right, the dome of Sir Christopher Wren's St. Paul's Cathedral, a phoenix rising up resurgent from the devastation of the Great Fire, which had so thoroughly destroyed its predecessor. Farther south again, the Monument commemorated the Great Fire itself, built in Pudding Lane where the flames had first begun. Beyond that, in turn, the rising skyscrapers of the City of London, the nation's financial heart; and farther on again, the even larger, blocklike towers of Canary Wharf.

Looking round, her gaze passed over the recently built but familiar Jordan Television Tower (familiar because she worked there), then turned back to the West End, to Centre Point and the old Post Office Tower (now headquarters of the Eye), before circling down to Westminster Abbey and the Houses of Parliament, and farther south, the Thames. All laid out before her like a map, or some moonlit model of the way the city really ought to be, its crimes and vices, terrors and suppressions, hidden in the dark, its beauties highlighted by a heavenly radiance. No wonder someone (she thought it was Dr. Samuel Johnson, long ago, but couldn't quite remember now) had said that "he who's tired of London is tired of life." Or something like that, anyway. Her father had said it to her on a sightseeing expedition once, which meant she must have heard it a long time ago.

"It's beautiful up here," she said, finally coming out of her absorption in the scene and turning round toward V, who stood beside her looking contemplatively toward the Old Bailey.

"A more perfect stage could not be asked for," he said softly, almost as if he too were enraptured by the setting.

"Still, I don't see any instruments," remarked Evey, puzzled.

"Your powers of observation continue to serve you well." Now the smile that was fixed there on his mask seemed somehow to be a real smile, as if the more she got to know him, the more his voice and body language brought expression to the expressionless. "But wait . . ."

And then, with the swiftness of a professional stage magician, V stepped toward the parapet and whipped out a slim conductor's baton from his sleeve, using it with a grand gesture to center her attention on the Old Bailey.

"The Old Bailey," he began, "was built in 1907 on the site of the notorious Newgate Prison, a hellhole where you were lucky to survive long enough to be strung up. The famous highwayman Dick Turpin was once imprisoned there, among so many others awaiting their last day on earth; a conclusion which for many must have come as a relief. Just across the road is The Magpie and Stumps where 'execution breakfasts' were served to the near-hysterical crowds who gathered to watch the mass public hangings held not far from here, cheering wildly every time some poor wretch was 'taken off,' until the executions were finally brought to a halt in 1868. And all that was back in the good old days, when England still had a judicial system and a functioning constitution. Back long before the latest war, with everything that's happened since."

The irony wasn't lost on Evey. Since the war, things had got far worse than that, and the Old Bailey had seen a countless number condemned to execution. It was just that nobody felt like cheering anymore.

Finally, returning to the subject of the evening's entertainment, he continued, "It is to Madam Justice that I dedicate this concerto, in honor of the holiday she seems to have taken from these parts . . . and in recognition of the impostor that stands there in her stead."

Looking again at the statue, Evey couldn't help thinking how things had changed. Though both remained in Justice's hands, these days it was all sword and no scales.

"Tell me," he asked, interrupting her contemplation, "do you know what night it is tonight, Evey?"

"Uh . . ." She had to pause and think. "November the fifth?"

And no sooner were the words out of her mouth than, back behind her down at Westminster, Big Ben began to chime the midnight hour, the instant when this most significant night was at its deepest. And with a slight nod of the head acknowledging the perfect timing of the bells, V continued, "And the meaning of the date?"

She knew, of course, but also knew the date was no longer celebrated. After all, the official line was that Guy Fawkes had been nothing more than a terrorist attempting to overthrow the state. And even if, ever since, the populace had burned the traitor in effigy every year in eternal punishment for his crimes, it had all come to seem too much of a celebration for the current government. And anything remotely suggesting the celebration of terrorism had rigorously been stamped out. That was too much like free speech and couldn't be allowed at all.

Then, almost as if the distant tolling of the giant bell were occurring for no other reason than to accompany his voice, the masked man began to declaim . . .

> Remember, remember,
> The Fifth of November,
> The Gunpowder Treason and plot.
> I know of no reason
> Why the Gunpowder Treason
> Should ever be forgot.

As the last note of the chiming midnight bell faded softly on the cooling air, V finally began his performance, tapping his baton on the stone parapet and then raising both arms above his head, as if calling his unseen orchestra to attention.

"First," he declared, "the overture."

And then his arms began to move, slowly and gently at first, as if he were trying to coax music from silence. There was nothing to be heard, though, and Evey began to wonder if he really was crazy, and the music only existed in his head; or if all his "performance" would be nothing more than mime. Somehow what he was doing reminded her of an old Bugs Bunny cartoon she'd seen as a child, before everything American was banned.

"Listen carefully," he said then, his soft voice reclaiming her attention. "Do you hear it?"

Puzzled now, for there was obviously more to this than first appeared, Evey tilted her head and listened, while all the time she kept watching V's baton, moving, summoning . . .

"I hear it," she said suddenly, a childlike wonder in her voice; this, after all, was magic, and perhaps it was less a conductor's baton he held than a conjurer's wand. Although, even then, she wasn't quite sure whether she might just be imagining it after all. But, no, it was definitely there . . . the soft strings of the opening bars of Peter Tchaikovsky's "1812 Overture," rising slowly like a thin, white mist emerging from the darkness of the London streets and alleys. As the music swelled up louder and picked up its well-known theme, she couldn't help dashing forward to the parapet and looking down, trying to locate its source.

Finally, she thought she'd tracked it down to a nearby loudspeaker, one of the myriad now strung across London and all the other cities of the country that filled the days with announcements and propaganda and control orders. But, no, it wasn't just one speaker. It was *all* of them.

Right across London, Tchaikovsky's musical portrait of Moscow's heroic resistance to the invading Napoleonic hordes sang out, growing louder all the time. And interwoven with the theme, although the composer had intended them to represent nothing more nor less than the enemy, were extracts from the "Marseillaise," that paean to the now-forgotten values of Liberty, Equality, and Fraternity.

That revolutionary call to arms: *"Aux armes, mes enfants . . ."*

And across the city, children woke and, startled, asked their mothers what it meant; while people spilled out into the moonlit streets to listen, curfew quite forgotten. For this was loud enough now to wake the entire city, loud enough perhaps to wake the dead . . . for were not most of the city's population now dead, indeed, to so many things that mattered? Liberty, Equality, Fraternity . . .

And in the offices of the security services, and police, and even there in Downing Street, all hell was breaking loose.

"How did you *do* that?" Evey asked, a smile of astonishment all across her face.

"Wait," said V, still conducting, his gestures growing more frenzied and extravagant still. "Here comes the crescendo."

Now the theme returned, far more powerful than at its first appearance, swelling inexorably toward its climax, with all the battle fury of drums and cymbals and timpani, to the point where, upon its premiere, Tchaikovsky had had real cannon fired as part of the performance.

And when that point was reached, the night sky over London was suddenly rent by a shattering explosion, perfectly timed with the music, and the statue of blindfolded Justice was simply blown apart in shards of melting metal, her sword and scales vanishing in a ball of angry smoke and flame.

Evey could only stare in shock as the music rose again, and, once more timed to match the original cannon fire, a further series of thunderous explosions smashed the Old Bailey into myriad fragments.

"Beautiful, is it not?" asked V as the monstrous echoes of the collapsing building faded, and he turned to take a conductor's bow before his utterly startled audience.

Evey just couldn't believe what she was seeing. That massive pile of stone and metal, one of the landmarks that had defined the face of London for a century or more, with all its history, all the memories of its criminal trials, for the most part just ones though recent others rather less so, was simply *gone*. Shattered, crumpled, and all but obscured in billowing clouds of smoke and dust. And V had provided a ringside seat at the spectacle, just for her.

But still the performance wasn't quite over, for as the roaring in her ears subsided, she suddenly heard the whoosh of fireworks and another, far less voluminous, explosion. But this was not the usual starburst of an exploding rocket; rather it was the performer's credit, writ large across the starry sky. Up there, in a pattern of bursting light, a single sparkling letter:

V

Eyes wide with awe and surprise, Evey turned toward the perpetrator of the evening's entertainment . . . but he had already disappeared.

"V?" she asked an empty rooftop. Asked again the empty, silent air, "V?"

Then, all around, from those same speakers that, mere moments before, had provided the musical accompaniment, the harsh, discordant sirens began to wail . . .

# THREE

The tension in the room was like the thick, black smoke of a sacrifice to evil gods, but none of the men gathered round the large table at its center could bring himself to say anything to relieve it. This too was a room of gloom and shadows, but quite unlike that which lay hidden underground an unknown distance away, this contained nothing to lighten the oppressive air: no posters, books, or music . . . certainly no bust of Shakespeare.

For this was the new, modernized, and thoroughly up-to-date Cabinet Room in Downing Street, now decorated in a totalitarian palette of gray, steel, and black. And here, where once elected Cabinet ministers gathered to debate and discuss the country's fortunes and direction, sat the appointed department heads that these days represented the new body politic; or rather its repression, for political life, like Guy Fawkes himself four hundred years before, had now been hung, drawn, and quartered, and afterward thrown to the dogs. These were hard-faced, ruthless men for the most part who, despite their power, still couldn't quite avoid the caricaturing humor of the British public they did so much to stifle and suppress. And so these remnant travesties of supposedly legitimate government departments had their nicknames: the security services, The Finger; visual surveillance, The Eye; audio-surveillance, The Ear; criminal detection, The Nose; propaganda, The Mouth. All, collectively, known as The Head, despite the apparent anomaly of including the Finger among them. But then the Finger was the most feared of all, and no one wanted to feel that particular digit's tap upon his shoulder. And here they all were, gathered round that large central table, haggard with lack of sleep, their faces lit only by small reading lamps upon the tabletop and the concrete-colored glow of a large monitor at the table's end. Waiting, like the monitor, for someone to appear. For the head, in fact, of The Head itself.

At last the monitor blinked into life, and then, as smokes were hurriedly stubbed and backs were suddenly straightened, the face of High Chancellor Adam Sutler glowered into view. And Chancellor Sutler was not at all a happy man.

"Gentlemen," he began coldly. "You've had four hours. You'd better have results."

An uncomfortable shuffling, for they all knew that the multiple cameras in the room would be returning their images to Sutler, just as his was reaching them. Who was going to get it first?

"Mr. Creedy!"

Peter Creedy leaned forward out of the darkness, the lamp illuminating a face of stone, the eyes displaying all the emotion of a gun barrel. A hard bastard, harder even than the men who served him.

"The Old Bailey area is quarantined," the head of the Finger said coolly. "All significant witnesses have been detained."

And, he might have added, were currently having whatever information they might possess beaten out of them at that very moment; but Sutler would know that anyway. The Finger wasn't renowned for subtlety; just for efficiency of a peculiarly unpleasant kind. Which was why there were some who referred to Fingermen as the Gestapo; but never aloud, and never to their faces.

"Good." Sutler nodded. "Mr. Etheridge?"

The small man with large ears that seemed so naturally to match his position rather nervously began to speak. "A recording device was found wired into the Central Emergency Broadcast System. The DCD was Tchaikovsky's '1812 Overture'—"

"Add it to the blacklist," cut in Sutler decisively. "I don't ever want to hear that music again."

"Yes, sir," Brian Etheridge replied, hurriedly making a note on a pad before him, seeming rather flustered as he felt the eyes of all the others present turn upon him. No wonder the man's nickname was Bunny, Sutler thought contemptuously. A rabbit caught in the headlights. If it wasn't for the man's obvious technical ability, he'd have been replaced long ago.

Just the sort of man that Sutler no longer wished to have to mix with at all, in fact. Although when it came right down to it, the High Chancellor didn't want to have to deal personally with any of them, let alone the hoi polloi out on the streets; thus the video-link, rather than personal contact with his own Cabinet. Human beings couldn't be trusted to behave themselves in any logical fashion, no matter how strictly you kept them under control. Not like the computers, whose company he'd come to prefer more and more, over the years, to human interaction. Machines at least obeyed physical, scientific laws that were forever immutable. Human beings, no matter how rigidly you enforced the most logical of man-made laws, continued to break them. Well, if anyone broke *his* laws, like this terrorist who'd committed last night's outrage, he'd break *them,* as surely as God had given him the power to. And the right.

"We've also doubled our random sweeps," Etheridge gulped next, hating to ever have to report anything remotely like news his leader wouldn't want to hear, "and are monitoring an increased amount of phone surveillance, indicating a high percentage of conversation concerned with the explosion."

"Mr. Dascombe, what are we doing about that?" Sutler asked, razor sharp as ever. From long experience, no one gathered here in the Cabinet Room ever let his attention slip for an instant. Others in the past who hadn't stayed on their toes just hadn't stayed in their jobs.

Roger Dascombe, however, was not one of those likely to be on their way out anytime soon. Sleek, tanned, and immaculately dressed in a bespoke suit without the slightest wrinkle, he looked every bit as perfect as he obviously thought he was. In fact, right now he looked rather peeved that anyone, even the

Chancellor, should think it worth asking him what he was going to do about a situation he'd had fully under control within an hour of the explosions. The Mouth didn't just hang around with its jaw dropping open, after all.

"We're calling it an 'emergency demolition,' " he explained, unable to avoid a smug glance round at his companions. "We have spin coverage on the Network and throughout the InterLink. Several experts have been lined up to testify about the Old Bailey's lack of structural integrity."

On the monitor screen, Sutler nodded, paused for just an instant's thought, then added, "I want Prothero to speak tonight on the dangers of these old buildings, and how we must avoid clinging to the edifice of a decadent past. He should conclude by saying that the *New* Bailey will become a symbol of our time, and of the future that our conviction has rewarded us with."

Then, almost as if he were searching for his next victim in the dark, Sutler leaned closer to the camera and pronounced, "Mr. Heyer."

Conrad Heyer was difficult to even notice, hanging back as he did in the shadows. Not so much a man of mystery as one who thought the best way to stay out of trouble was not to be noticed, unless it was really necessary; quiet efficiency was the image he wanted to project. "Our surveillance cameras captured several images of the terrorist," announced the head of the Eye, "though the mask obviously makes retinal identification impossible. We also managed to get a picture of the girl that Creedy's men were . . . *uh* . . . detaining."

"Who is she, Mr. Finch?"

"Not sure yet, sir, but we're working on several leads." Eric Finch was a longtime career policeman who really had no time for all this "Nose" stuff and preferred to just think of himself as still holding his old rank of Chief Inspector, before they'd bumped him up, not entirely willingly, to department head. *Chief Constable* would have been a more appropriate title for the rank he held now, but they'd shot the last Chief Constable of London when he'd tried to revolt against the Party takeover and abolished the title thereafter; shot him in public too, to make an example of the "traitor." Almost sixty now, lined and worn, Finch had that sagging, world-weary look of a professional bloodhound. And frankly he couldn't wait to be out of the place. Police work and detection were the things that interested him, not politicking and hanging round in Cabinet offices.

"Anything else?" Sutler asked him.

"We located the fireworks launcher and found traces of the explosives used at the site. Unfortunately, it appears that despite the heavy level of sophistication, these devices were homemade with over-the-counter chemicals, making them very difficult to trace. Whoever he is, Chancellor, he's very good."

"Save your professional annotations, Mr. Finch," said Sutler coldly, uninterested in praise for fallible human beings. "They're irrelevant."

Finch bit back an oath and filed away several expletive-laden thoughts for later conversation about the ironhearted, inhuman bastard he had to answer to;

then said what he knew he had to say. "Apologies, Chancellor."

On the screen, Sutler could be seen sitting back in his chair, obviously satisfied that, by now, he'd heard all the relevant reports. After a moment's thought, he leaned forward toward the camera once more.

"Gentlemen, this is a test," he said in his best politically lecturing, religiously sermonizing voice. "Moments such as these are matters of faith. To fail is to invite doubt in everything we believe and in everything we have fought for. Doubt will plunge this country back into chaos, and I will not let that happen. I want this terrorist found, gentlemen, and I want him to learn what terror really means."

And then, as always, the Chancellor's concluding words: "England prevails."

And with varying degrees of enthusiasm and belief, those around the table chorused back the same response.

"England prevails!"


And indeed England prevailed nowhere more so than at the Jordan Television Tower, the veritable mouthpiece of the government's "information" service, and one that Roger Dascombe regarded very much as his own private domain.

Sitting there in the control booth an hour after his return from Downing Street, he couldn't help but experience a feeling of smug satisfaction. All the other "Head Men," such as Finch and Creedy, were jumping through hoops right now, and here he was with everything perfectly under control. An operation so slick it could just slide through any crisis and still come out sparkling on the other side.

And there in the studio before him, sitting casually on a sofa just close enough to suggest a certain intimacy (and raise that age-old question in the viewer's mind "Were they at it when the cameras disappeared, or not?"), were the immaculately dressed Dick and June, the nation's darlings, selling the morning news wholesale to a captive audience. No surnames, no accents, no previous convictions, no whiff of scandalous behavior, and not a single hint of personality, they were absolute perfection, young, gorgeous and, as everyone just *knew*, completely trustworthy.

And, no, they *weren't* at it. Offscreen they hated each other's guts like fury; refused even to have their dressing rooms on the same floor. And the viewers never knew.

True professionals, the pair of them.

A glance at the autocue, and then Dick grinned with effortless plasticity and, with perfect enunciation, delivered Dascombe's perfect lines.

"On the lighter side of things, it seems that the crew responsible for the demolition of the Old Bailey wanted to give the old girl a grand, albeit improvised, send-off . . ."

Back in the control booth, Dascombe's senior assistant, Patricia (no surnames behind the camera either; everyone was part of "Roger's family" here, except perhaps for Gordon Deitrich), glanced away from the monitors and whispered to him, just a little nervously.

"You think people will buy this?"

"Why not?" Dascombe smirked. "This is the British Television Network. And BTN's job is to *report* the news, not fabricate it.

"That's the government's job."

Back out on the sofa, June had picked up Dick's link with effortless ease and now continued, "Though the demolition had been planned for some time, the music and the fireworks were, according to the crew chief, 'definitely not on the schedule.' "

Then, with perfect simultaneity, the perfectly pitched chuckle from the duo. "All is well with the world," it said. "It was just a tiny joke by an overenthusiastic crew member that got a little out of hand. Trust us."

And after a few seconds for the message to sink in, there was Dick: "We'll be right back . . ."

"Do you believe that bloody load of bollocks?" asked Evey's friend Vicky as they sat together in the room where they worked, farther down the corridor on the same floor of Jordan Tower, a pair of young PAs intent on working their way a lot higher up. And if there was an odd little smile round Evey's lips as she sifted through the schedules and the mass of daily paperwork, then Vicky was too busy looking up at the monitor in the corner of the room to notice.

"That was no bleedin' demolition," Vicky continued,

betraying her East End roots with every word she spoke. At times Evey half-expected her to break into Cockney rhyming slang and refer to "goin' up the apples-an'-pears" or "talkin' on the ol' dog-an'-bone," but somehow it never went beyond a litter of swear words and working-class crudities. Though to give Vicky her due, she was trying her best to improve. "I saw it," added Vicky. "The whole thing. Everyone in my flat did. Did *you* see it?"

"No," said Evey, suddenly just the slightest touch nervous. She didn't need anyone asking her about the previous evening, even Vicky. But something had to be said. "Last night, I—"

"Oh, that's right!" pounced Vicky gleefully, blue eyes sparkling. "You went to Daddy Deitrich's last night, didn't you? Come on. Spill, spill . . ."

Fortunately, before Evey could even think about what to say, the door swung open and there was Patricia bustling into the room; not exactly angry, but not exactly pleased.

"Evey, there you are!" she began immediately, businesslike as ever. "You are still working for me, aren't you?"

A moment's confusion, and then Evey noticed the small personal radio she used as an intercom between floors sitting on her desk. Somehow, after the night's excitements, she'd managed to forget to switch it on this morning.

"Sorry, Patricia," she said contritely.

That apology seemed to be enough, and Patricia was never one to waste time on useless chatter. Now that she'd found her missing minion, the task list just spilled from her lips in no time at all.

"I need two espressos and three filter coffees from downstairs. And Deitrich is ready for his tea."

She turned to go, already intent on the next item on the day's agenda. "And we'd like them just a little sooner than yesterday, please."

And Vicky, suddenly seeming enormously busy, glanced up and smiled briefly as Evey leapt to her feet, blushing, and dashed away through the door in Patricia's wake.

Over at New Scotland Yard, Chief Inspector Finch was starting to feel as rumpled as his old suit. He'd been out of bed as soon as the music started and the sirens went off: a couple of hours at the Old Bailey; a couple of hours at his desk; then that bloody Cabinet meeting; then back to his desk again.

And the desk was no more of a pretty sight than he was. A litter of reports, a mess of notes, a keyboard and a monitor, a couple of phones; and he'd piled up more empty coffee cups there than he had leads right now. And still the reports came in, 95 percent useless but needing to be checked anyway, and if he wasn't careful, they'd topple over again, and then he wouldn't know where he was or what he'd already read. If it had just been something simple and comprehensible, like a bank raid . . . but, no, it had to be a terrorist attack, with incomprehensible trimmings like fireworks and bloody concertos.

A cooperative operation between the Nose and the Finger this was supposed to be, whether he wanted it or not, and duplicate reports to be faxed as fast as WPC Barnden could send them. Poor girl had been sending out stuff all morning. Not that he was getting much from Creedy and his Fingermen. But that was typical. Take everything, give nothing back. Bloody Creedy. Well, two could play at that game. Maybe he'd tell Lizzie Barnden to go sick tomorrow and then be "too short-staffed" to find anyone to replace her for a while.

"I don't get it," remarked Detective Sergeant Dominic Stone, Finch's lieutenant—"DSDS" as he was usually known to the Yard's canteen staff, whom he somehow charmed into giving him all the prime cuts and extra helpings. The younger man looked up in puzzlement from a desk that was far, far more organized than his boss's. Almost clean, Finch thought disgustedly. But he'd grow out of that. At least he hoped he would. Not like the last DS he'd had, who'd had half his head blown off in that Scottish Nationalist Army terror attack a couple of years ago. Finch liked Dominic Stone for his personality as well as his efficiency and always thought of him as "Dominic" rather than "Sergeant Stone." Probably liked him a bit too much. After all, if Finch's son, Peter, hadn't died along with his mother, back in the troubles at the time of the Reclamation, he'd be . . . well, thinking about that didn't help him get on with the job.

"Why does he wear a Guy Fawkes mask and then

blow up the Old Bailey?" Dominic continued. "Didn't Fawkes try to blow up Parliament?"

"It's not too late," Finch told him wearily. "Maybe he's just getting started."

He almost added, "But let's not go there." But before the words could reach his lips, the phone rang on Dominic's desk. Finch looked up at him as he took the call. Young, handsome, well-groomed, smart, and eager. He'd grow out of all of those things if he stayed in this business long enough. The hair would be the first to go, falling out with worry while trying to solve just this sort of case. For a moment, Finch wondered if he was looking at himself when he was young; but then decided it was just stupid, wasting time thinking about things like that.

Instead, he turned his attention back to the photo of the terrorist that one of the CCTV cameras had picked up the previous night. And who, or what, was he looking at here? The mask. The grin. The whole bloody pantomime outfit. A joke? Or a nightmare?

The train of thought was suddenly interrupted as Dominic slammed down the phone and leapt to his feet excitedly.

"A lead on the girl!"

And so, with the gravity that his age and position had earned him, and the weariness that being up all night brought as well, Finch dropped the photo back on the desk and heaved himself out of the chair. Maybe there was something here for an old dog to get his teeth into after all.

• • •

The girl in question was, just then, about to encounter another older man; the one she was supposed to have met the previous night.

Gordon Deitrich was a longtime producer and variety-show front man from the old multichannel days, back before everything had gone to hell and there was nothing left afterward but the British Television Network, whether anyone liked it or not. He'd spent a while in the wilderness while the new powers-that-be were getting themselves set up, which he'd at first put down to the idea that the programs he used to make were far too coarse for present tastes . . . and then suddenly he'd got the call to produce a new, weekly, government-approved variety show. Only when he read the brief did he realize that he'd actually got the job because now they couldn't possibly find anyone coarser. Even so, there were limits. But as long as he provided enough cheap laughs and syrupy pap to keep the mindless masses entertained . . . well, it was a living. Frankly, it was a damned good living.

And living was what a lot of the media people he used to know just weren't doing anymore. The ones who used to flounce into the office every morning and call everybody "darling" and "sweetie." Not since the Reclamation.

"Look, don't get me wrong," Deitrich was saying as Evey approached his open door, tea tray in hand. She had to smile at that. Like every other producer in the building, he was *always* on the phone.

"I love it," he continued. "A cow getting crucified . . . it's hysterical. But we'll never get it approved."

He looked up then, a slightly wolfish glint in his eye as he saw Evey enter the room. "You've gotta rewrite it, okay?" he told the hapless script man at the other end of the line. And before there was time for further argument: "Gotta go."

Hanging up as Evey put the tea tray down on his desk, he got to his feet and walked round to join her. A big-boned and large-featured man who was probably in his fifties, Evey thought, and with what he preferred to think of as a "fairly well-rounded figure" . . . not quite fat, but he obviously lived well . . . he was well-known to have an eye for the younger and more attractive office staff. There were two ways to regard a man with a reputation like that; and Evey preferred to look upon him as a source of potential opportunities.

"I can't recall ever being stood up by a more attractive woman," he said, though the smile playing round his lips was intended to lessen the accusation just a little.

"Mr. Deitrich—" Evey began, blushing with embarrassment, but he cut her off.

"Gordon, please. I don't need *Mister* to make this body feel any older."

That, of course, just made her feel even more embarrassed, but she knew that something had to be said before the peach flush on her cheeks turned into something more like beetroot.

"Gordon, I was on my way last night, but there

were Fingermen about. And I got a little scared and went home."

Deitrich paused then, looking thoughtful for a moment. "Sadly, I think after last night our curfew will only get worse."

A sigh before he added, "But you're probably right. In days like these, home is probably the safest place to be."


Not for Evey Hammond, though. Not anymore.

The once-safe haven of her apartment was breached forever as Finch and Dominic kicked in the door, bursting in with guns drawn.

A few moments tension as they checked the shabby rooms that swiftly drained away as they realized no one else was there. Pistols put away . . . that always made Finch feel better, remembering how, when he'd joined the force, only special units had carried guns. They began to look around, checking drawers and closets for anything that might help. Letters, an address book, an answer-phone, anything . . . not that there was much here that suggested this was the home of a dangerous terrorist. Certainly no bomb-making equipment, no lists of targets or plans of action. The place looked as if it could have belonged to any young woman of relatively little means: student, office worker, shopgirl. The clothes were cheap; the decor was worse.

It was Finch who noticed the mirror, with the photos tucked in all around the frame. And there amongs the others, of course, was one of Evey herself. A perfect match for the rather more blurry image picked up on the CCTV cameras. A glance toward Dominic, and then . . .

"Gotcha," he said to the photo. And meant it too. This was just the confirmation of identity they needed.

# FOUR

The more she thought about it as the morning progressed, the more Evey wished she'd managed to make it to Gordon Deitrich's the previous night, nocturnal adventures notwithstanding (though it had to be said, the more she thought about those nocturnal adventures, the more hair-raising they became). After all, the grand-sounding "junior personal assistant" was just a joke really; they might just as well call her "gofer number two." Fetch the coffee. Go and find this. Send out for that. Now it was, collect the latest delivery from the main entrance. If she could actually work up to really being *someone's* personal assistant, instead of *anyone's* assistant, she might actually stop being run off her feet all the time. One day, she thought . . . well, maybe one day she'd go a lot further than that. After all, she'd always wanted to be in front of the cameras, not behind them. But with her background, she'd never had the opportunities for that sort of thing. If she could just get herself noticed by someone . . . someone who might be interested in her . . .

Right now, though, she was all alone in the elevator with a handcart stacked with perfectly uniform FedCo boxes, every one alike with their green-and-black stripe emblazoned on the side. Typical government mail system: everything the same; regular size; regular weight; regular color. Typical of the entire government itself, in fact. It was just a surprise that everyone didn't have to wear the same regular uniforms, the way they used to do in China back in the days of Chairman Mao. Best not to think about that sort of thing, though. Every time she thought of a way that things could get worse, they usually did.

As it was, the only uniformed people around Jordan Tower were the security guards, and there was one before her as the elevator doors opened and she pushed out the handcart. Fortunately, this was one of the friendlier ones, unlike the shoot-to-kill goons they had on the main door. A timeserver, just putting in his hours and taking home his paycheck, and far more interested in watching the latest episode of *Storm Saxon* than his security monitors.

"Hey, Fred!" called Evey cheerily, dragging his attention away momentarily from the Brylcreemed Aryan hero of "England's future nightmare," when the degenerates and terrorists were back and they had to be severely dealt with, just as they'd been before, only this time using Laser-Lügers and Rocket-Racers.

"All that stuff been x-rayed?" the big security man asked casually, his eye wandering briefly from the screen to run over the boxes, lingering a little longer on Evey, and then going back to where it had started.

"Nope," joked Evey, knowing full well she'd passed them through the machine herself. "They're filled with bombs."

"Well, wait till the commercial to set them off, okay?" Fred Thorpe said complacently, a faint grin on his round face as he held out a docket for her to sign.

"I can't believe you watch that shit," said Evey, scribbling her name.

"What?" he exclaimed, finally reacting in just the same, startled way she expected he would. Almost as if she'd suggested that football had no importance in the greater scheme of things. Or pinup girls. "But . . . Laser Lass is just . . . *banging!*"

Stifling a giggle and deciding this must be some masculine epithet she hadn't come across before, Evey gave the handcart a shove and went on her way. After all, "banging" wasn't anything that was shown on TV these days, even if some of Gordon Deitrich's shows did get pretty near the knuckle sometimes.

A couple of minutes later she'd arrived at her destination, the wardrobe department. The racket that hit her as soon as she opened the door was almost overwhelming after the quiet of the corridor, but when twenty nubile young women were hurriedly dressing up in showgirl costumes, it really wasn't surprising. And somewhere in that noisy mass of blond wigs, corsets, fishnet stockings, high heels, ostrich feathers, and sequins, Evey finally managed to find the wardrobe mistress, a woman far less interested in her own appearance than that of the girls she was trying to dress. In fact her own appearance had gone to hell long ago; but when she'd gone through three husbands and had five kids, that sort of thing didn't seem to matter much anymore.

"What's all *that?*" she asked bad-temperedly, eyeing the stack of boxes suspiciously and thrusting a handful of safety pins into her pocket.

"Not sure," Evey told her, not really caring. As far as she was concerned, this was just one more job to get out of the way before she went to lunch. "They just arrived, marked for Stage Three."

A sour expression crossed the older woman's face, which quite plainly said, "As if I don't have enough problems already, without this." And after that she jumped to a conclusion that didn't improve her temper one iota.

"Must be Prothero," she snapped. "I wish someone had the balls to tell him this station isn't his own personal bloody playground!"

With that, she grabbed one of the boxes from the stack and ripped it open.

"What the hell is *this?*" she asked, pulling out a long black cape and a mask. A mask that Evey instantly recognized. A Guy Fawkes mask.

V's mask.

Evey could hardly breathe. She felt the blood draining from her face, feared the shock would give her away immediately, started to panic—a return of the same sort of overpowering fear that had dominated her whole life since she was a little girl, that only ever left her when she was too busy to think.

But if the wardrobe mistress saw anything in Evey's expression at all, she seemed to take it only as incomprehension. Stuffing the mask and cape back roughly into the box and tossing it back on the pile, she turned away disgustedly and said, "Just put them over there until I can figure out what they're for."

And then she was off among her charges once again, straightening feathers and fixing diamanté brooches, snapping and yelling in the Babel of voices that filled the room.

And not noticing at all how Evey had left without uttering a word. Without being *able* to utter a word.

A minute later she was back in the JPAs' room, burdened with a secret she wished she didn't have and almost choking on a rising sense of desperation.

"What is it?" Vicky asked with genuine concern, immediately realizing something was wrong. "What happened?"

"I—I don't feel very well," stammered Evey, white-faced and looking every bit as sick as she said she was. "I think I have to go."

Hoping desperately that Vicky wouldn't ask her anything else, Evey began grabbing her things and stuffing them into her bag. It was a forlorn hope, of course.

"Was it Deitrich?" probed Vicky. "What did that old pervert say?"

"No, it was nothing like that," Evey said hurriedly, wanting to tell Vicky to mind her own business, but knowing that would only make things worse. "I just have to go."

And she did.

• • •

Sitting in the car while Dominic sent it hurtling from Paddington toward the Jordan Tower, Finch had got Evey's record up on the dashboard computer system and was intent on having something to concentrate on instead of the young man's hair-raisingly dangerous driving. Whether it was lunacy or confidence or just that "boy's toy" feeling of having a police car to drive around in, regardless of the limit, Finch never really knew; he just had a nasty feeling that if ever he came to a sudden end, it wouldn't be a terrorist bullet that did it. It would be Dominic's driving.

Still, in this case, there did seem to be a compelling reason for it.

"This looks serious," Finch remarked, not wanting to glance up at the street hurtling far too swiftly past the window, at the trucks Dominic insisted on weaving around, at the pedestrians who stood gawping in disbelief. "Her parents were political activists. They were 'detained' when she was twelve."

"What happened to her?" Dominic asked, turning his head in a way Finch didn't like at all.

"Juvenile Reclamation Project for five years."

"Shit," said Dominic, having read far too many criminal records that started off in the brutal hell of a JRP, and just went downhill from there. Usually until they suddenly stopped. Dead.

"We're going to need backup. But let's keep it minimal. I want to stay under Creedy's radar."

"You sure about that, sir?" Dominic asked in surprise, and now his eyes were definitely not on the road.

"I just want a chance to talk to her before she disappears into one of Creedy's black bags. And, for Christ's sake, look where you're going!"

Back at the security station in Jordan Tower that Evey had passed by only a few minutes before, Fred Thorpe was still devotedly watching *Storm Saxon* and licking his lips in anticipation. After all, Laser Lass was a big girl, and one day she was bound to have an accident and fall out of that skimpy costume, and he wanted to make sure he was watching when it happened. If only he were Rex Ranall, the lucky bastard who played Storm Saxon . . .

So he wasn't looking round at the security monitors when the first of them fritzed out into static.

Or the second.

In fact, by the time he noticed anything at all, Laser Lass having temporarily disappeared from the scene, more than half the screens were dead, including just about all the ones covering the immediate area round his security station.

"What the hell—?" he gasped, swinging round in his seat and starting to get to his feet. The last thing he needed right now was to have to go and find an electrician, right in the middle of *Storm Saxon*. Or, worse still, start some sort of full-scale security alert, just because of a blown fuse somewhere.

The soft ding of an arriving elevator cut across his thoughts, and by the time the doors slid open, he hardly had a moment left to think at all.

"Who's that?" he shouted, seeing only a grinning white mask, a wide-brimmed hat, and a floor-length cloak wrapped round a form that moved with supple swiftness. It could be an actor in costume, of course; that was the obvious conclusion. But somehow he didn't think it was. And besides, since last night's bombing, everyone around here had been nervous as hell, even without the loudspeakers urging vigilance and announcing new security measures.

Vigilance, he had to admit, that he hadn't actually been too hot on the last half hour. And somehow the guilt over that . . . or was it fear his lapses would be discovered? . . . meant that he was suddenly completely on the ball, and angry about it too.

"I ain't playing!" the security guard yelled next, reaching for his gun. A gun he'd never had to use and had always hoped he never would. "You show me ID, or you get the bloody *Storm Saxon* treatment! Right now!"

The dark figure before him said nothing, and that, in itself, was far more frightening than if he had. Instead, he merely opened the cloak to show the little party trick he'd brought along to provide some entertainment.

A heavy vest of dynamite sticks strapped all around his chest, the detonator nestling in his black-gloved hand.

"Fucking hell!" was all that Thorpe could say to that.

And the masked but smiling figure nodded, as if to say, yes, indeed, it was.

From outside, the sound of approaching police sirens could be heard, but V seemed quite unmoved, almost as if he didn't believe they could be coming here. With swift and silent efficiency, he disarmed the security guard, then delivered precise but whispered instructions. And they made their way off down the corridor, the one as cool as ice, the other chilled with fear.

A minute or two later, Evey passed the security station on her way to the same elevator and paused at what she saw. Or rather, what she didn't. This wasn't right at all. Fred was never missing from his post, especially not during *Storm Saxon;* the corridor was never this eerily silent. A dread anticipation made her gut clench.

She had to get out of here. And she had to get out *now*.

Not far away, the door to the main news studio suddenly swung open, and everyone within froze to statue stillness. The only motion was from the two figures that entered, the one familiar, the other quite the contrary. His cloak swishing the ground, the detonator in his hand, the dynamite in view, V floated in with a serene silence . . . accompanied by the plainly terrified Fred Thorpe, who pushed along the handcart filled with FedCo boxes that Evey had earlier delivered.

And at the instant that Evey was about to press the elevator button, V stepped across to the studio wall and hit the fire alarm.

Down in the lobby, Finch, Dominic, and their assembled backup of armed and uniformed officers suddenly reeled as the air filled with thunderously loud alarm bells . . . and all the building's elevators promptly shut down. And to a man, the company of police pulled out their guns.

"You two cover the elevators," Finch ordered, heading for the stairwell. "The rest of you, follow me."

Many floors above, while the studio staff cowered in terror, V used an electric drill to drive a heavy bolt through the metal entry door and into the jamb, sealing it shut. And no one made a move to stop him.

Evey, meanwhile, frustrated by the elevators' sudden seizure, found herself surrounded by a crowd of the tower's employees heading urgently toward the stairwell. Having no alternative, she let herself be swept along with them; and maybe it was for the best. After all, being one of the crowd was probably the easiest way to cover her tracks until she could, she desperately hoped, get out of the building and make her way home. And after that . . . well, she had no idea what to do after that.

Stricken with fear as she was, she couldn't help noticing how different the crowd's behavior was to when they'd carried out their practice drills. Those had been quiet, orderly affairs, with people heading calmly for the exits. As soon as the alarms had unexpectedly gone off and the loudspeakers had said, "This is not a drill!" everything had changed. Now she was in a frightened, jostling mob, some of them swearing, most of them yelling, demanding the people ahead of them move faster, asking what the hell was happening, calling for friends. The one advantage, Evey thought, was that in a crowd of panicking people, no one would notice how terrified she was herself. Keep going, then. Flow along in the river of people, like everyone else, and hope to wash up safe in the street outside.

One man who was fighting against the direction of the crowd was Roger Dascombe, making his way toward the news studio that was his normally untouchable pride and joy. A small group were already gathered by the door, mostly his personal team of security men, and it took only a moment for Dascombe to shoulder his way through them.

"What the bloody hell is going on here?" he shouted furiously, barely able to make himself heard above the alarm bells.

"It's jammed," one of the security men told him flatly, as if it were so bloody obvious they couldn't get in, it hardly needed saying. If they could have done, the bullets would have been flying long ago.

"Then break it down!" screamed Dascombe, a note of hysteria creeping into his voice. This shouldn't be happening. Not in his precious studio. Not in his perfectly regulated private domain. Not to *him*.

"*And turn those fucking alarm bells off!*" he shouted raggedly, to no one in particular, just about reaching the end of his tether now.

Back in the corridor, Evey had nearly reached the stairwell door when the crowd streaming toward it was suddenly sent staggering aside as Finch and his police came bursting through.

For a moment she thought they were just here in response to the alarm or, perhaps, to whatever mis-

chief V was cooking up now. Though *mischief* probably wasn't a strong enough word for whatever it was V
had planned. *Chaos* was much more like it. Or even
*complete anarchy*.

Only, Evey suddenly realized, *she* was the one who
was in trouble.

Finch looked directly toward her, then suddenly
pointed at her as well and yelled, "Dominic!" at the
top of his voice. And a younger, lither, far more ener-
getic man suddenly began to push his way through the
crowd in her direction.

"Oh my God," she thought, suddenly completely
panic-stricken and twisting round to push her way back
through the mob. "They've found me. They *know!*"

*"Police!"* Finch was shouting furiously now, following along in Dominic's wake, fighting his way through
the ever-more-agitated mob in the corridor. "Get out
of the bloody way!"

Sick with terror, pushing, shoving, and clawing at a
hand that tried to restrain her, Evey fought her way
back to a corner and managed to slip round it, out of
sight of her pursuers.

Only a moment later, Finch and Dominic rounded
the same corner, but that was a moment too late. The
quarry had completely disappeared.

"Damnit!" grated Finch, and stood a moment regaining his breath. Both of them knew what they had
to do next, and a few seconds later they started hurriedly opening office doors and continuing the search.

In the news studio, V had now reached the control
booth and, detonator still brandished, pressed a DCD

into the sweaty palm of a young technician. The grinning mask said nothing, hinted nothing, but somehow the young man knew exactly what was wanted. A sick expression passed across his face, almost as if the intruder had asked him to shoot himself.

But then, as he did seem to be confronted by a mad bomber, that might have been the easy option.

Desperate for someone else to take the responsibility off his shoulders, the technician turned toward a group of suited executives who cowered in the corner, at least one of whom looked to be on the verge of a heart attack. No help from him, then. But one of the others nodded slowly, and with an almost audible sigh of relief, the younger man slipped the disc into the player. If old Jenkins had told him to go ahead, at least he wasn't likely to get tagged as being the terrorist's collaborator. Assuming there was anything left of him to tag when this was all over. Or of any of them.

Dominic, meanwhile, came barging through the door of the JPAs' room, the corridor still alive with motion behind him, to find himself in empty stillness. The only sound was the laugh track of a sitcom, coming from a monitor screen on one wall. For a moment he felt as if the set were laughing at him and the futility of his search.

And perhaps it was, for as soon as he slammed the door behind him and left, Evey emerged from her hiding place beneath a desk, shoving aside the boxes of files she'd drawn in around her for cover.

Then suddenly the laugh track stopped dead, swallowed up in a buzz of static. And when Evey looked up toward the screen, the image had disappeared as well.

All across London, television screens large and small went blank in just the same way, from the tiniest portables to the most gigantic JumboTrons suspended high above the crowds in Piccadilly Circus. From retirement homes where old men fiddled grumpily with their TV antennae, through pubs and clubs where a blank screen meant an opportunity to get another pint before the picture came back or the lunch was served, to family homes where small boys asked plaintively, "Mum, what's gone wrong with the telly?" everything was silence and signal-less snowy screens. And puzzled anticipation.

But not for long.

In the JPAs' room, Evey was getting to her feet and preparing to make another break for freedom when the monitor suddenly winked into life once more. And there was V's familiar mask grinning down at her, his face almost filling the screen, as if in a parody of Sutler's overbearing political broadcasts. In one corner of the screen appeared not the usual BTN logo, but VTV instead. And in a calm, almost professional announcer's voice, he began.

"Good morning, London."

And Evey could only shrink away. This was getting too much for anyone's nerves, let alone hers, after the previous night's events. Fear was starting to make her feel nauseous by now.

Roger Dascombe wasn't taking things well either. Even though the alarm bells had been turned off now, he was getting more and more wound up by the failure of his security men to get through the door. Then, to his horror, he noticed the on-air light was glowing and V's voice was echoing everywhere throughout the building.

"Allow me, first, to apologize for this interruption."

"That's the emergency channel!" screamed Dascombe, knowing full well it'd be overriding every broadcast in the land. And with that he bolted away to find a set on which to watch, leaving his minions to sort out the problem with the door.

"I do," V's voice continued, "like many of you, appreciate the comforts of the everyday routine, the security of the familiar, the tranquillity of television. I enjoy them as much as anyone."

"Bloody hell," said Finch, looking up at the screen in the wardrobe department where he had been searching for Evey. Well, that'd have to be left to the ordinary coppers now, he thought, heading back toward the door. Right now he needed to get along to the studio and get this sorted out. Or more to the point, get this stopped.

At the same time, a part of him didn't want to leave the screen; which told him that even if he did get it stopped, the terrorist would almost certainly have escaped by then . . . after all, this was a man who was obviously too smart to commit real or potential suicide for the sake of a single broadcast . . . and that he might be better using his time to watch his enemy and perhaps learn something of the way he'd think and act. One thing was certain: he knew enough about television to exploit the medium for his own purposes.

On screens across the land, the camera pulled back away from the close-up of V's mask to show him sitting at a desk, hatless now but still masked and wigged, while behind his shoulder the BTN logo that usually appeared with the normal newsreaders had been sprayed over with a circle containing the letter V. He began to speak again.

"But in the spirit of commemoration, whereby those important events of the past, usually associated with someone's death or with the end of some awful, bloody struggle, are celebrated with a nice holiday, I thought that this year we could mark the fifth of November . . . a day that sadly is no longer remembered . . . by taking some time out of our daily lives to sit down and have a little chat."

By now Dascombe had withdrawn to his private office, with Patricia and several armed guards, and was pacing up and down in front of the TV set, looking almost ready to start tearing out his perfectly groomed hair by the roots.

"Let me think," he said to no one in particular, as if it were a mantra that, said aloud, would somehow help him do so. "Let me think!"

And all those around him stood in silence and let him get on with it. Except that V's continuing voice wouldn't let him think at all.

"There are those, of course, who do not want us to speak. In fact I suspect that right now orders are being shouted into phones, and that men with guns will soon be on their way."

As if on cue, a cell phone rang on Dascombe's

desk. Patricia picked it up, listened for a few seconds, then thrust it out toward him.

"It's Chancellor Sutler," she said nervously, looking almost as if the phone were too hot to handle, or likely, at any moment, to turn into a venomous snake.

"Goddamnit!" grated Dascombe, and snatched it from her hand.

"Anything and everything will be done to stop me talking to you," V was saying, this time on the monitor in the security station that had previously been showing *Storm Saxon*, where Finch had paused and now stood watching as Dominic ran up to join him.

"We're going to need a torch," Dominic told him, obviously referring to the problem with the studio door. But Finch merely nodded, leaving his lieutenant to sort it out, having decided by now that he was far more interested in the voice of the man he'd already come to regard as a personal opponent. And when the face was not to be seen, every nuance of the voice needed to be absorbed, of the body language, of the thought behind the words. "Know your enemy." Just as relevant now as it ever was.

"Why?" asked V. "Because while the truncheon may be used in lieu of conversation, words will always retain their power."

Still not leaving the JPAs' room, Evey stood transfixed, looking at the screen and feeling almost as if V were talking directly to her. That same magnetic voice that she'd heard last night continued to hold her in its thrall.

"Words offer the means to meaning, and for those

who will listen, the enunciation of truth. The truth is, there is something terribly wrong with this country, isn't there?"

In his office, a sweating Roger Dascombe was trying to listen to Sutler with one ear and V with the other, though obviously only one of them needed a reply.

"*You* designed it, sir," he pointed out, trying to sugar the pill of truth with as much of a tone of obsequiousness as seemed appropriate. And to shift the blame as much as possible. "You wanted it foolproof. You told me every television in London—"

But then V's voice cut across his train of thought, becoming more powerful now, more strident. "Cruelty and injustice . . . intolerance and oppression. And where once you had the freedom to object, to think and speak as you saw fit, you now have censors and systems of surveillance, coercing your conformity and soliciting your submission."

Roger Dascombe, forgetting for an instant whom he was talking to, looked round toward the open door of his office and saw several policemen hauling a large acetylene torch along the corridor toward the still-unyielding studio door.

"Cameras!" he screamed suddenly. "We need cameras!"

And facing another camera, V opened out his gloved hands expressively, to match the questions in his words. "How did this happen? Who is to blame? Certainly there are those who are more responsible than others, and they will be held accountable. But again, if truth be told . . . if you are looking for the guilty, you need only look in the mirror."

V paused then, and all across the city, viewers did the same as the words sank in. In varying degrees, of course.

"I know why you did it," he continued. "I know you were afraid. Who wouldn't be? War. Terror. Disease. Food and water shortages. There were a myriad problems . . . which conspired to corrupt your reason and rob you of your common sense."

Somehow, then, even the mask couldn't hide V's obvious sense of disappointment. "Fear got the best of you, and in your panic, you turned to the now High Chancellor, Adam Sutler, with his gleaming boots of polished leather and his garrison of goons. He promised you order. He promised you peace. And all he demanded in return was your silent, obedient consent."

Another pause from the masked man of a myriad screens, during which Dominic returned to the security station to update Finch.

"Inspector, they're almost through," he said, and Finch nodded uncertainly before turning his back on the screen and following him down the corridor. They arrived just as Dascombe did, accompanied by a small video crew.

"Last night," V said, picking up the thread, "I sought to end the silence. Last night, I destroyed the Old Bailey, to remind this country of what it had forgotten. Four hundred years ago, one of our citizens wished to embed the fifth of November forever in our memory. His hope was to remind the world that fairness, justice, and freedom were more than words. They are perspectives. So, if you have seen nothing"— and here the voice sank in an obvious expression of distaste for anyone so obviously blind—"if the crimes of this government remain unknown to you, then I suggest that you allow the fifth of November to pass unmarked. But if you see what I see"—and now the magnetism was back as V started into his rousing finale—"if you feel as I feel, and if you would seek, as I seek, freedom from their tyranny and an end to this oppression . . . then I ask you to stand beside me, one year from last night, outside the gates of Parliament. And, together, we shall give them a fifth of November that shall never, *ever*, be forgot!"

With that, the recording ended, and V's masked face was lost in static. And those of his audience mesmerized by what he had to say, and there were not a few of them spread across the city and the country, suddenly found they had the power to move restored to them.

And among the first to move was Evey Hammond, who, snapping out of her trance and looking round thankfully to find herself still alone, bolted from the room.

# FIVE

With a spray of melting metal, a hissing roar of flame, and more smoke than anyone might reasonably have expected, the acetylene torch finally sliced through the last section of the heavy, soundproofed studio door, and a hefty police boot immediately kicked it in. It hit the floor, flat, with a loud thud, but before another boot could be laid on top of it, a thick cloud of fog belched out into the hall, engulfing police, security guards, and studio staff alike.

Finch, newly arrived on the scene, tried to peer through the dense gray blanket but could see absolutely nothing, all the lights having been extinguished as well. In the sudden quiet following the end of V's broadcast, the hum of a small motor broke the almost-eerie silence of the dim, beclouded studio.

"Kerosene fog," Dascombe remarked, appearing at Finch's shoulder. "He's using our smoke machine."

Not particularly grateful for information he could have figured out himself, Finch turned to Dominic and softly instructed him to cover the exits. Was that to have the best man on that particular job, or to save him from whatever might be waiting in the studio? Finch found he couldn't really say. As the younger man left, going about his task with quiet efficiency, Finch turned to his gathered band of coppers, wondering just how many of them would get out of this alive. Or, looking at the barely disguised thuggery that gleamed in many a slightly glassy eye, hopped up as they were on the prospect of violence, how many of them deserved to get out alive. The police service wasn't anything like it used to be in his younger days; and these were just the wimps who couldn't make it into the Finger.

Still, right now there was a far more important question in his mind: Would *he* get out alive?

"You two stay here," he told a disappointed pair, though they did look a little more encouraged when he told them, "No one gets out.

"The rest of you," he added, beckoning the others forward, "follow me."

And Dascombe and his camera crew tagged along behind as well. No one was going to keep him out of his own studio, especially when that studio was at the center of the news.

The fog still billowing around them, they began to pick their way cautiously into the cavernous studio, edging past the shadowy forms of camera dollies and long-extinguished lighting gear, of director's chairs and the telescopic arms of drooping microphone booms.

A familiar cool chill ran down Finch's spine, while a cold sweat made the palm of his gun hand greasy, though the last thing he was going to do right now was change hands to wipe it. He was jumpy as hell, and if that was how *he* felt, nearly forty years a copper, he could only conjecture how the young thugs behind him were feeling in their turn. He just hoped that the one with the itchy trigger finger wouldn't turn out to be standing directly behind him.

Ahead, in the gray blankness, there was the sound of movement; a vague thrashing noise.

Guns and cameras zeroed in, each, in its way, ready to shoot.

Next came the sound of footsteps, stumbling at first, then running . . . running toward them.

A shout in the fog: "Don't shoot! Please don't shoot!"

And a dark figure emerged from the blanketing grayness, cloak flapping around its shoulders.

A grinning white mask upon its face.

Behind Finch, before he could even think and certainly before they had, the police gunmen opened fire. And the Inspector threw himself flat and prayed.

Twisting in the air like an unstrung doll, the caped figure flipped and went down, twitching and jerking in a cacophonous hail of bullets.

And lay still. Quite still.

Hoping no one would shoot it off, Finch raised a hand, barking an order as he started to get to his feet, and the guns fell silent. Then, with extreme caution, he stepped forward.

Leaking blood, the man lay strangely twisted on his side. The shooting having stopped, he began to writhe in pain, yet somehow seemed unable to get his hands to any of his wounds. Only then did Finch notice his wrists were zip-tied behind his back.

With a horrible sinking feeling in his gut, the Inspector reached out and pulled the mask away from the man's face. An old man's face, white with terror and with pain.

"That's no terrorist!" exclaimed Dascombe, appearing suddenly at Finch's shoulder, camera crew close in turn. "That's Brownleas, one of our studio executives!"

"He . . . he put masks on all of us," the man managed to gasp out weakly, then lapsed into silence, his eyes closing, his teeth gritted in a rictus of pain.

"Jesus—!" yelled Finch, appalled.

More shuffling and stumbling noises emerged from the slowly clearing fog, and another shout: "Don't shoot! Dear God, don't shoot!" A theme picked up, with multiple variants, by a multitude of voices.

And then the men themselves appeared ahead of Finch, all caped, all masked, all tripping over their own feet in terror. And behind him, the police began to mutter and stamp their feet, their growing sense of uncomprehending panic almost palpable. It would take only one nervous trigger finger, one shot, and all hell would break loose. A police massacre. Not as uncommon as they used to be, but still something they could do without right now.

"*Freeze!*" shouted Finch, as loudly and commandingly as he possibly could, an order directed at those both before and behind. "Nobody move!"

The shadows in the mist came to a ragged halt, stumbling awkwardly, one of them falling helplessly to the ground.

"If you're wearing a mask, get down on your knees," Finch ordered next. "*Now!*"

The caped forms crumpled to the floor, and behind Finch one of the police hissed through his teeth softly, releasing his own tension and, somehow, doing the same for the rest of them.

"Get their masks off!" Finch said more calmly, pointedly saying nothing about releasing their hands. And, accompanied by his men, he began to slowly and cautiously move forward.

"Please hurry!" said the kneeling man Finch approached first. A different voice, this, lacking the elderly tone of the others; the voice of the same young technician who'd been forced to play the intruder's recording. A voice that next pronounced a doom-laden message of terror.

"He's got a bomb wired to a timer in the control booth!"

"Oh, no!" groaned Dascombe, still standing forgotten behind Finch and suddenly white-faced. People getting shot was one thing . . . news . . . but his beloved studio . . .

"Bloody Christ!" muttered Finch, as Dascombe bolted for the booth, camera crew still tagging along behind. "Jones! Get anyone not wearing a mask out of here!" Then, glancing back at the wounded, possibly dying executive who'd been cut down in the first volley: "Marshall, help carry this man."

With a horrible sinking feeling in his belly, he started after Dascombe, beckoning the rest of his men to keep searching the studio for the real terrorist. "Everyone else, let's go!"

His every move being taped by the pursuing crew,

Dascombe had reached the smoke-filled control booth . . . and paused in horror.

"Good God," he breathed, his knees suddenly threatening to give way beneath him as he looked through the fog at the red LED lights of a clock, already passing four minutes and rushing inexorably back toward three. From an open panel in the side of the clock, wires snaked away to the vest of dynamite sticks that V had earlier been wearing. And somewhere in Dascombe's head, a voice was whispering that it wasn't electricity running along those wires. It was *evil*. Evil on a cosmic scale that threatened to overthrow whole worlds of order. Most particularly, *his*. And destiny had picked him out, like a knight in shining armor, to do battle on behalf of the forces of light and save the world from darkness. Or, at least, to make sure it still had the nine o'clock news.

By the time Finch arrived in the booth, shouldering aside the camera crew (they protested, of course; this was great television, and what could be more important than *that*?), Dascombe was down on his knees before the bomb, almost as if in prayer. But it wasn't a rosary or a prayer book he had clutched in his hands. It was a pair of wire cutters.

"Dascombe!" yelled Finch sharply. But before he could say anything else, Dascombe had turned to face him, and something about his face now stopped the words on his lips. For Roger Dascombe was a man transfigured, a man who, forced to the greatest decision he'd ever had to make, had almost reached a state of grace. Which was the most important, his life or the studio? But somehow he'd transcended the opposites: quite plainly his life *was* the studio. There was no question to answer. Anything else to be decided could be rendered up to God . . . and the almost-sanctified pair of wire cutters he held in his hand.

"Do you have any idea how long it would take to rebuild this facility?" Dascombe asked, with a near-supernal calm and a strange luminescence in his eyes.

"Do you have any idea what you're doing?" Finch grated harshly, hoping that some word would shake Dascombe out of this state that, to an honest copper like him, looked close to madness.

"Pray that I do." Dascombe smiled, turning back to the device.

And Finch, knowing that any race to get a disposal unit here in time would be won hands down by the bomb, began to pray very earnestly indeed.

Outside the studio, Jones had managed to shepherd the unmasked studio executives past the two police-men left guarding the torched-down door and so, he hoped, to safety. He was about to go back in and get himself a piece of whatever action was left when he heard another shout from the still-befogged studio.

"Wait!" came the cry. "Don't shoot! Wait for us!" Two more masked men, like all the others wearing capes, came rushing through the door. Jones jumped back, uncertain which of the two to train his gun upon, hoping desperately that the other two guards would cover the one he didn't. Damnit, he thought, this wasn't a situation for poor bloody infantry like them to sort out; but no superior officer was in sight.

Seeming to shove each other aside in their haste to escape, the two masked men lurched into the hall, the first suddenly pushed somehow by the second and, desperately trying to retain his footing, barging into the three cops and scattering them. By the time they'd regained their wits, the second man had stumbled awkwardly, his hands still fixed behind his back, and gone sprawling on the floor.

And then he began to yell. Yell words that, just then, were the last things that Jones wanted to hear.

"Shoot!" he shrieked, looking up toward his standing companion. "Dear God, it's him! *Shoot!*"

The upright man hurriedly spun round . . . though, strangely, did nothing more than that . . . to face the three policemen who had by now regained their composure sufficiently to ensure that all three pistols were pointing dead straight in his direction. But that was about as far as their composure went. The wonder was that none of those three pistols had yet gone off.

"On your knees!" screamed Jones, the note of rising panic obvious in his voice. "Get down on your *knees!*"

And, to his enormous relief, the man actually did. Slowly. Awkwardly. Silently.

No one moved.

Someone had to.

Blowing out a breath and then sucking in an even larger one, Jones raised his free hand, gesturing for the other two to stay back and cover him. Then, holding his gun before him, almost as if it were a crucifix with which to fend off a vampire, he took a slow pace forward . . . another, yet more slow . . . then tentatively, nervously, reached out to pull off the man's mask.

And, ripping it away, revealed Fred Thorpe, the security guard, his eyes stretched wide with terror, his mouth stuffed full of gag.

And before any of them had time to react . . .

V had risen from the floor as swiftly as a striking cobra, all pretense now thrown aside—the real V, his hands not bound in any way behind him, but rather holding long knives.

So sharp those blades, and such a silvery glint along their edges, it was almost beautiful to see . . . until they suddenly crimsoned for a moment, and after that were never seen again.

It was over in an instant. Jones never got off a shot, being closest as he was, though his companions did. But all their bullets found was a billowing cloak swirled out around their target, confusing their aim like a bullfighter's cape: no red rag this, but simply formless shadow. And then there was no time for further shooting.

There was only time for screaming, and the noise of cracking bone, and the wicked, slicing sound of sharp knives sinking into human meat.

And falling bodies. And sightless eyes. And slowly spreading pools of thick, coagulating gore.

Poor, *bloody* infantry . . .

• • •

It was only sweat that was pouring from Finch's brow back in the studio control booth, as he watched Roger Dascombe, still somehow bathed in that glow of serenity that Finch himself was desperately wishing for, almost certainly about to bring their lives to a shattered, shredded end. And if he didn't, the clock, now rapidly nearing 0:00, quite definitely would . . . the clock and the bomb attached. How did it feel to be blown to bits? Finch didn't really know, but was rather afraid he'd soon find out. And it wasn't much comfort to think he wouldn't be alone in the discovery. Or that it would almost certainly be quick.

Two or three minutes had passed while Finch had assumed that Dascombe was examining the bomb; but then he realized he was doing nothing of the sort. He was simply using the last moments of his life for some sort of demented contemplation, until there was no time left for anything else but decisive action. And now that time had finally arrived.

"Here we go," said Dascombe coolly, and clipped a wire. A tiny noise, but in the frozen silence of the room, more than enough to make Finch jump. He blew out a nervous breath and raised a thankful glance toward heaven . . . then realized that no one else had made a move or said a word. Looking back toward Dascombe, he saw the man still down there on his knees, his eyes still fixed religiously on the clock. The clock that still continued to tick down the last few seconds with a horrid, glacial slowness.

4 . . . 3 . . . 2 . . . 1 . . .
Zero.

Nothing.

No explosion. No screams. No noise. No pain.

No death.

And then the tension broke, restoring Roger Dascombe to almost human form.

"I did it!" he exclaimed, face alight with quite another excitement now. *"I did it!"*

"Damn," muttered Finch, there seeming nothing else to say. And leaving Dascombe to his triumph, he turned away and began to push his way through the crowd at the door, some laughing, some looking nauseous, some just slumping to the ground, depending on how the stress and its relieving took them. He was sure he'd never like Dascombe, but he had to admit that, when it came to the things he sincerely thought were important, the man certainly had balls. Not much sense, perhaps, but balls. And because of Dascombe's demented foolhardiness, they'd managed to put a stop to one of their foe's relentless attacks.

"And now I've got to catch him," he added, to no one in particular.

Not far away, Evey Hammond was hurrying along the corridor toward the elevators, hoping desperately that now the fire alarms had been switched off, they would have been restored to full function as well. But not far from Fred Thorpe's still-vacant security station, she suddenly glanced up. And there, coming from the direction of the studio in silent haste, was V.

All her guts knotting up at the sight of him, Evey

ducked into a doorway and simply hid. Ridiculous as those old stories were about ostriches hiding their heads in the sand, now she could see the logic behind them after all. If it wasn't the police, it was V, and she just wanted all of them to go away. Wanted to get home and hide her head under the bedcovers, then to wake up tomorrow morning and find that everything was once again the way it had been yesterday . . . and for today, and last night, to have simply never happened.

Yes, there was something enormously attractive about V, despite that she had no idea of his looks. A sense of wildness and freedom, and the potential to be so much more than any normal person ever would . . . but at the same time that wildness, and that freedom, were terrifying. And the violence only made it worse. Especially to one who feared the world as much as she did.

So hide, then. Wait until he'd gone, and then try to slip away before he or anyone else noticed. But to know when he'd gone required risking a glance round the corner before she dared to make a move.

No, not yet. She'd guessed the timing wrong, and he had only just arrived at the elevators, reaching out to press the button and summon up a car. But when his finger was a mere inch away—

*"Freeze!"*

Dominic Stone's voice rang out first, and then the young policeman himself appeared, emerging from his hiding place behind the security desk. His gun was firmly held in a two-handed grip, and it was pointing with absolutely unerring aim directly between the masked man's eyes. And there was something in his handsome bravery that she had to admire. Or would have done, anyway, under any other circumstances. Right now, though, he was the last person she wanted to see.

"Get your hands on your head!" he shouted harshly, tension edging a voice he was, with some small success, struggling to control. "Do it now or I shoot!"

As if her previous terror weren't enough, by now Evey was thrown into a complete panic. A few seconds ago, the course of action had seemed obvious: just wait a little longer for the situation to clear, then escape. But what on earth was she going to do now? If V was arrested and the rest of the police came back here to this landing, she'd never get an elevator; probably never reach the stairwell either. Whether they got V or not, they'd still be after her as well.

And besides, if V was arrested now, things would never change. No wildness, no freedom, no potential. Just eternal Adam Sutler, and Fingermen, and terror.

And which of those alternatives was actually the more terrifying?

"I must say," V declared, a few paces away and with his hands now firmly placed behind his head, "that I'm rather astonished by the response time of London's Finest. I hadn't expected you to be so Johnny-on-the-spot."

"We were here before you even got started," Dominic told him, eyes and aim never wavering from the target, concentration never lapsing for an instant. No

point in telling him they'd come here looking for someone else entirely and that him being here had just been
a fortunate coincidence. "Bad luck, chummy."

"Oh, I don't know about that," V told him calmly,
not moving a muscle, but looking past the young policeman and farther down the corridor.

Still the gun didn't waver, nor the concentration.
Even so, Dominic couldn't prevent the images that
were rising up unbidden in his mind. *The man who
caught the terrorist.* His picture in the papers. The
television interviews. Celebrity. Promotion. Maybe
even the Police Medal, though that didn't mean as
much these days as it used to.

When the hand tapped him lightly, almost tentatively, on the shoulder, Dominic jumped so much it
was a miracle his jerking finger didn't pull the trigger;
but that much he did manage to achieve. Looking
round, though, was something he couldn't prevent.

And there was Evey, right behind him, and looking
absolutely terrified at what she was doing, the pepper
spray held up and little more than six inches from his
face. Right before his widening eyes.

And then she pressed the button.

Screaming, blinded, retching in pain and shock, he
reached out instinctively and managed to grab her
wrist, twisting the spray away before she could do
any more damage, making her yelp with the bone-
crushing tightness of his grip. And then he was spinning toward her, attacking sightlessly, swinging the
pistol like a club.

Cold metal cracked against Evey's temple and her

legs buckled, sending her collapsing to the floor just as V moved forward and dragged Dominic away from her.

No time for steel now; just instant, unarmed retribution. A straight-fingered knife-hand jabbed viciously into the policeman's solar plexus, taking his wind and doubling him over in exactly the right position for a hammerlike elbow straight down on the base of his skull.

Dominic was unconscious before his head hit the floor.

And then, for the first time in a long, long while, V stood there over the prone pair of bodies, staring down at Evey and quite uncertain what to do next.

Not long afterward, television screens across the land blinked into life once more, reappearing with a somber and obviously hurriedly constructed caption: SPECIAL EMERGENCY REPORT.

And in those same retirement homes, pubs and clubs, and middle-class family homes that, only a short while ago, had hosted V's interruption to the schedule for an audience both puzzled and enthralled, expectant viewers held their breath and wondered what they'd be getting next.

What they got was Dick, this time without June, without the viewer-friendly sofa, and definitely without the reassuring, all's-well-with-the-world smile. But with a banner logo in the corner of the screen saying CRISIS AT JORDAN TOWER.

"We are interrupting your regularly scheduled program," he began, as if the program hadn't already been interrupted, "to bring you this terrifying report of a terrorist takeover of Jordan Tower, which ended only moments ago."

All this was said with a grim and dour expression to match his tone of voice, Then a pause, just to make sure everyone had got the point: the takeover had *ended;* there was no longer any crisis; normal order was rapidly being restored. Professional as ever. And with a script written, almost instantly, by Roger Dascombe himself, who now believed that there was nothing beyond his power to do.

"A psychotic male terrorist identified only by the code letter V attacked the studios and control booth with high-powered explosives and other weapons, used against innocent, unarmed civilians, in order to broadcast a message of hate. We have just received this footage of a daring police raid."

At this point, the screen began to display an edited extract from the handheld, grainy video footage that Dascombe's crew had shot on entering the studio behind the police. Cinema verité, it looked, with its swirling fog and cacophonous volley of gunfire, its twisting, bleeding body, and its screams. And cinema verité it was, except that the cry of "Don't shoot!" had been edited out, and no one mentioned how *many* men in masks had been found in the studio, or that this one, now on life support in a nearby hospital but fading fast, was not, in fact, the right one.

No one would know about that, of course. The

main thing was to show the audience the gunshots, and the blood, and the obvious evidence that the terrorist was *dead*. Threat over. See how efficient the police and security services were. Feel safe. More to the point, heed the warning: *Don't try it, buster.* You too could end up like dead meat in the butcher's shop, the same as the masked poltroon who'd been talking all that crap a few minutes before. And getting shot dead like that, he was *lucky*.

"This is only an initial report," Dick's voice-over continued, until the camera returned to him and his now much more reassuring smile, "but at this time it is believed that during this heroic raid the terrorist was shot and killed."

And then, with just a hint of triumph and much more emphasis, as if the louder it was said, the much more obviously it would be true: "Again, from what we have been told by the authorities, the danger is now over and the terrorist is dead."

And somewhere on a hill in southeast London a little girl who could have been Evey a dozen years before, and whose parents were already suspected of being dangerously free thinkers, said precisely what she thought. And what her parents thought. And half the population of the city too.

"Bollocks!"

# SIX

Evey woke in darkness, a dull, throbbing pain in the side of her head that felt as if someone were thumping it insistently and sadistically with a rubber mallet, only to realize a little later that the throbbing was actually caused by the pumping of arterial blood through the bruised and sensitive skin where she'd been hit by the policeman's automatic. She'd always known there was a pulse there, but this was more like the crack of doom; a doom that just kept repeating itself, over and over, forever and ever. Reaching up to touch it, she found a cool, damp compress over the welt and wondered who on earth could have put it there.

With that memory of how she'd been rendered unconscious, and all that had happened before it, came first horror and then the realization that she was lying in a bed, still fully dressed. But not her own bed. Not in her own apartment.

A weak ray of light was leaking into the windowless room from a door that stood slightly ajar; a warm, candlelike glow that spilled across the bed, and, as her eyes adjusted, allowed her to take in just a little of her surroundings.

The room seemed to have no walls; or, rather, every inch of wall was hidden by bookshelves, all of them stacked horizontally so that even more volumes could be crammed into the available space. Book upon book upon book, rising up with the density of bricks so that it almost seemed that they and nothing else were supporting the low and vaulted ceiling that loomed above the bed like a stone canopy. More books than she'd ever seen, outside of a library.

And quite apart from the shelves, there were more stacks of books rising from the floor, occasionally falling back to spill in untidied chaos, like breaking waves in a vast sea of literature. And near at hand, that soft light from the door picked out a few gold-decorated spines and gave their authors' names a hallowed glow: Oscar Wilde. Radclyffe Hall. William Beckford. Banned authors, every one. Or so she had to think; some of the names, such as Pierre Louÿs, she'd never even heard of before.

Beside the light there came soft music from beyond the door. For a moment, she wasn't sure what it was, but then she remembered it from long, long ago. The sort of music she'd last heard when she was just a little girl. The kind her father liked. Blues. Black American music. Banned like the books around her.

And then she almost choked on a memory, rising up out of the past and threatening to strangle her with its sweet, cloying loveliness, of lying in bed on a Sunday morning with Teddy in her arms, warm and safe and five years old, entranced by the dust motes floating in a beam of golden sunshine, recovering from a childhood illness and smelling Mummy's roast beef and Yorkshire pudding, and Daddy's pipe smoke rising from the downstairs living room as that same song was played on an ancient hi-fi. And how Daddy always mowed the lawn on Sunday mornings, and how there was wisteria growing against the garden wall, and there was always, always sunshine.

And then she knew she was going to have to get up and find out what this was all about, before she burst into salty, melancholic tears.

Beyond the door lay a short passage that somehow reminded her of a wine cellar, leading to a larger room, more startling and more wonderful even than the bedroom book-room in which she'd awoken. But windowless, just the same.

Like some sort of storeroom from a museum or art gallery, or both combined, the place was packed with artworks from the Renaissance to the modern, from art for art's sake to the commercial, from Titian to the comic book cover. Comic books themselves as well, abused as they were, though mostly of the under-ground, political, or artistic varieties that never quite received the treatment they deserved. Still more books too, with fictions from *The Iliad* to Raymond Chandler, philosophies from Plato to Foucault, works of the now-eradicated Neo-Pagan religions, and histories by the hundreds containing tales that it seemed no one ever paid any attention to anymore.

More than this, there was all that could be saved of the popular culture, swept away by Sutler's fascist imperialism: the DVDs and videos, CDs, cassettes, and even old vinyl albums. Blues, soul, Tamla Motown. Gypsy music. Protest songs. An endless cornucopia, now tossed away like a fistful of dead roses.

Again, there were movie posters, papering the wall behind all these foreground piles: Humphrey Bogart. George Raft. James Cagney. Old gangsters never die . . . but it seemed they'd been asleep for longer than she could remember.

And in a corner, gleaming brashly with its chrome and plastic and electric lights, a 1950s jukebox, from which that same old blues came gently crooning forth.

And Evey could only stand there like Alice in Wonderland, choking up with mingled melancholy nostalgia and equal portions of delight. So many things she thought were lost; so many things preserved.

From out of the shadows, V silently emerged, capeless now, but still masked and wigged, still dressed in the same Jacobean tunic, britches, and boots.

"Oh!" yelped Evey, startled. "You scared me."

"My apologies," he said gently, a genuine concern quite obvious in his voice. "Are you feeling alright?"

"Yes, thank you," she told him warily, a little reassured by his tone but still uncertain about so many things, including his intentions. "What is this place?"

"My home," he replied, and artificial as it obviously was, there seemed to be something genuine about the smile upon the mask; or perhaps the smile was in his voice. "I call it the Shadow Gallery."

"It's beautiful." Evey turned to let her eye run over the assembled treasures once again, always spotting new things she hadn't seen before. Was that really an

Egyptian mummy case over there in the shadows, or just some movie back-lot prop? And those strange wooden carvings, like the ones she used to see in The Africa Shop before Sutler's thugs had burned the place down. Japanese woodblock prints. Buddhas. It just seemed endless. "Where did you get all this stuff?"

"Here and there," he said lightly as the blues tune came to an end, idly starting to wander round the room and taking in the display with a single, all-encompassing wave of the hand. "Much of it comes from the vaults of the Ministry of Objectionable Materials."

"You stole them?" Evey asked, wide-eyed, suddenly afraid once more. Was there nothing this man wouldn't dare? Theft, violence, terrorism . . . and here she was with him, in his headquarters, consorting with an "enemy of the state." What would they do to her if ever anyone found out?

"Heavens, no!" A gentle laugh added unexpected warmth to his voice. "Stealing implies ownership. You cannot steal from a censor. I merely *reclaimed* them."

"God, if they ever find this place—" Evey began, but didn't quite complete the thought.

"I suspect that if they do find this place," V told her, making light of the thought, "a few bits of art will be the least of my worries."

"You mean, after what you've done," replied Evey, and then all the events of the previous day came flooding back, and the floor seemed to tilt beneath her feet. "Oh, God . . ."

Suddenly all the wonderland around her didn't look anywhere near so wonderful at all, and her head, forgotten for a while in overwhelming novelty, began to throb once more.

"What have I done?" she asked, mainly to herself, a hand raised to massage her forehead, as if that would somehow make her brain work the better. "I maced a detective." A groan of despair. "Oh, no . . . why did I do that?"

"You did what you thought was right," V told her in an almost-fatherly, reassuring tone.

"No," said Evey, shaking her head in rejection. "I shouldn't have done it. I must have been out of my mind."

"Is that what you really think," he asked, and now somehow he reminded her of one of her old school-teachers, "or is that what they would want you to think?"

Actually, though, now that she thought about it, she remembered that particular schoolteacher, intriguing though he might have been, was one of the ones she couldn't really bring herself to like. The one with the harsh, uncompromising view of the world, who saw everything in black and white and had no time for comfortable moral shades of gray. Who had principles. The one who made her think too much. The agitator who would, undoubtedly, have been among the first to have had his head put in a black plastic bag. Not the bags the Finger used as blindfolds when they took you away, though God knew she was terrified enough of those. The sort of bag they put a bullet through. That prevented the brains splattering everywhere.

And then she couldn't help but feel, deep down in her bones, that the man standing before her, his true face hidden by the smiling mask, was exceptionally dangerous.

Not just to the police, the state, or the world at large . . . but to *her*, personally, as well.

"I think I should go," she said abruptly, trying to suppress a sudden feeling of panic, looking round hopefully for an exit door.

"May I ask where?" he said in a calm, calming, and oh-so-reasonable voice.

"Home," she told him, unable to think of anything else but all the safety and comfort that it represented, tawdry as it was. Strange how she'd been wanting to get out of the Paddington area for ages, to move to somewhere better; now she couldn't wait to get back there. "I have to go home."

"You know they're looking for you," he said slowly, patiently, as if he were having to explain things to a small child. "If they know where you work, they certainly know where you live."

"I have friends," said Evey desperately. "I could stay with them."

"I'm afraid that won't work either."

She'd known he was going to say that, even as she mentioned the idea. Knew, as well, that he was right. She couldn't drag her friends into this by asking for help. Or rather, she couldn't drag them in any more. Undoubtedly they would already have been pulled in for questioning, and not at all of a pleasant sort; and these days innocence was no excuse, no protection.

"I want you to understand, Evey," V continued, turning away from her now as if the words he had to speak were rather too hard to say directly to her face. "I didn't want this for either of us, but I couldn't see any other way. You were unconscious and I had to make a decision. If I'd left you, right now you'd be in one of Creedy's interrogation cells. They'd imprison you, torture you, and, in all probability, kill you in pursuit of finding me."

Evey knew that every word he said was true, but still they sounded like a death sentence. And in many ways they were, for whatever happened now, the old life she'd had was over. Irrevocably and forever.

"After what you did for me, I couldn't let that happen." V's words cut once again across her train of thought. "I picked you up and carried you to the only place I knew that you'd be safe. Here. To my home."

"I won't tell anyone," Evey pleaded, desperation giving way to terror now. "I swear. You know you can trust me—"

"I'm sorry, but I can't take that risk." He turned back to face her now that the worst had been said and everything else would only emphasize the point. "Have you ever been tortured? People say things they'd never believe they would."

Looking at her, he could read exactly what she'd do. She was so frightened and confused she'd say anything they wanted to hear at the first sign of a threat, if only it would save her. She wouldn't want to. She'd never forgive herself afterward. But her resolve would just completely collapse as soon as they started to question her.

"But I don't even know where this is," she countered, trying to convince herself that after all the things she'd already had to go through in her short and miserable life, torture couldn't be that much worse, but knowing deep down, of course, that it would be. "We could be anywhere!"

"You know it's underground. You know the color of these stones. That would be enough for a smart man."

"What are you saying?" Evey shouted, close to losing all control. "That I have to stay here forever?"

"Only until I'm done," V replied, trying to calm her down again. "After the fifth, I no longer think it will matter."

"The fifth?" she said, puzzled for a moment, until she realized what he was talking about. "You mean a year from now? I have to stay here for a *year?*"

"I'm sorry, Evey," he told her, suddenly seeming deflated in the face of her angry rejection. "I just didn't know what else to do."

"You should have left me alone!" she yelled, losing it at last, yet knowing, even as she screamed at him, that she didn't really mean it, knowing he had no other choice. "Why didn't you just *leave me alone!*"

Then, with tears blurring her vision and streaming down her face, Evey spun around and dashed from the room, back along the passage to the bedroom, which it seemed she was now going to have to think of as "home." Because it was either that or think of it as a prison; and she had no other home to go to now, or perhaps forever more.

And V, surrounded by all the treasures of the past,

all those things that made a solitary life worthwhile, could only stand and listen as the stillness of the night was rent by painful, uncomprehending sobs. And know that Evey Hammond's wasn't the only life that had changed forever.

Windowless as the Shadow Gallery was, the only indication of the coming morning was that the lights had been turned up a little more brightly. And the smell of frying eggs.

It was the eggs rather than the light that woke Evey, though if truth were told, she hadn't slept much at all anyway. And crying herself to sleep was one of those things that she'd hoped was long behind her now. Still, no matter how much pain or grief the heart and mind might bear, the stomach always has demands, quite independent, of its own. And Evey had always been prepared to get up for fried eggs.

In the Shadow Gallery's kitchen, V was smiling to himself beneath the mask, preparing what the Americans had called eggs in a basket, though, in the part of England where he'd come from, they were always called an Egyptian fish-eye sandwich. Quite why he never knew, but he treasured the picturesque name as another fine survival from the past.

Evey found him standing at the stove, the eggs starting to sizzle in the middle of the toasted bread before him, masked and dressed pretty much as usual, except for the cloak. And an apron tied around his waist, which she found at once both ridiculous and touchingly homely. A mother and a father figure, both combined.

"V?" she asked tentatively, not really certain how his mood would be after their contretemps the night before.

"Oh, good morning," he said pleasantly enough, turning round and holding the pan and spatula away from the stove a moment while he talked.

"I just wanted to apologize for my reaction last night," Evey said nervously, trying not to stumble over the speech she'd been rehearsing every time she'd woken up in the latter part of the night. "I understand what you did for me and I want you to know that I'm grateful. . . ."

And then the words just tailed off and refused to say themselves anymore as she looked, appalled, at his hands. For V, too busy with his cooking, had neglected to put on his gloves.

The skin of both hands was horribly scarred, as if from severe burn damage, and that not treated very well besides. What was left of the flesh was healed over now, but the resemblance to normal skin was marginal at best.

"Your hands?" Evey questioned softly, but there didn't seem to be anything else to add.

"Oh, yes," said V, quickly putting down the pan and grabbing his gloves from the kitchen counter nearby, turning away from her and hiding his hands as he pulled them on.

"There," he said a moment later, turning back toward her. "That's better. I hope I didn't spoil your appetite."

"No, please," Evey put in quickly, suddenly filled with a sympathy that, the previous day, she'd never have thought to feel for this strange and baffling man whose unrevealing reserve disguised almost as much as his mask. "It's just . . . are you . . . alright?"

"It's fine," he told her briefly but by no means abruptly. "Fine."

"Can I ask what happened?"

He turned his attention back to the eggs. "There was a fire." V raised his head as if looking off into the distant past. "A long time ago. Ancient history, for some. Not really very good table conversation."

And then, with little more than a mental shrug, he glanced round toward her, changing the subject. "Would you care for a cup of tea and some eggs?"

"Yes, thank you," she said eagerly, as if she thought he'd never ask. "I'm starving, actually."

With that, he nodded toward a small breakfast table and skillfully slid the eggs out of the pan onto a plate, picked up a knife and fork, and turned to set the simple feast before her.

"Please, enjoy," he said, adding, after the slightest of pauses, "I've already eaten."

Of course, she thought: to eat in her company would require taking off the mask, and there might be more than simple reasons of identification for avoiding that. And if his face was anything like his hands, did she really want to know what he looked like? But by then the eggs were hot in her mouth and there was something else to think about apart from other people's features.

"Mmm, delicious," she sighed softly, mouth full and already forking up some more.

"Good," he remarked with all the satisfaction of a chef who'd just served up an eight-course banquet.

"Oh, God," said Evey suddenly, recognition dawning of a long-forgotten taste and bringing back a flood of memories. "I haven't had real butter since I was a little girl. Where on earth did you get it from?"

"A government supply train." V's voice betrayed the smirk that obviously played about his lips. "It was on its way to Chancellor Sutler."

"You stole it from Chancellor Sutler?" Evey spluttered, almost choking on a bit of egg. Was there anything he wouldn't risk? "You're insane!"

" 'I dare do all that may become a man,' " V quoted at her sententiously, " 'who dares do more is none.' "

"*Macbeth*," Evey tossed back at him, determined not to be outdone.

"Very good," said V, casting a glance out into the Shadow Gallery, toward his favorite bust; then nodding his head a little bit, to indicate a query.

"My mum," she explained, finishing off the eggs. "She used to read his plays to me, and ever since then I've always wanted to act. Be in plays or movies. When I was nine, I played Viola in *Twelfth Night*. Mum was very proud."

A little smile played, unbidden, round her lips. Memories as sweet as that were few and far between.

"And where is your mother now?"

"She's dead."

"I'm sorry."

Evey nodded, well used to receiving this kind of sympathy; but then she was hardly alone in that. She couldn't think of anyone she knew who hadn't been touched by this sort of loss somewhere among their family or friends. She took a mouthful of tea, and they sat there for a moment, looking at each other across the table in silence, wondering what other secrets might still remain. Everyone, she knew, wore masks of one kind or another; it was just that V's was far more obvious than most.

"Can I ask you about what you said on the telly?" she said at length, although she wasn't really sure she wanted to go back over the previous day's events. But if she was going to have to live here and with him for a whole year, she needed to know what was going on. What made him tick. "Did you mean it?"

"Every word."

"You really think blowing up the Houses of Parliament is going to make this country a better place?"

"There is no certainty. Only opportunity."

Aphorisms and quotations. They seemed to make up half his conversation, Evey thought; maybe even more. Sometimes she was impressed, though probably not as impressed as he thought she ought to be; at other times she just found it downright annoying. Was he really just a know-all with a photographic memory? Or was his manner of speaking just another mask, to hide his real self? Or was he, as had occurred to her on the first night they'd met, actually some sort of lunatic? Well, the only way to find out about that real self would be to keep him talking, and to listen to the bits that weren't just learned recitation.

"I think you can be pretty certain that if anyone does show up to join in," she said a moment later, "Creedy'll black-bag every one of them."

"People should not be afraid of their government," he said, slipping back into his teaching mode. "Governments should be afraid of their people."

"And you're going to make that happen by blowing up a building?" she asked, rising to the challenge now.

"The building is a symbol," said the man whose face was nothing more than that besides, "as is the act of destroying it. Symbols are given power by people. Alone, a symbol is meaningless, but with enough people involved as well, blowing up a building can change the world."

"I wish I believed that was possible." Evey put down the empty teacup. "I really do. But every time I've seen this world change, it's always been for the worse."

She stood up then, adding, "Thanks for the eggs."

And with that she walked away and headed back to her room, leaving V still sitting there at the table, the expression on his mask as enigmatic as ever.

"Right there. What's he thinking?" asked Chief Inspector Finch, more to himself than Dominic, even though the younger man sat there right beside him. Both of them were staring intently at a small monitor showing security-camera footage from the Jordan Tower fiasco of the previous day, from one of the few cameras that the terrorist had somehow neglected to disable on his way in. Looking with total concentration at V standing contemplatively over the unconscious bodies of Evey and Dominic, sprawling at his feet. "Is he considering leaving her? After she just saved him?"

"He's a terrorist. You can't expect him to act like you or me," Dominic said shortly, still red-eyed and raising a hand to feel the bruising at the back of his neck. Understanding the man wasn't his major priority at the moment, just catching him. Catching him and getting him alone in a cell where he could kick nine kinds of living shit out of the bastard. And as for the girl . . . well, Dominic wasn't the kind who'd normally go around beating up women, but for women with pepper sprays he was prepared to make an exception.

On the monitor, V finally bent down and scooped Evey up in his arms.

"Some part of him is human," Finch pointed out. "And for better or worse, she's stuck with him."

Watching V carry Evey to the elevator one more time—and he couldn't remember how many times he'd watched the masked man do the same before—Finch finally turned the monitor off and swiveled his chair round to face Dominic, noticing the folder his assistant had brought when he'd come over to join him. "You got anything else on her parents?"

"Yeah." Dominic spread papers on the desk. "And it's not good. They were both interned at Belmarsh."

"Oh, no," groaned Finch. The same old story again. How many thousands had disappeared—good people for the most part, he was sure—just because they'd disagreed with the Party policy line or protested at the takeover? How many families had been broken up while they were establishing the New Order?

Still, there'd been worse places than Belmarsh, he knew. Belmarsh was just where they took the "politicals"; there'd been other, fouler hells during the Reclamation, for the "degenerates," the "immigrants," the "heretics," and all the other labels they'd used to dehumanize the victims. How easy it was to forget that one was dealing with real people when they just became categories, to be sorted, filed, and then forgotten when they'd been "removed from the records." It was still going on to this day. After all, nobody in the media or the government news releases spoke of this "V" as a man, as someone who might have feelings, a family, a history: he was just "the terrorist."

Of course, of all the "categories" who'd been "dealt with" in the Reclamation, it had been the politicals who'd been the most troublesome, who'd put up the most resistance.

"Yeah," Dominic continued, a little more sympathy in his voice now that the subject had changed away from his particular bête noire and back to Evey's parents. "She died during the hunger strike and he copped it when the military retook the shed."

"That's terrible."

"That's not the worst of it. Her brother was at St. Mary's."

"Christ."

"Nothing but bad luck there," the younger man concluded, with a shrug that implied "But what could anyone do?"

"So we know her story. Now we need his."

# SEVEN

To say that Lewis Prothero had an apartment worthy of a man in his position would be something of an understatement. The penthouse overlooking the Thames was more of a *monument* to a man in his position. Or more to the point, a cathedral raised entirely in celebration of its owner. Lewis Prothero is God, it said; there is no other God but He. And this is where Lewis Prothero retires at night, for worship of Himself.

The large and lavish bathroom reflected this no less than any of the other rooms. Indeed, right then, it reflected nothing but Lewis Prothero, for his face and robed figure were to be seen looking back from gleaming mirrors all around the room; and where there were no mirrors, monitors projected from the walls instead, each screen wired back to a central video unit that was repeating the evening's earlier *Voice of London* broadcast on a continuous loop.

Somehow, then, the bathroom became a vast kaleidoscope, combining past and present, audio and visual . . . a myriad starry aspects of the divine Lewis Prothero, too wonderful for simple words ever to quite express.

What more could a man wish to contemplate,

stripped naked and leaving behind all the dross of the everyday world, than himself, the star and marvel of his age?

And what better voice to provide accompaniment to his own than, again, his own?

"I'll tell you what I know!" the Prothero of the monitor was shouting to the London mob; and Prothero of the bathroom joined in: "I know this is not a man!"

The broadcast was, naturally, about that stupid terrorist who'd almost managed to blow up the studio; almost taken the great Lewis Prothero off the air. A mask-wearing clown, he thought, that's all he was.

"A *man* does not wear a mask!" cried television Prothero, as his living counterpart flipped open a mirrored cabinet to reveal row upon row of prescription medicine bottles, for none of which he had any legal prescription at all.

"What is he?" cried Prothero, sorting out his drug list for the evening.

"A *man* does not threaten innocent civilians!" the tape continued.

"What is he?" Prothero threw back the feed line again, now with better timing.

"I'll *tell* you what he is!" the monitor responded with precision. "What every gutless, freedom-hating terrorist is . . . a goddamned *coward!*"

Strange how they always wrote that line for him to say, he thought, even when he was talking about suicide bombers, who dared far more than even he, the heroic Lewis Prothero, would do. After all, he might *say* whatever was necessary in defense of what he believed in, but to actually *die* for it . . . no, thank you very much. He was officer class, and they had cannon fodder for that sort of thing. Still, calling other people cowards had never affected his ratings, and those were far more important than anything else.

As the "audience" broke out into "spontaneous applause" just as they always did, Prothero paused to gobble a handful of pills, chasing down the cocktail with half a tumbler of Scotch. Ah, yes, that should do it.

Before he could take another swig, the phone began to ring.

Using the remote to pause the tape, Prothero picked up the handset and listened for a moment. That prancing, self-important little piece of shit Roger Dascombe. Just because Dascombe attended Cabinet meetings (and that was unjust in itself; it was quite obvious that Prothero himself was the only person fit to talk to Sutler on behalf of the Mouth . . . no, actually, he should be telling *Sutler* what to do, not receiving instruction from on high) and just because he dressed up like a nonce . . . and what was this drivel he was talking about now? Oh, *that* again.

"There will be no negotiation, Roger," he said flatly, disregarding that Dascombe was nominally his boss. "When I come in tomorrow, the Paddy will be gone. I'm looking at the tape right now and he has no idea how to light me. My nose looks like Big fucking Ben."

Dascombe began to whine, but Prothero was no longer listening, instead carefully checking his nose in the mirror against the one on the monitor. Definitely the thick Irishman's fault.

"Listen to me, you bleeding sod!" Prothero cut in. "England prevails because I say it does! And every lazy sod on this show is there because *I* say he is . . . and that includes you. Find another director of photography, or find yourself another job!"

That told him, Prothero thought, clicking off the phone. Then, picking up the remote and setting *The Voice of London* rolling again, he headed for the shower.

Dascombe. The terrorist. Everybody. Fuck them all.

"I'll tell you what I wish," the taped voice came again, more brash, more bully-boyish by the moment, as Prothero turned on the faucet. "I wish I'd been there. I wish I'd had the chance for a face-to-face . . . just one chance, that's all I'd need . . ."

And as the shower began to stream, down in the lobby the elevator doors opened with a faint, mechanical ding, while a black-gloved hand swiped an ID through the security panel. An ID with a familiar name and face, though not the one belonging to the hand: Evey Hammond's.

Prothero, of course, knew none of this, sluicing down his well-rounded form in the enormous shower while watching none other than himself upon a waterproof monitor, placed there specially for the purpose.

"This so-called V," his voice re-echoed, "along with his accomplice, Evey Hammond . . . neodemagogues, spouting their message of hate . . ."

Nice delivery that, he thought, as clouds of thick

steam rose around him, coagulating like ectoplasm. But Prothero was wrapped up in far more than that by now. He was wrapped up in himself.

"A delusional and aberrant voice," said his television self.

"Aberrant and abhorrent," he chimed in, embroidering on the theme. Ought to be writing his own scripts, obviously, as well as doing everything else.

"Delivering a terrorist's ultimatum!"

*"Treason!"* cried Prothero, taking the audience's part, responding to himself.

"An ultimatum that was met with swift, surgically precise justice!"

*"No mercy!"*

"And the moral of this story, ladies and gentlemen?" his electronic persona asked, dropping now into a calm, reassuring voice that sought to put all the troubles of the past few days behind them.

Prothero, smiling and winking to his own reflection as he stepped out of the shower, didn't wait for the recording, but delivered the punch line on his own.

"Good guys win, bad guys lose, and, as always, *England prevails!*"

And as the tape re-echoed that triumphant declaration, he clicked off the monitors, watching that much-loved image of himself fade to gray . . .

And saw another face reflected in their glass. And in the mirrors.

A bone-white smile. A fixed, mustachioed grin, hideous in its implication.

A mask.

Partly shaded beneath a broad-brim hat, mounted on black-caped shoulders; a combination of the Puritan and the joker, an image of the grinning night.

A seventeenth-century incarnation of the Grim Reaper, come back to haunt the twenty-first.

V.

"Holy Christ!" cried Prothero, half a shout of terror, half a gasp of despair. As he spun round to face the intruder, his foot slipped on the slick marble floor, his legs collapsed, and all those extra pounds of flesh accrued through years of increasingly good living slapped down wetly at V's feet. He lay there for an instant, gasping for breath like a beached whale as the sobering adrenaline pumped through his veins; then looked up terrified at his uninvited, most unwelcome guest.

"Good evening, Commander Prothero," said V calmly, though rather less than pleasantly, looking down at him as if he were some pinned and wriggling insect, awaiting examination. Or dissection.

"Oh my God!" groaned Prothero, suddenly and desperately hoping that there might be another deity beside himself. "How did you get in here?"

Disdaining to reply, V seemed to be giving him a moment to recover from his panic before commencing with the evening's entertainment. And Prothero, still looking to retain some scrap of dignity despite his terror, took advantage of the pause to scramble away and grab a bath towel. The phone on which he'd been speaking to Dascombe earlier, however, seemed too far away to reach.

"Don't worry," V told him, following the direction

of his glance, "I've made sure our reunion won't be disturbed by any annoying late-night phone calls, Commander."

"Stop that!" snapped Prothero, annoyance mingling with his confusion. And something a little more than annoyance. "Why do you keep calling me that?"

"That *was* your title, remember?" V stepped closer, looming over him like the shadow of impending death. "When we first met, all those years ago."

Cooling droplets of shower water now began to mingle on Prothero's quaking flesh with even colder sweat.

"You wore a uniform in those days," said V, a sudden hardness edging his voice. "You looked very good in it."

And then the images began to come back. Not video footage this time . . . *no one* saw any footage from those days anymore . . . but memories, emerging from their long-suppressed hiding place in Prothero's dank and rank unconscious.

Larkhill Resettlement Camp.

Latest in a long line of venerable institutions— after all, the very concept of the concentration camp was a British invention, dating back to the Boer War— picked up by others, with enthusiasm . . . Auschwitz, Dachau, the Gulags, Guantánamo Bay . . . Larkhill . . .

Not that anyone called them concentration camps after the Second World War, of course. They were "detention centers" or "resettlement camps."

Different names. Same nasty institutions.

The razor-wire fences. The watchtowers and

searchlights. The brutes in boots with the soulless faces and the automatic weapons. The doctors with the scalpels, not bothering with anesthetics.

The wire cages where the naked prisoners huddled together, regardless of their sex or age (don't call them human beings; don't even bother with their names; the numbers forcibly tattooed upon their skin were surely quite enough), unwashed and wallowing in their own filth and praying to their varied gods. Not *the* God, for, as everybody knew, the true God was an Englishman and had no time for Johnny Foreigner.

The punishment beatings. The sexual abuse and humiliations. The photographs to laugh over in the officers' mess afterward. The torture rooms. The executions.

The cremation ovens.

And, yes, the human skin lampshades that one of the guards had made. A joke, he said, to keep up the old traditions. Besides, anything Hermann the German could do, be sure that Tommy Atkins could do far better. Of course the man had been disciplined for that, but all that meant was transfer to another camp, where he probably did the same sort of thing all over again. Being a psychopathic sadist wasn't the problem; quite the reverse. As they always used to joke in the mess, with the jobs they did, camp guards needed to be more than a touch pathological to stay sane. It was just that this one had got a mite . . . frolicsome.

And there, bestriding his world like a colossus . . . his little hell on earth and kingdom of his own . . . Commander Lewis Prothero. So fine in his perfectly tailored uniform (and tailored then to fit a rather leaner and more muscular body, the sort the ladies liked; or so he told himself, but perhaps it was just the power), his mirror-polished boots, his horsewhip. His first delusions of grandeur—delusory in that his notions of his own grandeur had simply been far too humiliatingly modest—before he rose to the godhead that only television could bestow.

Strolling along the bloodstained and ceramic-tiled floors in that special block, the one that only the top brass were shown. But only after the floors had been sluiced clean so he didn't soil his boots.

The cells where the experiments were . . .

Or at least the ones who'd survived the ordinary horrors of the medical block.

The experiments. One particular experiment.

"You . . . ?" gasped Prothero, terror almost freezing the word upon his lips.

A final image then, from when it had all come to an end. A faceless silhouette against a howling inferno of flame, stalking his nightmares to a sound track of explosions and screaming men. The heart of the darkness that had haunted him ever since.

The horror. The horror . . .

"It *is* you," said Prothero flatly, finally, knowing there was nothing more to be done, and nothing more to say.

Not wet ceramic tiles beneath him now, but marble. Not bloodstained. Yet.

"The ghost of Christmas past," said the voice behind the mask.

And then the figure stepped forward, became silhouetted against the bathroom lights.

Became as black as death itself . . .

Across town in Lambeth, south of the Thames, a phone began to ring in a night-darkened apartment. Nothing here of the overblown grandeur of Prothero's place; this was a small studio flat suited to a man living alone, a man who'd lost his family long ago and whose existence, as a consequence, was little more now than work. With his salary, the occupant could have afforded something better, but all he really needed was a place to sleep that was close enough, when the fuel shortages got bad, for him to leave the car behind and walk to work. Or at least a place to sleep when he was allowed to. Some time passed before the figure in the bedroom stirred, fumbling in the dark and cursing under his breath, then finally flipped on the light and reached out for the handset.

"Yeah?" said Eric Finch, barely awake, eyes half-open, completely unaware of the time but knowing that this was not the time for routine calls.

"Finch!" a panic-stricken voice bleated in his ear. "It's Dascombe."

"Dascombe?" queried Finch uncomprehendingly. Why was that slimy little prat phoning him in the middle of the night? "What—?"

"I've already called the Chancellor," Dascombe cut in hurriedly, almost tripping over himself in his desperate urgency to get the words out. "We have to get control of the situation."

Finch couldn't figure this out at all. He had no idea what Dascombe was talking about, and more than that, he'd never heard him in such a state before. Rubbing the sleep from his eyes with a knuckle, he asked: "What situation?"

Half an hour later, and still waiting for forensics to arrive, Finch and Dascombe stood side by side in Prothero's bathroom, looking down at the former star's lifeless, naked body. Cold and paling as the blood, no longer pumping against the pull of gravity, sank down toward the floor, his was a two-tone corpse, white above and pink beneath. No knife wounds on this corpse to let the blood escape, no messy human meat exposed to view; a "clean" death, as far as murders ever went.

By the body sat a single floribunda rose, petals open in full bloom, salmon pink but blending into cream and yellow.

And looking round the gilded palace of sin that was Lewis Prothero's bathroom, Finch was sure as hell that the man who'd been the Voice of London wasn't the type to put it there. Jesus Christ, what sort of life was the man living anyway? The bathroom was bad enough, but the other rooms . . .

"Chancellor Sutler agreed, for obvious reasons," Dascombe cut across his train of thought, "that we have to keep this discreet, Inspector. Cast in the wrong light, the loss of the Voice of London could be devastating to our credibility. You understand?"

Finch understood alright. No thought of the man who was dead, of the man who'd killed him, or of bringing the murderer to justice. Bloody media people. Let's just cover our arses and get out of this mess with our jobs and pay packets and status still intact. Looking good and smelling of roses, like the one here on the floor.

Unfeeling bastard.

Roses. This one obviously had some significance, though right now Finch had no idea what. He knelt down to look at it more closely. Not a familiar color, but then flowers weren't his forte anyway. He'd need to find someone who could tell him more about it.

"Perhaps a stroke?" Dascombe continued, merely thinking aloud now, as he realized that Finch wasn't going to give him any audience feedback. "No, no, too horrific. A quiet, dignified death in his sleep."

Not that there was anything dignified about being poisoned, Finch thought, glancing back at the green foam that had bubbled from Prothero's nose and mouth, at the empty eyes staring fixedly at the ceiling. No mirrors up there, Finch thought. But then Prothero obviously never thought he'd end up lying on his back with poison eating into his nerves and brain, unable to see himself in the last few seconds before he was unable to see anything at all.

With that green gunk coming out of his nostrils, he probably wouldn't have wanted to see himself anyway.

Footsteps clicking on the marble floor attracted

Finch's attention. He looked up to see Dominic enter the room, pause to glance around, a little bleary-eyed, in bewildered disbelief at the sybaritic luxury all around, then come over to join him. He too looked down at the body for a moment. Not a pretty sight, but young in the service as he was, he'd quickly become used to seeing a large variety of corpses. Especially in days like these.

"Got any eyes or ears on this one?" Finch asked him, rising once again to his feet.

"Camco's were cut," Dominic replied. "Same MO as before. But we've got an elevator log ID."

"Let me guess," Finch remarked wearily, already knowing the answer as well as his assistant.

"She's in deep, Inspector," Dominic confirmed.

# EIGHT

Terror. The old terror, the one she tried to suppress, the one she hated to think about and mostly didn't dare. The one where she woke shortly before dawn . . . and heard . . .

Was she back there now? Was the old terror repeating itself? Or was this a new one?

Whatever it was, Evey woke to the sound of a violent struggle, as she'd done so long ago. And that wasn't the only terrifying part. The predawn violence was bad enough, but it was always, she knew, the precursor to a chain of events that grew more terrible still. But surely that couldn't be happening here. Not again. Not here, in V's underground home. Not unless . . .

Unless someone had discovered the location of the Shadow Gallery.

"V?" she called quietly, hardly daring to shout in case it gave her position away. The noise continued, but then she realized there'd been nothing like the barking report of gunfire. Only the clash of metal, the sound of stamping feet, and shouting.

Slightly reassured, but still nervous, Evey tumbled

out of bed, hastily pulled on a robe, and then silently and cautiously made her way along the passage to the Shadow Gallery's poster-littered living area.

Creeping into a gloomy corner of the hall, she looked . . . and felt her jaw drop in astonishment.

For there was V, his cloak thrown back over his shoulders, wielding a rapier in one hand, leaping and stamping as if in a deadly duel, cutting, parrying, and lunging toward a hopelessly overmatched opponent. A stationary suit of armor.

Had he gone completely mad? The previous day she'd thought him dangerous, but that sort of threat receded into nothingness compared with this completely uncontrolled behavior.

But then she realized that, actually, he wasn't entirely alone. Or, at least, not entirely unaccompanied.

On a television set behind him, an old black-and-white movie was playing. A swashbuckler that looked as if it went back to the 1930s, with a dashing hero also fencing for his life, and more besides: for love. And V was mimicking all the hero's moves in perfect synchronization, and speaking his lines as well—words he quite obviously knew by heart.

With a last flurry of clicking, metallic blows, he finally vanquished the helpless suit of armor and sent its helmet crashing to the floor. Evey could only smile to herself at the complete and absolute commitment of his lunacy.

As the echoes of the tumbled helmet eventually faded into silence, he realized he was being watched.

"Oh . . . ," said V quietly, quickly adjusting his

mask, though whether that was to make sure his identity or his embarrassment was covered, she couldn't tell.

"I'm sorry," he continued. "I hope I didn't wake you."

"No," she told him, though that wasn't quite the truth. "I just thought you were fighting . . . I mean, fighting for real . . ."

Whether there was concern in her words for him, for herself, or for the both of them was something neither of them could quite decide. Leaving the question hanging, V turned and gestured toward the TV set, using the rapier to do so.

"It's my favorite film. *The Count of Monte Cristo*, with Robert Donat as Edmond Dantès. It gets me every time."

"I've never seen it." After all, it must have been made at least fifty years before Evey was even born, and now that there were far fewer TV channels than when she was a little girl, it wasn't surprising she hadn't come across it.

"Really?" asked V. Then, with a rather charming eagerness: "Would you like to?"

"Does it have a happy ending?" she asked tentatively, feeling somehow that, after all she'd been through in the last few days, happy endings were now the most important things in the world.

"The Count finally finds peace in the arms of the beautiful Mercédès," he assured her.

"A happy ending?" she asked again, still not quite certain what "finding peace" might imply.

"As only celluloid can deliver."

"Okay," she said, smiling with just a little relief. Then, looking at what he still held in his hand and remembering how carried away he'd been a few moments before, she added, "But put the sword away."

Finch had returned to his desk at New Scotland Yard and begun to drain a steady succession of coffee cups. He ought to be used to losing sleep after all these years on the force, but on balance the older he got, the harder it got to take. And in spite of the continuing "law and order" clampdown by Creedy and his goons, the sort of crime that ordinary coppers had to deal with didn't seem to be going down at all. The more you took away the things that were important in people's lives, he guessed, such as liberty and freedom of movement, the more desperate they became. And desperate people didn't worry about what was right or wrong, only what they could get away with.

He looked up then from the computer monitor, where facts and figures were blurring into meaningless symbols before his aching eyes, as Dominic came into the office, flicking through a sheaf of printouts.

"Forensics just wrapped things up," the young detective told him. "No prints, no hair, no fibers. The guy is like a ghost. But you wouldn't believe the shit they found in Prothero."

"Drugs?"

"Could've started his own hospital."

"Interesting," Finch beckoned him over.

"Why?" asked Dominic, coming round to join him behind the desk. Finch indicated the monitor, where the meaningless symbols he'd been looking at a moment earlier now began to make a little more sense.

"Did you know that Lewis Prothero was one of the richest men in the country before he became 'The Voice of London'?"

"Drugs?" Dominic's eyes lit up as they always did when there was even the slightest hint of a hot lead.

"Legal ones," Finch said. "A major stockholder in Viadox Pharmaceutical."

"Whoa . . . ," breathed Dominic as the link snapped into place. "Viadox and St. Mary's in less than a week. Coincidence?"

Finch shook his head, the faintest of smiles upon his face; *his* usual reaction to a hot lead. "When you've been at this as long as I have, you stop believing in them."


In the black-and-white world of the TV screen, which had somehow had all the color of magic to Evey for a couple of hours, the final romantic swell of music was coming up, with Edmond Dantès, the Count of Monte Cristo himself, nestled in the tree of happiness with Mercédès de Rosas.

"Find your own tree," he addressed a final remark to the viewer, and as "The End" came up, Evey could only sniff. They certainly didn't make them like that anymore, and she didn't care if that was a cliché.

"Did you like it?" asked V, looking round for the remote.

"Yeah." To simply sit in safety on a comfortable couch and watch a movie, after the last few days that she'd been having, was a pleasure in itself. "But it made me feel sorry for Mercédès."

"Why?"

"Because he cared more about revenge than he did about her."

V nodded, as if this was an acceptable female point of view but not one that carried a great deal of weight with him, and clicked off the DVD player. BTN's regular news programming reappeared on the screen.

And June, far more serious than usual (though it had to be admitted that, in the last few days, serious-faced newsreaders were becoming more and more the norm), was making yet another grave announcement.

"Fans nationwide have been devastated as news of the most popular . . ."

V started to reach out to turn off the set, but Evey put a hand on his arm. "Wait. What's this?"

". . . most awarded stars in the history of the BTN," continued the familiar face and voice, "a man known to the entire nation as The Voice of London, passed away late last night from apparent heart failure."

A black-bordered photo of Lewis Prothero appeared next on the screen.

"She's lying," Evey said flatly, her conviction absolute.

"How do you know?" asked V, though obviously he knew well enough that she was.

"She always blinks a lot when she does a story that she knows is false," Evey told him softly, still trying to concentrate on the words of the announcement.

"An extraordinary talent, he had dedicated his life to his country and his beliefs, working tirelessly at his profession. It came as no surprise to those who knew him that his body was found at his office where he often worked long hours after everyone else had gone home. Lewis, you will be sorely missed."

Evey could feel her hackles rising as V reached out to turn off the television. Something about all this just didn't seem right. So many things had happened in the last few days, and she couldn't quite put her finger on how they connected up. Except that, she began to suspect, they all linked back to V.

And then she became aware that he was silently watching her, the mask's expression as unreadable as ever.

"V," she began hesitantly, hardly wanting to bring up the subject, as she didn't know where it would lead. "Yesterday I couldn't find my ID."

Still he sat there, regarding her in enigmatic silence.

"You didn't take it, did you?" she asked nervously, dreading the answer as soon as she asked the question. She found she couldn't quite sit still, and the couch that had seemed so comfortable a few minutes before was starting to feel more like a bed of nails.

"Would you prefer a lie or the truth?" he asked her in a neutral voice, suggestive of nothing but making the answer absolutely clear.

"Oh my God," gasped Evey, jumping up from the couch and staring down at him in shocked disbelief. "Did you have anything to do with . . . that?"

A gesture toward the TV set made it quite plain what the *that* she was referring to was.

"Yes," he told her calmly. "I killed him."

"You—?" Evey didn't believe she was hearing this; yet at the same time, she knew, she had to believe she was. "Oh, God!"

"You're upset." V quite plainly stated the obvious. One of those facile pieces of phrasing that suggested he thought that acknowledging she was upset might somehow calm her down. Unfortunately, it had quite the opposite effect.

"I'm upset!" she cried, trying to fight down a growing sense of near-hysterical panic. "You just said you killed Lewis Prothero! *Lewis Prothero!*"

"I might have killed the Fingermen that attacked you too." He inclined his head in what she'd come to recognize as a gesture of inquiry. Usually uncomfortable inquiry. "But did I hear any objection then?"

"What?" She almost choked on the word, suddenly taken aback. Why was he suddenly changing the subject?

Or . . . *was* he changing the subject?

"Violence can be used for a higher purpose."

Here it came again, that sense of being tutored in unpleasant truths. She took a couple of paces backward, suddenly nervous. "What are you talking about?"

"Justice."

"Oh." Evey paused as she thought of the movie they'd just watched. Of the injustice done to Edmond Dantès, of the illegal imprisonment in the Château d'If, and, although she had no liking for the principle of revenge, of the admittedly justified payback his enemies had finally received. And how, in the end, yes, she *had* thought there was a happy ending.

"I see," she breathed softly, understanding but still wishing to sound noncommittal. At times V's view of the world was just too raw and uncompromising, too hard for her to take.

"There is no court in this country for men like Prothero," V told her, though he didn't actually tell her what the crime had been that merited such final and fatal retribution.

"Are you going to . . ." A pause. A deep breath. A question she didn't really want to ask: ". . . kill more people?"

It hardly seemed necessary to answer, but he nodded anyway.

"Are you going to kill me?" The question just slipped out.

"Of course not, Evey." He rose to his feet and started toward her, almost as if he wanted to take her in his arms and reassure her. But then, of course, he would say that, whether he intended to or not.

"No, don't," she said, backing off a pace to match the one he'd taken toward her. Then, turning away in a gesture that effectively ended the conversation, she said, "I think I should go back to my room now."

• • •

Finch, meanwhile, hadn't left his room at all; hadn't left his desk; hadn't left that same screen where he was dredging through the Nose's data-retrieval system.

"Take a look at this," he said, summoning Dominic, who'd been doing much the same. "Prothero's military record. What do you see?"

Dominic leaned forward, squinting at the screen. "Hmm . . . Iraq, Kurdistan, Syria before and after. Sudan. Busy boy."

"Yeah." Finch swigged coffee. "But after all that, they put him in charge of a detention facility at Larkhill."

"No good deed goes unpunished," put in Dominic contemplatively.

"Right," agreed Finch, though he silently added to himself, "or bad deed unrewarded." Though he found it hard to think what the reward might have been in a place like Larkhill. Maybe Dominic was right; maybe it was some misdemeanor that had got Prothero sent there. But that wasn't what his instincts said. So maybe Larkhill had been more important than it first appeared.

"You think there's a connection between Larkhill and our boy?" asked Dominic after a few seconds' thought.

"It might explain the connection between him and the Hammond girl," Finch replied, though he recalled that the girl's parents had been sent to Belmarsh, rather than Larkhill. Still, detention camps were detention camps. But maybe it wasn't the camps that were the connection. It was Viadox who'd come up with the cure for the St. Mary's virus, and Prothero was a major shareholder in Viadox . . . and in charge of Larkhill. And V had killed Prothero. No, it all went round in circles somehow and didn't quite add up. But the name *Larkhill* was eating into his gut now, and he knew he was going to have to find out more. Such a pleasant-sounding name, redolent of birdsong and woodland and rolling English countryside. But then people probably used to think that Belsen was a nice place name before they built a concentration camp there. Larkhill . . .

"Problem is," he added, "I can't find any other record of the place."

They looked at each for a few seconds, but, as Finch had suspected all along, Dominic didn't surprise him with a brilliant idea. Instead, the expression on his face just said, "What do we do next?"

Sometimes the boy was *such* a disappointment, thought Finch ruefully, smiling slightly to himself. But, no, that wasn't really true. He had no more right to expect Dominic to suddenly solve things for him than he did the Almighty. And in the last forty years, the Almighty hadn't come through once. Yet . . .

It was just that, unfortunately, Finch knew exactly what they had to do next, and he was absolutely sure it was going to be absolutely futile. But they had to go through the procedures anyway. Sighing, he got slowly to his feet and started toward the door, gesturing for the young man to follow. At least the journey he had in mind probably wouldn't take long enough to give Dominic time to kill them.

STEVE MOORE

A couple of hours later, Finch's frustration was starting to approach boiling point. He'd had quite enough of dead ends and stonewalling, as he'd also had enough of traipsing along what seemed to be end-less miles of corridor on his redirected way from one filing clerk to another, and now here he was sitting in an office at the Department of Military Records in the Ministry of Defence; the office of, he'd been told, "the man who'd been there." The man in charge. Who'd be "just the blighter" to sort out the problem for him.

Fat fucking chance.

Major Wilson had some of that same military pom-posity that the unlamented Lewis Prothero had had, though he still had the form and style to carry it off convincingly. An officer and a gentleman. Sitting there behind his desk with his back ramrod straight (and probably all the straighter in response to Finch's bat-tered, weary slouch), he obviously had no time for civil-ian interference. Damnation! If this was what a career policeman looked like, he'd show him what it was like to go up against a career military man. Damned nosy bastard anyway. And the boy with him looked as if he could do with six months' worth of square-bashing to knock him into shape. Young puppy had actually had the damn nerve to ask him a direct question a couple of minutes ago. Shouldn't be allowed.

"Larkhill?" Wilson queried, military bluster min-gling with an apparent desire to help as Finch brought up the name yet again. "Larkhill? I don't recall that particular facility, Inspector, but of course you're wel-come to review our records."

"We've been through your records, Major," Finch said through gritted teeth, struggling with no great success to maintain a dignified calm. "All they say is that there was a detention facility at Larkhill, approximately ten miles north of Salisbury."

"Well, then, there you have it," Wilson said smugly. That'd show these civilian johnnies. Military records. Absolutely reliable. At New Scotland Yard they probably couldn't tell the difference between a criminal record and a laundry list. If they could find either.

Finch sighed and rubbed his forehead wearily, looking up at Wilson's completely false, but oh-so-helpful, oh-so-condescending smile. And the bastard hadn't even offered them a cup of coffee.

"This is a matter of some urgency, Major Wilson," he said with exaggerated patience, determined that he wasn't going to fall into that old English routine where, if someone didn't seem to understand what you were saying, you simply repeated it louder and louder until he did. "We need to know if there was anything different about this facility."

"I'm sorry, Inspector," came the supercilious reply, "but I really cannot remember."

"Was there a specific profile for those being sent there?" Finch probed doggedly, exasperatedly.

"Usual undesirables, I should think."

"But do you *know*?"

"Of course not," snapped Wilson, his own patience starting to wear thin. A breath to regain his composure; couldn't let these damned civilians get under his skin. "I wasn't stationed there myself."

"Do you know who was?" Like a dog worrying a bone, Finch wouldn't let it go.

"I cannot recall any specific names," Wilson stone-walled again. "But if you look through our records—"

"Your records are either deleted, omitted, or missing," growled Finch, voice rising, patience finally exhausted. "As you were the head of the Detention Programme at that time—"

"Before you go any further, Inspector," Wilson barked back, face starting to flush with anger, "let me remind you that things were very chaotic back then."

Finch groaned inwardly, while Dominic looked on in helpless frustration. How many times had they heard that line already this morning?

"Right now we don't have the problems we had back then," Wilson continued flatly. "We all did what we had to do, and under the circumstances we did the best we could."

Then, finally, shortly, and in the act of rising to his feet: "And that's all I have to say about that."

A couple of paces round the desk, a hand gesturing toward the door, a tight-lipped expression, and silence. That really *was* all that Wilson had to say.

Wearily, frustratedly, Finch shrugged and got to his feet, accompanied by Dominic; saying nothing, but giving Wilson a contemptuous glare that all too eloquently said, "Roast in hell, you pompous bastard." And left.

An officer and a gentleman.

Fuck off and die.

# NINE

"**Y**ou can do this," Evey said to herself, taking a deep breath and looking down at the small piece of paper she had clutched in her hand. The same piece of paper with the address written on it that she'd taken from its place in the frame of her makeup mirror, the night that all this had started. The night that had changed her life.

Funny how you held on to things like that, even when everything else had descended into complete chaos.

Well, if she was going to do it, it was time to make a start. Time to overcome that feeling of nervousness that, she knew, was only the surface symptom of an underlying dread she'd always felt: a fear of the world and all its parts. But sometimes that fear just had to be overcome, if only for a little while. Getting up off the bed, she left the room that had become "hers" and returned along the passage to rejoin V. She found him sitting quietly, listening to soft music, masked and inscrutable as ever.

"Hello," she said tentatively, not even sure if he was actually awake behind that mask. And if he wasn't, was this the opportunity for one of those *Phantom of the Opera* moments? The unmasking . . . the hideous face . . . the horror? No, when she started to think of the possible consequences, it didn't seem like a good idea at all. And anyway, the nod of greeting he gave her showed he wasn't asleep at all.

"I've been thinking," she said hesitantly, sitting down on the couch and looking toward him like an actress not quite sure of her next line. "I want to ask you something, but I don't think you'll understand why unless you know a few things about me."

Another nod from V, and now he sat up straighter, quite obviously giving her his full attention. That, at least, was encouraging; but still she found herself picking nervously at a thread on the couch. What she wanted to tell him brought back unpleasant memories that she preferred not to think about. The past—her own past particularly—didn't make for idle conversation.

"My father was a writer," she continued after a deep breath. After all, he'd been so dear to her, with his unruly hair and glasses, his gangling frame and lopsided smile, that since he'd been . . . gone . . . it was always painful to even think of him, let alone talk about him. "You would have liked him. He used to say that artists used lies to tell the truth, while politicians used them to cover the truth up."

"A man after my own heart," V remarked briefly, softly.

"He always told the best stories until . . ." A pause. Another deep breath. "Until my brother died. That was when everything changed. My brother was one of the pupils at St. Mary's."

And then the memories really did come back, with an overwhelming power. Memories so poignant they almost made her weep now, just as she'd wept so much then, so many years ago.

The intensive care unit at the hospital, where she hadn't really understood what was going on, but they'd all had to wear masks over their mouths and noses, and it wasn't the sort of mask you wore to play games in. And Mummy had been crying, and Daddy had been trying not to as he held her in his arms and did what he could to comfort her. And Evey had been standing there trying to get her fingers under the mask to wipe away the tears that kept streaming down her cheeks as she looked through the plastic tent at little Timmy, whom she'd been angry at the day before for kicking his football at her, and who was lying there gasping for breath and covered with purple sores. And she'd never had the chance to say sorry for the nasty things she'd said to him about the football, and he'd never had the chance to forgive her for them, and she'd never forgiven herself for saying them in the first place. And she didn't understand it then, and she still didn't understand it now.

But that was the last day she'd ever had with Timmy. They hadn't even been allowed to attend the cremation. And Timmy had been one of the "lucky" ones . . . one of the pupils they'd got out of the school alive, if only for a little while. As for the vast majority of the schoolkids, who'd died on the spot and whose bodies had just melted together in a rotting, deliquescent mess before they could be identified . . . they'd just gone straight into a hole in the ground, pretty much there on the spot where they'd died. A throwback to the old plague pits in the days of the Black Death. Only this time, it was purple.

"After he died," Evey told V, pulling herself together as she moved on to memories less raw, yet only a little less painful, "my parents became political."

A bit of fun it had seemed to her at the start, standing in the street with her placard-bearing parents, wearing her school uniform and with her hair carefully braided into pigtails, handing out flyers to passing businessmen, who usually promptly threw them away. And picking up the discarded leaflets, and handing them out again. And again. The ones no one paid any attention to. The ones that were headed, "Viral Weapons Developed by U.S. Military for Use in the Middle East." That was another thing she hadn't quite understood at the time, but obviously it had meant a lot to her parents. Nobody stood out in the cold and rain and got shouted at, or worse, by passing crophead youths unless they thought it was important. That wasn't fun at all.

She hadn't understood the leaflets demanding "Stop the Government Lies!" either. After all, only bad people told lies, and why would anyone vote for bad people?

"They protested against the War and the Reclamation," continued Evey, remembering how she'd been ten years old at the time. That was when the Americans, after all their apparent successes in the Middle

East ("Creating a desert and calling it peace," Daddy had said, quoting some ancient author she couldn't remember), had finally overreached themselves and were forced to pay the price. Fortunately by then, successive British governments had got into such hot water with their own electorate for their unthinking support for American military adventures that they'd closed the U.S. bases here and sent the missiles home, pretty much as the rest of "Old Europe" had some years before. And the NATO alliance being defunct was probably what saved the country when the Taiwan crisis came.

Of course, no one had really expected what happened then, when it turned out that the American military hammer failed to smash China apart like the crockery their propaganda machine kept comparing it to. It was the hammer that broke on the porcelain instead, though not without immense loss of life on both sides. Then the hand that wielded the hammer had broken too, and the Second American Civil War had begun. And hadn't finished yet, though both sides seemed to have fought themselves into an exhausted stalemate now. It was one of those situations that cried out for international intervention, but before the war the Americans had destroyed the United Nations when it wouldn't just roll over and do what they wanted it to.

England hadn't been immune to the chaos that had washed across the entire world like a tsunami after the War, with the collapse of international trade, the transnational banking system, and the food supply.

With the oil crisis and the petty wars in South America, as the various states struggled for supremacy in the power vacuum left when the United States followed the United Nations into functional oblivion. And perhaps worst of all, the changes to the global weather system. Evey could still remember how the Thames Barrier had burst and flooded most of London. More people had died then than from the St. Mary's virus. But that had been a *natural* disaster, so no one could make much political capital out of that, except for the religious right. But they saw the hand of God in everything, so everyone regarded them as a joke. And they were, compared to what was coming next.

Because then the fascists had won the election and started the Reclamation, that hideous excuse for an orgy of ethnic, political, religious, and moral "cleansing" in the name of "reclaiming England for the English" and its appeal for "Victorian values." The sort of values that had prevailed when the British Empire had still straddled half the globe and maps of the world were printed mostly pink, that harked back to times when it was "the white man's burden" to bring enlightenment to the heathen savages. Only this time around the white man was disburdening himself of the heathen savages as rapidly and brutally as he could. And everyone who didn't believe in the one true God whose name was Jesus Christ, and who didn't have the right "family values," and who was principled enough not to swallow the Party line.

"When Sutler was appointed High Chancellor," Evey went on, "they were at the riot at Leeds. I watched it on the telly, thinking I was going to see my parents killed. I remember them arguing at night. Mum wanted to leave the country. Dad refused. He said that if we ran away, they'd win. Win. Like it was a game."

And then there was the other memory, the second of the two that she always did her best not to think about, especially at night, especially just before dawn; the one that kept coming back anyway. The worst one, more awful yet than Timmy. The one she'd remembered that very morning, when she'd confused it with the sound track of *The Count of Monte Cristo*.

She'd been asleep too when that had started. Started with the sound of breaking glass and the sound of a heavy iron ram, battering in the front door. The heavy footsteps of metal-shod boots. The shouting. The gunshot.

They should have expected it. It had been happening all across the country, and to people they knew as well. But when friends stopped getting in touch, it was far easier to delude yourself that there must be some minor reason for it, other than what you knew in your heart to be true. And always there was the feeling that these things only happened to other people, that it would never happen to *us*.

But then, nobody had really expected a fascist government would happen either.

It was just after the gunshot—no more than a warning shot, as it turned out—that her mother had burst into her bedroom, nightdress-clad, and slammed the door behind her.

"Evey, quick!" she'd said with quiet desperation,

hoping the intruders might not hear. *"Hide!* Under the bed!"

And she had, though not without her favorite Teddy, the one she'd always talked to in her troubles, the one who knew the magic word that took them off on dream adventures to a world where everything was lovely, now grabbed one-handed, without thought. Then the door had been broken in, knocking her mother to the floor and revealing not the police they'd always half-expected, but soldiers. Brutal, coarse, laughing among themselves as they ogled her mother in her nightdress, dragging her to her feet and pinning her arms behind her back, speedily fastening her wrists with plastic zip-ties. And not caring where they put their hands as they did so.

Evey, huddled desperately beneath the bed and overwhelmed with panic, found she could hardly breathe at all, only managing tiny mouselike gasps. She looked up in absolute desperation to see her mother looking straight back at her, as if to fix her daughter's image in her mind forever, just before they pulled the shiny black bag down over her head.

Then Evey had screamed, helplessly, all control completely lost. And the flashlights had stabbed under the bed.

And the soldiers had found her and taken her away.

"I never saw them again," Evey told V, struggling with things she never talked about; and remembering then, with pathetic absurdity, that she'd never seen Teddy again either. "It was like those black bags erased them from the face of the earth."

Erased the magic word as well, and all the magic that had ever been in the world; and then there was nothing left but fear. Cold, dark fear that lived somewhere near the bottom of her spine and, at the slightest opportunity, would suddenly rush up and engulf her entire brain and seep throughout her mind.

"I'm sorry, Evey," V said gently and with an obvious sympathy that transcended the usual platitudes.

"No, I'm the one that's sorry," she said, trying to gather herself, only to fall prey to another memory: of how, at times like these, so near to tears, her mother would always smile and tell her, gently, to "blow your nose and pull yourself together"; but ever since she'd said that for the last time, it seemed somehow that nose-blowing didn't help.

"I'm sorry that I'm not a stronger person; I'm sorry I'm not like my parents. I wish I was, but I'm not. I wish I wasn't afraid all the time, but I am."

She sucked in a deep breath then, steeling herself to say the words that all this had been leading up to: "I know this world is screwed up. Believe me, I know it better than most. Which is why I wanted to ask . . . if there's anything I can do to help make it right, please, let me know."

"If you wish," murmured V quietly. "If you wish . . ."

Another request, meanwhile, had been made at another ministry; this time one of the civilian—and infinitely more civil—ones. But still Finch and Dominic waited with growing impatience at the issue desk. How long did these things take? The rain had been coming down so hard when they'd arrived—"in stair rods" as Finch's old Mum had used to say, which was a stage quite beyond the usual "raining cats and dogs"—that they'd got soaked just walking into the building from their parked car. Now they'd been waiting so long they were almost perfectly dry again.

Mind you, it was Saturday morning, and though he and Dominic were prepared to put in the extra hours, they'd had to call out someone specially to help them here. And no doubt the man would be putting in for time and a half for Saturday work, so maybe it wasn't surprising that he was dragging it out for as long as he could. Or maybe it did just take this long.

"You really think we'll find something here?" Dominic asked the elder man, as much to make conversation as anything else.

"Worth a shot," Finch told him, wondering what it was these days that seemed to have deprived the nation's civil servants of coffee. "One thing is true about all governments: their best records are tax records."

At last a door opened on the other side of the room, and the gray-haired, bifocaled filing clerk they'd first spoken to, a forgotten age ago, reappeared. Stooping slightly, he meandered across the office toward them, carrying a large box-file. The expression on his face didn't look at all hopeful.

"It appears that the original electronic records have all been lost, probably during the Reclamation," he said apologetically, seeing disappointment slide across the faces of the detectives like curtains closing on the casket at a crematorium. "A lot of things went missing back then. But I found this hard copy filed down in the vaults."

Still with a rather apologetic expression, he handed the box to Finch. "Everything we've got on Larkhill is in there."

And then he glanced up, almost in wonder, to see the look of grateful surprise dawning on Finch's lined and world-weary face.

"Thanks," Finch told him, for once meaning it quite sincerely. "This is a big help."

Christ, he thought, if only things *always* turned up like this. . . .

Somewhat later, Evey made a discovery of her own. Passing the time until there was something for her to do and trying to make her bedroom look a little more like home, she'd found some fabric to hang over the small amount of bare brick wall that was visible between the book piles and had now turned her attention to cleaning the dressing-table mirror. As she scrubbed away the dust that V had allowed to accrue in what was, after all, little more than a storeroom with a spare bed in it, she found a motto carved in Latin on the frame. Peering at it through the gloom that nothing seemed able to dispel, so dark the walls and ceiling were, so dark the books that gathered there before them, she finally managed to pick the words out enough to read them.

"*Vi Veri Veniversum Vivus Vici*," she said aloud to

herself, though as she did so, she noticed V appear in the mirror there beneath the words. And she could only gasp in amazement.

For a moment, her mind reeled. This was like the old days when she was a child, like the tales in the storybooks her father had read to her, like . . . like the times with Teddy . . . for it seemed to her that she had spoken the magic words, and V had suddenly appeared, genie-like, in the magic mirror. And then she realized that he had really entered the room behind her, and his appearance at that exact moment was just one of those amazing coincidences. Yet such a strange one . . .

" 'By the power of truth, I, while living, have conquered the universe,' " he translated for her, moving forward into the room. She turned to face him.

"Personal motto?" she asked, knowing his penchant for all things related to the letter V.

"From *Faust.*"

Of course, she thought: a magician. Who else would have the magic words? "That's about cheating the devil, isn't it?" she asked, after a pause to gather her thoughts. Cheating the devil indeed. . . .

"It is." A certain warmth in his voice expressed his pleasure at her knowledge. "And speaking of the devil, I was wondering if your offer to help still stood."

"Of course," said Evey, her pulse quickening as she put down the cleaning cloth.

"It appears that unforeseen circumstances have accelerated my original plan. As a result I am in need of someone with some theatrical skill."

"I'll do my best." She smiled, not a little pleased at his appreciation of her talents and the opportunity this presented.

"I believe you will," V told her, preparing to coach her in her script.


"Another doctor?" queried Finch, not entirely sure whether he was asking himself or Dominic or the empty air. Or maybe the rain, which was still battering against the windows. It never used to be like this, before the weather collapsed. Now it was weeks of drought, followed by a month's worth of rain in a single weekend. No wonder what water they had was so rigidly controlled. With it falling so heavily, all this would be running off down the sewers and into the Thames before anything useful could be done with it . . . if the sewers didn't back up again and flood the streets with sewage as they had a couple of months ago. And that hadn't been the first time either.

"What does a detention facility need with so many doctors?" Finch continued, picking up his coffee cup and, finding it empty, putting it down in disgust. They'd been here throughout the night, sorting through the tax files, sleeping occasionally in their office chairs, sending out for sandwiches when the canteen closed. And here it was on Sunday morning, and they didn't seem to be getting any further.

The latest doctor was a Dana Stanton, one of a list that he couldn't quite remember the length of. The tax records they'd brought back from the ministry contained plenty of food for thought, even if a lot of it just didn't seem to fit together. Interesting, suggestive . . . but puzzling.

"I don't know," Dominic replied to his question, going through a folder of his own. "But this is interesting. The highest-paid person in the camp was a priest."

"What?" *Puzzling* wasn't the word anymore; that latest nugget of information seemed just completely incomprehensible.

"The Reverend Anthony James Lilliman," Dominic told him, seeming as baffled as his superior. "He was paid almost two hundred grand a month."

"That *is* interesting." Finch typed the name *Lilliman* into his computer search engine.

"Looks like he was promoted," he added when the information came up on the screen. "He's a bishop now. Officiating priest at Westminster Abbey."

Why on earth would a priest, whose official role at the camp appeared to be to ensure that rules and rights weren't violated, be paid that much?

Unless it was some sort of hush money?

"I guess we're going to confession tomorrow then?" smirked Dominic.

"Yeah," Finch agreed, allowing himself a little smile of satisfaction as it seemed they were finally starting to get somewhere on this case. "And I'll bet his confession will be a lot more interesting than ours."

# TEN

**E**arly Sunday evening in the Deanery at Westminster Abbey, now Bishop Lilliman's private living quarters, found two men, one young, the other considerably older, with rather different things on their minds.

"Your Grace," the young man called, his voice somehow retaining a reverent hush while still carrying along the echoing corridor as he sought to catch up with the bishop. A marvelous opportunity for a young priest, he'd thought this position as personal assistant to the bishop would be; until he'd realized just how personal some of his duties actually were. Still, needs must when the devil drives, even here in God's house at Westminster, and once he'd got used to the notion, and some of the perks and side benefits involved, it still was a marvelous opportunity. Just not quite the way he'd thought it was going to be.

"Ah, Denis," the bishop said softly, pausing and turning to look back as the young priest caught up. "Has everything been arranged?"

"Yes, Your Grace," said Denis hurriedly, eager to please as ever. "I've just received your InterLink itinerary, and you should arrive in Perth in time to celebrate Communion."

Lilliman smiled, but it was a smile much more suggestive of reptilian descent than pleasure, of tested patience rather than fatherly pride in his assistant's accomplishments. The sort of smile that went with his thin, lanky body, with the receding hairline, and the almost-shriveled, skin-on-a-skull face. All he really needed was a forked tongue to complete the look, but Denis had soon realized that the old hypocrite spoke with one anyway, regardless of what he physically had in his mouth.

"You are most diligent, Denis," he began, with a hint of sarcasm. "A noble example for all those who labor in the name of the Lord. But . . ."

"Your Grace?" queried Denis nervously, realizing from the bishop's tone of voice that the conversation was veering toward an area where, today anyway, he didn't really want it to go.

"It wasn't labor that I was speaking of," the bishop said with barely concealed impatience. Surely the boy should have come to understand him by now. And why was he looking so nervous?

"It was rather," Lilliman continued, "my final remittance that I was interested in. My last little joy . . ."

"I'm sorry, Your Grace," said Denis more quietly yet, unable quite to meet the bishop's eye and shuffling closer as if, alone as they were, he was still afraid they might be overheard. "She's arrived, but there was some confusion at the agency, and they've sent a new girl." An inquiring look from the bishop, and here, at last, was the crux. But it had to be said anyway: "A new girl who, I'm afraid, is a little older than usual."

"Older?" Lilliman asked, annoyance in his eyes but still with marvelous control in his perfectly modulated preacher's voice. "Oh, dear. Not *too* old, I trust?"

"That is for Your Grace to decide," said Denis, dropping his gaze deferentially, hoping the explosion he half-expected would never come.

"Ah, well," the bishop sighed, casting a glance heavenward. "If Job could bear his trials, I suppose I must bear mine."

And with that he turned away, opening the door to his bedroom, revealing something quite the opposite of a monk's penitential cell. Thick Persian rugs, antique and purloined from the storerooms of the Victoria and Albert Museum, were strewn across the parqueted floor; the double bed was king-size (or "bishop-size" as he preferred to think of it), and round the walls were not the images of religion, but icons of the grossest lust. Child pornography. Young girls painted in the roles of whores. Very young. The sort the agency usually supplied, and not just to the bishop; though not to anyone who wasn't somehow associated with the government or the Party. An exclusive agency this; after all, it was *run* by the government.

And there, a picture of innocence in the midst of decadence, blond hair braided into pigtails, wearing a frilly pink party dress quite plainly several sizes too small for her but which she'd forced herself into anyway, and little white ankle socks, stood Evey, a nervous smile upon her face.

"Oh, my . . . ," breathed Lilliman, stepping closer.

"Your Grace." Evey curtsied, holding the hem of

her dress pinched between her thumbs and fingers and looking up, appalled but hardly daring to show it, into the lined and aged face of the dog-collared pervert into whose hands she'd fallen.

"To think that I doubted your loveliness for an instant." The bishop leered, running his eyes down her body from tip to toe and then back up again. Not the veal he usually dined upon, but a young and tender lamb nonetheless. "Mea culpa, my child. Mea culpa."

"Umm, thank you," Evey said hesitantly, wondering whether this was such a good idea after all. Wondering how long there was to go before V arrived.

Not having to wonder, however, about whether the bishop was a quick worker, as he took her hand and led her over to the bed, sat her down, and plumped down by her side.

"Why don't you let me help you with your dress, my child?" he asked immediately, his tone of voice fatherly, his eyes burning with unsuppressed lust.

He started to reach for her shoulders, stooping forward, his sticklike figure closing in like a praying mantis . . . but she shrank away, pushing his hands aside. For a moment he seemed taken aback. Surely the agency had explained precisely what was required? He paid them well enough, after all.

"Please, Your Grace," Evey said urgently, trying to fight down a sudden attack of nerves. Now was the time to do what she'd been planning, not to get involved in the bishop's disgusting little games. "We don't have much time and I have to tell you something—"

"A confession?" Lilliman laughed, annoyance disappearing. Perhaps the girl had initiative enough to make up for her surplus years after all. And she was quite, quite delicious. Pretty in pink, and perfectly succulent.

"I love the confessional game," he told her lickerishly, entering into the spirit of things. "Tell me your sins."

"This isn't a game, Your Grace," she told him desperately. Why couldn't he understand? "Someone's coming, and I think he means to kill you."

There. She'd said it now. Taken the first step along what she hoped would be the path to redemption and escape. Hated herself for doing it and knew it was a betrayal. Felt exactly like the frightened coward she'd described herself as to V; knew that the description was absolute truth, and the only lie was that she wanted to do something about it. But if she could just keep her head out of a black bag . . .

"Pardon me?" said the bishop in confusion. People in his position just didn't get murdered. Who'd want to kill a man of God?

"I'm telling you this because I want some kind of protection or amnesty. I had nothing to do with the Old Bailey and I made a terrible mistake at Jordan Tower, but I think this should balance it out—"

"What on earth are you talking about?"

"My name is Evey Hammond," she said, trying to get the words out before he interrupted again. So much to say, so little time to say it; and then it all spilled out. "I am . . . I have been the prisoner of the terrorist named V for the past several days, and I'm telling you that any moment he's going to come through that door because I unlocked the window in the room where your man Denis told me to get ready."

He stared at her then, the whites of his eyes starting to brighten with fear, and she thought, perhaps, the message was at last starting to sink in. He'd surely have heard of V with all that had happened since the Old Bailey, no matter how cloistered his life was here. Must have known about the Jordan Tower incident too; the giant television in one corner of the room couldn't just be there to play the pornographic DVDs stacked up beneath it, even if that was its main purpose. And if he was on V's target list, he might be high enough in the scheme of things to have heard about the actual cause of Lewis Prothero's death.

But then he started to laugh. After all, weren't there two armed security guards outside the main door, provided by the government specially to deal with this current terrorist threat?

"Wonderful!" he chuckled. The child certainly had an inventive talent for this sort of thing. "A game I've never played! What a delightful mind you have. I hope the rest of you is just as interesting."

A hand settled on her thigh, his aging skin like parchment, and began to slide up between her legs with a serpentine motion.

"No, please," Evey protested, bringing her knees together hurriedly. This was all going terribly wrong. Not at all the way she'd planned it. "You have to believe me—"

"Oh, I do, I *do!*" the bishop told her wolfishly, forcing her back down on the bed. "Let me show you the firmness of my beliefs."

"Stop it!" she screeched. "Get off me!"

But Lilliman was playing the game to the hilt by now, delighted even more as she began to struggle.

"Seems like I've captured the dangerous terrorist," he said enthusiastically, pressing down on top of her. "Now, how to best procure her confession?"

*Rape* was the obvious first answer, and perhaps later, if she seemed amenable . . . or even if she wasn't . . . a little carefully administered pain until she was begging for the forgiveness of her previous sins and the opportunity to commit whatever new ones he might have in mind. Hmm, yes, he hadn't had one who'd really responded to a good thrashing since that little brown-haired minx in the school uniform a couple of months ago. How could he have felt disappointed earlier? This was going to be absolutely sumptuous.

Pushing and twisting, and with completely different ideas in mind, Evey finally managed to get one leg free beneath him, then brought her knee up between his thighs with all the force she could muster.

Like cracking eggs.

Lilliman screamed, automatically reaching for his crotch with both hands and rolling aside just enough for Evey to get in a right cross to the side of his head, sending him sprawling off the bed and tumbling to the floor. He lay there for a moment, gasping and wheezing; literally spitting blood and figuratively spitting venom.

"You little bitch!" he squealed, starting to crawl across the floor toward his nightstand. "You filthy little *whore!*"

Sitting up on the bed and massaging her aching knuckles, Evey watched and wondered. She wasn't quite sure why he was crawling away from her like this, but as long as it *was* away, that was all she wanted right at that moment.

But he'd never listen to her now. And somehow the fear that she'd been trying so desperately to escape from had only dropped her into even deeper trouble.

And then with a shriek of breaking wood, the door was kicked in, and there was V, a demon in black, the cloak flapping behind him, the smile forever fixed.

Still down on the floor, Lilliman's eyes grew wide with terror.

"Oh, my God, she wasn't lying!" he groaned, sick with pain and fear alike. "It's you!"

V paused then, struck by the significance of the words and looking round toward Evey.

"I . . . ," she began, getting to her feet and trying to think of some word of explanation. Of anything. Anything to express the guilt and shame she now felt, that somehow made her feel even sicker than her terror. "I . . ."

The mask tilted, oh so slightly. And by now she'd come to understand the expressions that supposedly inexpressive mask conveyed.

Disappointment. Understanding. And worst of all, perhaps, forgiveness.

"I'm sorry!" she almost sobbed. "I had to—"

And then the words wouldn't come anymore. All the ways he reminded her of her father came back to haunt her, counterbalanced against the awful betraying fear. Betraying him. Betraying herself.

She couldn't speak to him. She couldn't face him. She ran.

"Evey?" he said, looking after her as she fled. But by then she'd bolted from the room, and nothing would call her back.

Lilliman saw his chance then. The pain in his groin was still insufferable, but the pain of death would be far, far worse, and he found the energy to hurl himself toward the nightstand he'd been crawling over to before. Toward the big, gilt-hinged, and gold-edged Bible that sat there, closed, upon it.

A prayer before dying was the last thing he had in mind, however. Still doubled up with pain, he managed to flip open the book's ornately inlaid cover and reach into its hollowed-out interior, grabbing the ivory-handled revolver that lay hidden within. The word of God and the power of the gun: the two pillars of the bishop's meteoric rise to success, of his very faith. If one couldn't take care of this terrorist, the other certainly would.

Straightening up at last, he managed to spin round, pulling the trigger even as he did so. Two shots rang out, cracking open the silence of the evening like hammer blows.

But the shots came too late, for V had already leapt toward Lilliman, tiger-swift, as soon as he'd realized the man was on the move. He was already within the arc of the bishop's gun hand before the trigger was squeezed, the inky cloak flapping round the pair of them, making it difficult for Lilliman to see anything at all—only to feel V's gloved hand suddenly reaching for his own, grabbing, squeezing, wrenching.

And then there was another loud crack. Not gunfire, this time, but the dry snapping of bone as V's iron grip broke the priest's wrist, sending him screaming to his knees.

A moment, then, as the masked man stood holding the revolver, looking at it contemplatively.

" 'And thus I clothe my naked villainy,' " he quoted, " 'with odd old ends, stol'n forth of holy writ, and seem a saint when most I play the devil.' "

He tossed the gun across the room, far out of reach.

Lilliman, a wiry figure still hunched and kneeling, sobbing with pain and clutching his wrist, finally managed to raise his head, looking up at the dark, Death-like figure looming above him.

"Who are you?" he managed to gasp.

"You once said I was the devil incarnate," V reminded him. "Remember that, Bishop? You do remember Larkhill, don't you?"

Larkhill. The word almost stopped Lilliman's heart. But he'd hardly done anything there, he'd always told himself, except turn the blind eye that he'd been well paid to turn. And to avail himself for free of the same sort of pleasures he paid for now. It was the *others* who'd done the experiments, not him, even if he had amused himself at the expense of the victims sometimes. And that was all behind him a long time ago, a shadow in the past. Eradicated like the camp itself, the night it burned to the ground. Long gone, like the man who'd burned it.

Like the man who'd burned it. . . .

"Oh, dear God, have mercy!" he gasped, realization dawning . . . a realization more sickening than the pain.

"Not tonight, Bishop," V pronounced, the words a sentence too final to appeal. "Not tonight."

Outside in the rapidly darkening night, where the rain had thankfully stopped sometime before, Evey Hammond was fleeing along the still-wet streets as if her life depended on it, trying to get as far away from Westminster as fast as she possibly could. It hadn't worked out at all the way she'd hoped or planned; it had been a bad decision, motivated by fear, that ended in a bad result. There should have been enough of an alarm raised to scare off V, whom she hadn't really wanted anything terrible to happen to, whatever he might have done. And then it should have been a few hours' interrogation, perhaps a short sentence at the worst, a return to work and normal life. Instead they'd be hunting her even harder now, undoubtedly blaming her for the bishop's death besides. And, yes, although she'd escaped from V, she'd also given up the small amount of protection he provided; though looking back now from her new, even worse situation than before, perhaps that wasn't such a little amount of protection after all.

Wrong. Wrong. It had all gone horribly wrong, and now she was even more afraid than she'd ever been before.

Terribly frightened that she was going to end up, unseeing, in a black bag.

Just keep running, she told herself, but that too brought back horrid memories of that night when she'd been running through the alley, and the Fingermen . . .

And V coming to her rescue. But he wouldn't be rescuing her anymore. Not now. Not ever again.

A dark shape, turning a corner up ahead, sent her scrambling into shadow. Not a man this time, but one of the Ear's huge, armored surveillance vehicles. Black as night (the incoming fascist government had swiftly realized the symbolic and psychological significance of the color, when it came to keeping the population cowed), it sprouted aerials and dishes, directional microphones and the occasional camera besides, both visual and infrared. And she was sure that was a light machine gun over the black-glazed cab on an automatic swivel-mount. They didn't used to have those, she knew, but with the way things seemed to be deteriorating, who could tell where they'd end up. Tanks in every street, most likely, and the ever-present whiff of tear gas on the wind, the way it used to be back in the days of the Reclamation.

Threatening as a great black killer shark, the truck prowled slowly along the street toward her. And Evey, even though she knew it wasn't curfew yet and, so long as they didn't recognize her, there was no reason why she shouldn't walk the streets, cowered against the wall and prayed.

No one inside the truck, however, was paying the slightest attention to anything the cameras showed. They were Earmen, after all, and they were paid to listen. And the best listening in the Westminster area, they knew from long experience, was always early Sunday night.

"Oh, no!" they heard the bishop gasp throatily, breathlessly. "Don't do this. I beg you—"

"Children's hour at the Abbey," one of the operators said, grinning to his mate, who, smirking, fine-tuned the equipment. Any minute now there'd be the girlish giggles, then the warm elfin squeals . . . and then the little childish gasps that always set their imaginations racing . . .

Snickering, they listened more intently. But it was no young girl's voice they heard next. It was a man's. It was brutal, and it wasn't going to stand for any argument.

"Open your mouth and stick out your tongue," commanded V in a horrid parody of the Communion rite.

"What the fuck?" exclaimed the chief operator.

"I don't want to die," the bishop pleaded frantically in his headphones, that rich, sermonizing voice now reduced to little more than an amphibian croak.

And then, as Lilliman started screaming horribly, desperately, and ultimately pathetically, the Earman began barking hurriedly into his headset mike, "This is Surveillance One Zero Nine! We have an emergency!"

# ELEVEN

E ven though it was only the second time he'd seen it, Eric Finch was already becoming thoroughly fed up with the sight of green and white vomit, now foaming in the puddle of brackish, already coagulating blood that had stained and soaked into the Persian rug. A good old-fashioned shooting at least left the victim with more dignity. Or the same sort of knifing that had been done to the security guards outside, before they'd had a chance to draw their guns or even make a sound. But a dead man was still dead, no matter how he'd been done in. And ex-bishop Tony Lilliman had been done in very thoroughly indeed.

Perhaps he deserved it too, Finch thought wearily, looking round at the paintings on the wall, at the pile of magazines they'd found in the bishop's bedside drawer, at the hard-core DVDs. Little girls. Kiddie porn. The sort of thing that was supposed to have been stamped out when the New Order came in, that an ordinary mug in the street could be shot for these days. But which the rich elite could have for the asking, it seemed. Put that together with what he'd seen at Prothero's place and a sick world started to come into view, a new aristocracy full of decadence and corruption and hypocrisy. And these were the people who were supposed to be guarding the nation's morals, good, honest Christians to a man. Maybe V was doing the world a favor taking them out.

But now they'd never get the chance to ask Lilliman about that obscenely high salary he'd been getting at Larkhill.

On his chest lay a single yellow and salmon rose. Just like the one by Lewis Prothero. A calling card, then. Obviously some significance there that needed following up. And if they could just get something useful out of the young priest who was, at the moment, giving a preliminary statement to one of the junior officers.

Of course, by the time anyone could respond to the Earmen's emergency message, it had all been long over; but it was a matter of some pride to Finch that he and his coppers had been the first on the scene again. Even so . . .

"He's just ahead of us, isn't he?" Dominic remarked, looking down at the rose and the corpse, standing there opposite Finch on the other side of the dead bishop.

"Run every name in that file," Finch told him, suddenly decisive. "I want the whereabouts of every one of them. Tonight."

"Yes, sir," said Dominic smartly, then paused as he saw his superior's face fall.

"Oh, hell," muttered Finch, and Dominic turned to see several Fingermen entering the room. In a matter of moments, they'd insinuated themselves in between the police and Denis, uncompromising expressions on their faces and hands tucked inside their immaculate suits. Up there near the armpits, where the shoulder holsters were. No argument, their whole attitude said; and no argument was what they got.

And then Peter Creedy came through the door, heading straight toward Finch.

"Pucker up, here comes the Finger," whispered Dominic, eyes quite plainly saying he'd like to give the man the finger himself.

"Get going. I'll handle him," Finch told Dominic quietly, and looked up with feigned surprise at the newcomer. "Creedy, what are you doing here?"

"Several prominent Party members have been murdered, Chief Inspector," Creedy told him coldly, barely bothering to glance down at the corpse. After all, a dead bishop wasn't all that different from any other dead Party member. And Creedy had personally purged enough of them for corpses to become, to him, little more than statistics. He hadn't been known as Sutler's rottweiler for nothing, back in the Reclamation.

Now everyone called him Creepy Creedy behind his back, though never loud enough for him to hear. Finch couldn't help wondering what his fetish was. After all, if an apparently respectable bishop was into underage sex, Finch had to suspect that with Creedy it would be something far, far worse. Probably something to do with baths full of tarantulas. Or medieval torture instruments.

"This is no ordinary situation and requires more than your ordinary attention," Creedy continued arrogantly, as Finch began to bristle. "The Chancellor demanded my immediate involvement."

A flat statement, delivered in just about as unfriendly a fashion as it was possible to make it. Creedy had no time for the ordinary coppers employed by the Nose, for their chief, or their methods. What was the point of all that sodding about with detection, and evidence, and proof in court, when torture and terror and the secret tribunal were so much more effective? The gun and the black bag, that was the way to deal with troublemakers.

"It's going to be very hard to run an investigation if you're 'detaining' all my witnesses," Finch said sourly, gesturing toward Denis but looking Creedy straight in the eye, determined that he wasn't going to be cowed by anyone, especially the evil bastard standing there before him.

"The security of information is paramount," Creedy said flatly, as if it was a line learned by rote. "In these volatile times, mistakes such as Jordan Tower can no longer be tolerated."

That was it, then, thought Finch. He'd put one over on Creedy by getting his boys there first, before the Finger; worse, he'd got here first as well, and now it was payback time. The first thing to be done was to grab the witnesses and make things as difficult for Finch as possible, and after that all the supposed "collaboration" between their departments would grind to a complete halt. If only the Hammond girl hadn't maced Dominic, Creedy wouldn't have had a leg to stand on.

"*If,* in fact, Jordan Tower was indeed an accident," added Creedy with heavy emphasis.

"What does that mean?" Finch asked shortly, suddenly starting to get angry at the obvious, though not quite understood, insinuation in the man's words, despite his best intentions.

"The terrorist seems to have a rather intimate understanding of our system," Creedy said airily, now looking around the room for the first time, as if Finch's response were hardly worthy of his attention. "The Chancellor suspects there may be an informer."

"Are you saying I'm under surveillance, Mr. Creedy?" Finch asked flatly, fed up now with Creedy's game-playing and wanting to get to the heart of the matter.

"At this time it would behoove you to cease any investigation of matters that have long since passed," Creedy said brutally, "and concentrate on the concerns of the present."

Ah, *there* it was then. The annoyance about Jordan Tower was personal, but that wasn't the crux. That'd got Creedy's back up, but the real reason he'd arrived was to deliver a message; a message he particularly enjoyed passing on because it gave him a chance to get back at Finch. This wasn't about capturing terrorists. This was a warning.

"You mean Larkhill."

"Major Wilson is a friend of the High Chancellor," Creedy told him, with just the ghost of a malicious smile. So that was what it meant to be a "career military man," Finch thought. Whining and tale-telling to get the nasty police bogeyman off his back. But Creedy wasn't finished on the subject of Wilson yet. "His loyalty is not in question."

"But mine is?" Finch responded shortly, suddenly not liking where this was going. "I've been a Party member for twenty-seven years." And somehow he hated himself for saying that. It was true, but it rankled, and it wasn't anything he'd normally parade before others. Something he'd felt he'd had to do at the time, and he certainly wouldn't be where he was today if he hadn't. But not something he was proud of.

"Your mother was Irish, wasn't she?" Creedy cut in coldly, knowing exactly which nerve to hit.

"You bloody—"

"Terrible what St. Mary did to Ireland, wasn't it?" said Creedy, turning away and barely able to keep the gloating, evil laughter out of his voice. "If I were you, Chief Inspector"—and somehow Creedy managed to turn the title into a term of complete contempt—"I'd find that terrorist. And I'd find him soon."

Just for a moment, Finch started to take a step forward, fists bunched, almost tripping over the dead bishop in his eagerness to let Creedy chew on a knuckle sandwich, regardless of the consequences. But one small thought made him relax into a shrug instead.

Just a bloody messenger boy . . .

"Evey?" gasped Gordon Deitrich, opening the front door of his big, old, and very expensive Bloomsbury home and simply looking at her, stunned, standing there in the same pink party dress she'd been wearing earlier. "Good God!"

"I'm sorry," she said nervously, helplessly, looking up at him in almost-tearful desperation. "I didn't know where else to go. . . ."

That was true to a certain extent, though secretly she had to confess to herself that it had always been part of the plan. When she'd first suggested helping V, in the hope that he'd take her out of the Shadow Gallery and so give her the opportunity to escape, she'd always had it in mind to come to Deitrich, as he was the sort of man who had the status and influence to help her. Then, when V had involved her in the plan to assassinate Bishop Lilliman, she'd seen a much more obvious opportunity to make a deal with the authorities. But now that that had gone so horribly wrong, she'd really had no alternative but to fall back on Plan A.

It had taken her nearly two hours to get here, as she hadn't dared to make her way along Whitehall, which, being the seat of government with all its various ministries, was too well guarded these days for someone like her to risk, especially when she was so obviously dressed to catch attention. Instead she'd come along the Victoria Embankment down by the Thames, occasionally dodging into the Gardens to avoid passing patrol vehicles, then up through the backstreets around Charing Cross Station and so into the maze that was Covent Garden. She'd had to run for her life in Long Acre, though whether the man she was fleeing from was a Fingerman, a mugger, or a pervert, she really wasn't sure. But she'd shaken him off and finally she was here. And now there was still the big question that had been tormenting her all along: Would he take her in?

Deitrich scanned the streets quickly, seeing no one and nothing except an approaching FedCo truck, dawdling slowly along the street as if the driver wasn't quite certain of the address he was looking for.

"Come on, quick!" he said then, it never occurring to him that FedCo didn't normally deliver on a Sunday evening as he grabbed her wrist and drew her into the warm glow of the front hallway. "Come inside before someone sees you."

Moments later she was sitting on the couch in his living room, still hunched up with tension, knees pressed together, hugging herself despite the central heating, trying not to shiver. No, actually, that should be trying not to *shudder*. She couldn't stop gulping nervously, hoping desperately she wasn't going to be sick. Or worse. Actually, if she could just faint, right now, that would be a marvelous relief.

"Here, drink this," said Deitrich, approaching with two large glasses of single-malt Scotch, one of which he thrust in her direction.

Evey drained it summarily, in one gulp.

"Hmm . . . cheers," he added somewhat posthumously, eyebrow raised and rather taken aback. But there seemed nothing else to do but follow her lead.

"Gordon," she began as he brought the bottle near for a refill, and then the words all spilled out, uncontrolled and faster than either of them expected. "I know every cop in the country is looking for me. I know it's horrible of me to come here, to put you in this situation—"

"Evey—" he tried to interpose gently, but she wasn't to be stopped.

"If they find me here, you could be in terrible trouble—"

"Evey, listen to me," he said, much louder now, taking her free hand and almost shaking her as he sat down beside her. "If the government ever searched my house, you would be the least of my problems."

Evey could only look at him in blank incomprehension. What could be worse than what she'd done in the last few days? And thinking only of herself, she completely missed that someone had said something similar to her only a few days previously.

"You trusted me." He smiled, and she detected a fatherly and, despite his name, very English side to him that she'd never noticed before. "It'd be terribly bad manners for me not to trust you."

And when she still didn't seem to understand, he took the glass out of her hand gently and raised her to her feet. "Come along with me."

A few moments later he'd led her down the stairs to the basement and, when the click of a pull chain illuminated a single naked bulb, led her into a beautiful old stone wine cellar filled with racks of dark, dust-covered bottles. Obviously, *Deitrich's Half Hour* paid the bills, and for quite a lot more besides. Some of the wines here, she guessed, would cost more per bottle than she could earn in a month.

But exactly why he'd brought her down here, she couldn't figure out at all.

"I've always said in public that I don't make art, I make fun of it," he said, as if this explained why he was showing her his wine cellar. "But the truth is I love art, and I do whatever I can to protect it."

And then he stepped over to a rack by the wall and twisted one of the old bottles.

Slowly and with a slight electric hum, the entire rack swung away from the wall like a door, leaving a dark space beyond. He ducked down into the opening, reached out for another pull chain, then stepped aside and ushered her into the secret room ahead.

And Evey could only stare.

There was only one other room she'd ever seen like it. And that was underground too: the Shadow Gallery.

This was a smaller version, but it reflected much the same tastes, and definitely the same interest in preserving what was old and valuable, discarded, forgotten, and forbidden. Books, music, paintings, erotica of various persuasions, sculpture, and, though there was less of the popular, commercial stuff that V obviously treasured so much, row upon row of movies, on video, on disc, and even on original reels.

Remembering how she'd enjoyed *The Count of Monte Cristo*, Evey let her eye run over the movie collection. An amazing jumble, from all times and all parts of the world: *Easy Rider, Women in Love, The Golem, Dragon Inn, Woodstock, 1984*. And then she looked round toward the far wall.

"Oh my God!" she exclaimed, looking up at a large

and extremely satirical painting. "That's *God Save the Queen*! My parents took me to see it when they hung it at Gallery 12. I thought Sutler had it destroyed."

And that would hardly have been a surprise, for there was Adam Sutler standing on a balcony and giving something between a fascist salute and a royal wave with one delicately gloved hand, crowned and bejeweled and dressed like the late Queen Elizabeth II, only with far more décolletage. A painting made before he'd come to power, when he and his Norsefire rallies were still regarded as a bad joke by large sections of the population. Just *how* bad a joke only became apparent later, when those same large sections of the population were taken away in the night. They weren't laughing then, or ever again.

"He believes he did," Deitrich told her, smiling fondly at one of those little triumphs that still made living, even in a totalitarian state, worthwhile. "It cost more than this house, but no matter how bad I feel, it always cheers me up."

Evey turned away, letting her eye wander further round the room, noticing a large and obviously ancient book lying open under a glass case. She stepped closer to look but found the writing foreign and incomprehensible. Just squiggles.

"What's that?" she asked, gesturing toward it as she turned back to face him.

"A copy of the Qur'an. Fourteenth century."

Taken by surprise, she inquired, "Are you . . . a Muslim?"

"No, I'm in television," he joked. And there weren't

any Muslims in television. Weren't any Muslims in Britain, anymore. The lucky ones had been deported.

"But why would you keep it?" Evey asked, puzzled.

"I don't have to be a Muslim to find the images beautiful or its poetry moving."

"But is it worth it?" she asked with worried sympathy. "I mean, if they found that here . . ."

"As I told you," Deitrich said with a rather rueful smile, "*you'd* be the least of my worries."

A sudden sense of tremendous relief and gratitude overwhelmed her. And without really knowing what she did, or being able to stop herself, she stepped forward and kissed him tenderly on the cheek. Something she thought she'd never want to do, that night she'd started off to visit him.

And now, surrounded by all these treasures, she remembered where she'd heard that similar phrasing before. That too had been back in the Shadow Gallery, and the words had been spoken by V. And now she was starting to get something of that safe, protected feeling that she'd had there; probably more so, because if there was one thing she was sure of, it was that Gordon Deitrich didn't go round blowing up buildings or murdering people in some sort of vendetta. The only trouble was, she'd betrayed that protection the first time around. Well, she thought determinedly, not again.

"Thank you, Gordon," she said, smiling at his slightly bewildered, slightly embarrassed look. "Thank you so much."

"It's alright," he told her gently, relieved that, at

last, she was showing signs of relaxing, of letting the tension drain away.

"You know, this whole thing started the night he blew up the Old Bailey," she began, wanting to tell him everything, wanting his reassurance that it wasn't her fault, her blame, her guilt. "I was on my way here. . . ."

And then her words trailed off as she noticed what was hanging on the wall behind him, seen there over his shoulder. Gorgeously colored prints of the most explicit homosexual erotica, and displayed so prominently their importance was absolutely obvious. She tried her best not to stare, but Deitrich had noticed anyway, glancing back behind him and then smiling sadly in confirmation.

"Ah, yes. You see, we're both fugitives in our own way."

"But . . . ," she murmured, still not quite comprehending.

"You're wondering why you would be invited for supper here in the first place if my appetites were for less-conventional fare. Unfortunately, a man in my position is expected to entertain young and charming ladies like yourself . . . because, in this world, if I invited who I really desired, I would undoubtedly no longer have a home, let alone a television show."

"I'm sorry," Evey said with genuine sympathy, genuine concern. After all, whose business was it, in the end, what direction his tastes ran in? Surely not that of the government, the church, the judiciary, or, least of all, the police. If no harm was done to others . . . if they were adult and consenting . . . then whose business was it? But people like Gordon Deitrich got sent to the camps, while elitist reptiles like Bishop Lilliman got away scot-free. What kind of world were they living in? No need to ask that, really. A society that treated its citizens like that was a fascist society, and there wasn't any other way to describe it.

"Not as sorry as I am," he said, but the words that might have sounded bitter on the lips of a younger man were nothing more than resigned acceptance on his own.

"But there must be . . . others?" she asked, desperately hoping, on his behalf, that he wasn't quite so terribly alone as he appeared.

He merely shrugged, eloquently.

"Occasionally you read something delightful," he said wistfully, "or notice a rather well-designed woman's shoe, and you wonder . . .

"But the truth is, after so many years, you begin to lose more than just your appetite. You wear a mask for so long, you forget who you were beneath it."

# TWELVE

"**S**ame basic toxicology as Lewis Prothero," said Dr. Delia Surridge, pulling the sheet back up to cover the gaunt grimace frozen onto the face of the late Bishop Lilliman. "You could get these poisons from any house in London."

"Thanks, Delia."

In her early fifties, she was a smart, attractive-looking woman, Eric Finch thought, although he had to admit he was prejudiced. She was a friend, after all; sometimes, a little more. But right now he was talking to her in her official capacity: Chief Medical Officer. Pathologist. Autopsy specialist for the Nose.

Running the body back into its chilled morgue-drawer cabinet, she asked her next question without looking up at him, almost as if she didn't want to put him on the spot. Or perhaps, just feeling that she ought to ask but didn't want to meet his gaze. Maybe even not really wanting to know the answer.

"Any leads in finding this guy?" she said, presumably oblivious to the pun and unaware that the very word *guy* had its origin in the same Guy Fawkes whose mask V wore.

"Honestly, nothing yet. Nothing concrete." Finch

glanced round the brightly lit, clinically sterile room, where it seemed impossible to ever tell if it was night or day outside. Delia didn't seem to fit in this cold, empty domain of the dead. She was a warm, live human being, round-faced though occasionally with a slightly weary droop to the corners of her mouth, but somehow she'd ended up here in a room cut off from the real world outside. Almost as if she was running away from something or someone . . . people, relationships, he wasn't sure. Medics, helping people recover, he could understand. Forensic pathologists, poking about inside the bodies of the deceased, he didn't.

"But there is something else you can help me with," he added, reaching into his pocket. "You started as a botanist, didn't you?"

And then he pulled out a plastic bag containing the rose found at Westminster, told her he'd found another with Prothero. Looked at her expectantly, his eyes asking what it was.

And Delia Surridge stared as if she'd just seen a survivor from the dinosaur age, or the dead come back to life.

"It's . . ." She leaned closer, looked, and started off again, "It's a Violet Carson. I thought they were extinct."

Violet. The letter V. Well, that went some way to explaining it.

"He leaves them at the crime scenes," Finch explained, handing it to her. "I'd appreciate it if you could take a look at it. Any information could be helpful."

"Of course." She started to tell him how it was a hybrid, dating back to 1963 and named after a popular actress who used to be in the TV soap opera *Coronation Street*. Was there anything there? Finch wondered, vaguely remembering the show from when he was a kid. What was the character's name? Ena Sharples, that was it. A blunt working-class busybody whom he'd always, frankly, regarded as a bit of an old cow; but she'd been in the show for nearly twenty years and had made herself a household name. Probably nothing there, then . . . unless his man was somehow obsessed with popular culture from back before the Reclamation. But, no, it was probably just the letter V . . .

His phone rang before he could take the thought any further. Pulling it out of his pocket, he just said, "Yeah?"

Dominic was at the other end, and his tone of voice alone made everything sound urgent.

"I just finished going through the file, Inspector. You'd better get back here."

"My God," said Finch, staring as the list of names ran down Dominic's computer screen as if descending, inevitably, into hell. As, it seemed, they had. Beside every name was the word *Deceased*.

"He's killed *all* of them?" Finch asked, there seeming no other reason why the dates of death should all be so close together, so recent. Maybe one or two could have been natural, but as for the rest, no way.

That would have been too much of a coincidence, even in a coincidence-riddled case like this.

"All but one," Dominic told him, hitting *page down* and pointing out, "Dr. Stanton, Dana."

"Who's she?" asked Finch, a rising sense of urgency and excitement tingeing his voice. If they could just find her . . . get to the last victim before he did . . . perhaps even catch him in the act. Because if it was a series of revenge killings and nothing more, and he worked his way through to the end of the list . . . well, what then?

"Not sure who she is," Dominic told him. "She was clearly one of the people in charge at Larkhill, but after they shut it down, she disappeared for two years. Until she applied for an overseas visa, which was denied."

"Running away?"

"Probably. Because after that, all record of her seems to stop."

"She changed her name." Finch drew the obvious conclusion. One that Dominic had already reached.

"That's what I'm guessing," the young man said. "I put a call in to the Registry, but I haven't heard back. But it is late, after all. Or early . . ."

"Call 'em again," Finch said decisively. "I want that name."

And he sat there drumming his fingers nervously on the desktop, waiting as Dominic pestered and blustered his way through the usual succession of unhelpful, buck-passing civil servants until, finally . . .

"What?" the young detective exclaimed in surprise. "Are you sure about that? Okay. Thank you."

He hung up, then glanced toward Finch with a look of rather nervous bewilderment. This was news he didn't really want to give him. After all, there were some things his boss couldn't quite keep to himself, even if he'd never mentioned them aloud.

"Dr. Dana Stanton," Dominic said, hesitated, then continued, "changed her name to Delia Surridge."

"Jesus!" spat Finch, starting to reach for his own phone and then tapping out her number. "I just saw her!"

Absolutely nothing. No answer, no ringing tone: just nothing. A cold terror almost paralyzed his fingers as he tried again. Again. Then tried the operator.

"I'm sorry, Inspector," she said at last, "but I can't get a response from that number. There's a problem with the connection."

"Jesus Christ! He's there." Finch slammed down the phone and lurched wearily to his feet, then hurriedly reached for his coat. "Let's go!"

The night was still deep over Plaistow, where a bright moon shone through a gap in the breeze-rippled curtains of Delia Surridge's bedroom. Asleep, her face had regained all the peaceful innocence of a child's. Or the newly dead's. It was an irony she would surely have appreciated as a pathologist, if only she could have seen herself unconscious.

But finally she stirred, drew in a sharper breath, and woke.

Woke to the scent of roses.

And to a dark-cloaked figure in a broad-brimmed hat, standing silently in the shadows, barely visible in the moonlight.

"It's you, isn't it?" she asked, sitting up suddenly, but speaking with a calm, quiet voice. "You've come to kill me."

"Yes," said the intruder, floating toward her bedside like the angel of death, his calm tone matching her own. The hat tilted back slightly then, revealing the mask in the moonlight.

"Thank God," said Delia Surridge, and softly began to weep. It was to be a romantic death then, the sort she'd always hoped for but never dared expect, with moonlight and roses; not with fury and violence, but with quietness and peace.

And V, playing the perfect gentleman, stood there beside her in silence until she gathered herself, until the tears stopped flowing, and, finally, until she was prepared to raise her head and look him in the face. Or rather, the mask.

The mask that revealed nothing, but eloquently said so much.

"After what happened, after what they did," she began falteringly, "I thought about killing myself . . . but I knew one day you'd come for me."

She glanced round then toward the nightstand beside her bed, and the red leatherbound book that lay there. The book that, on some impulse, she'd felt the need, earlier in the evening, to get from the small safe concealed in the bottom of her wardrobe where it had sat unread for years. Not that she'd wanted to read it again herself, but because she'd known that there'd be someone who would, even if at the time she hadn't been quite certain who. Known as well that this, somehow, would be the night of revelations. And, oh, how she wanted the story to be known, to escape from all those years of government suppression and finally be brought to light. It wouldn't even matter to her if it was only shared with one other person, and the story was never made public. But if she could just pass it on to *someone* and lay down the burden of guilt that she'd been carrying for so many years, before she died. . . .

"I didn't know what they were going to do," she told him, as if some final confession, or at least an explanation, was necessary for her soul. "I swear I didn't. Read my journal."

She glanced toward the book, but if she hoped for some expression of sympathy, it wasn't forthcoming.

"What they did," V told her, unmoving, like a judge pronouncing sentence, "was only possible because of you."

A cold evaluation that, and hardly the clemency she'd hoped for. But truthful nonetheless. And truth was something to be treasured after so many years of lies.

"Oppenheimer was able to change more than the course of a war," she said meditatively, thankful if not for sympathy, at least for the opportunity to talk. "He changed the entire course of human history. Is it wrong to hold on to that kind of hope?"

"I haven't come for what you hoped to do, Delia," he told her gently, and the use of her new first name seemed almost like forgiveness. "Dr. Dana Stanton" would have struck her as much more accusatory, would have reminded her so much more of her guilt.

"I've come for what you *did*."

"Yes, I know," she sighed, shaking her head wearily. "It's funny. I was given one of your roses today. I wasn't sure you were the terrorist until I saw it."

And with that she managed a small, rueful smile. "What a strange coincidence, that I should be given it today."

"There are no coincidences, Delia," said V softly. "Only the illusion of coincidence."

And then he reached into his cloak, pulled out something that seemed to glow palely in the moonlight. "I have another rose," he said, handing it to her. "This one is for you."

She took it almost gratefully, held it close, and looked at it as if it was the last treasure in her life, and somehow the most valued one of all. A valentine from Death himself, come now to claim her as his long-predestined bride.

"Are you going to kill me now?" she asked at last, looking up toward him with genuine warmth in her expression.

"I killed you ten minutes ago," he said, showing her an empty syringe. "While you slept."

"Is there any pain?" Her doctor's voice, now. A last medical inquiry, in the spirit of professional curiosity.

"No," he said in a tone of obvious, reassuring truthfulness.

"Thank you."

Outside, on the still night air, a distant police siren began to wail. But if V felt even the slightest touch of concern about that, it was not at all apparent.

"Is it meaningless to apologize?" she asked. One last question while there was still time.

"Never," he said, and, at that, the mask seemed touched with something of a real smile.

"I'm sorry," she murmured as the rose slipped slowly from her fingers.

And then there was only silence, as an expression of peaceful innocence returned to her face.

Less than two minutes later, Finch's car screeched to a halt outside, the passenger door opening before it had even stopped. Cursing the amount of time it had taken them to cross east London to get here, even with the curfewed, empty roads and Dominic's dangerous driving, Finch ran toward the house and pressed the doorbell urgently, repeatedly. Waiting no more than thirty seconds for a response, a light, a sound, anything, he summoned Dominic forward and told him to kick in the front door.

They found her in the bedroom, lying at peace in the moonlight, the bedclothes pushed back where she'd first sat up, her eyes open and staring fixedly at the ceiling, the Violet Carson rose lying loosely in her lap.

Too late. Too late again. And this the occasion when Finch had wanted, most of all, to be on time.

"Damnit," he muttered with mingled anger and despair. He wanted to say much more, of course, to rage and shout and curse the entire world and the

God who allowed such things to happen . . . but somehow he couldn't bring himself to break the serenity that seemed to have fallen over Delia, her room, and all the moonlit night.

Almost as if the world itself were telling Delia Surridge, "Rest in peace," and he could only add the same, remembering the few times they'd drifted together, two lonely people in their middle age who'd gone for dinner and wound up once here and twice at his place, before drifting apart again the following morning with vague promises that neither of them ever really intended to keep. That bottle of Scotch they'd drained together when she'd told him pathologists had more to get drunk about than coppers ever did, and he'd told her plainly that they didn't.

But even when she couldn't stand up anymore and he'd had to carry her off to bed, she still hadn't mentioned anything about Larkhill.

And then his eye lit on the leatherbound journal, still there by the bedside, inviting attention.

Waiting to be read.

There was no way Finch was going to allow this particular piece of evidence to fall into Peter Creedy's hands, and the only way to prevent that happening—and to cover his exposed rear end at the same time—was to take it right to the top himself. So here he was, after a sleepless night's reading, alone in the Cabinet Room in Downing Street, looking up at the huge monitor, dwarfed by the televised face of Adam Sutler.

"It was found at the crime scene, beside the bed," Finch explained, gesturing toward the journal on the table before him, knowing that the multi-angle cameras around the room would be picking up a view of it well enough, along with every nuance of Finch's behavior. Difficult to conceal anything when every slightest movement, every trace of expression, could be picked up and examined from a multitude of different angles. And every word, every pause, every breath, and every silence was being taken down on tape as well.

Well, "tell the truth and shame the devil," Finch thought to himself. And that was pretty much how he was seeing the High Chancellor now, after reading the contents of the journal. And everyone else involved in this case, from those who were employed at Larkhill to the political masters they worked for. A rotten business, a rotten system, a thoroughly rotten world; and that he was just another compromised cog in this horribly inhuman wheel didn't make him feel any better at all. But he'd tried to keep all those feelings out of his presentation as he'd told Sutler something of the journal's contents. Whether he'd succeeded—well, only time would tell.

"The terrorist obviously wanted us to have it," he continued, looking up at the screen to watch Sutler's reaction to what he said next. "He wanted us to know the story, or at least a part of it."

The reaction was pretty much as he'd expected. First time he'd ever seen the evil old bastard even remotely discomforted. Well, life had its little triumphs, mixed in with its larger, far more widespread despairs.

"Am I to understand that you have read the whole of this document, Inspector?" Sutler said coldly, malignance ringing in every word.

"Yes, sir." Finch had and it would have been obvious that he had, or he wouldn't have known it was important enough to bring to Downing Street, so there was no point in lying about it. But there was still that gnawing uncertainty in his gut about what the consequences might be. He didn't want to end up in a black bag any more than anyone else.

"Has anyone else read it?" Sutler continued, trying to sound matter-of-fact, but somehow just suggesting he was looking for an excuse for further action. What they used to call, euphemistically, "executive action." With the emphasis on *execute*.

"No, sir." Finch waited.

It wasn't as bad as it could have been. After a few seconds of narrow-eyed contemplation, while he was obviously weighing the pros and cons of whether it was more useful to keep Finch alive or not, Sutler made his pronouncement.

"Then let me make this perfectly clear to you. The contents of this document are a matter of national security, constituting an assault on the character of several important Party members, as well as being a blatant violation of the Articles of Allegiance."

A pause, and then came the statement of denial that would, true or false, obviously be the official Party line.

"As the authenticity of this document cannot be verified," Sutler continued with heavy emphasis, "it could be an elaborate forgery created by the terrorist, as easily as it could be the deranged fantasy of a former Party member who resigned for psychological reasons. So any discussion of this document or its contents will be considered at the very least an act of sedition, if not a willful act of treason. Is that understood, Mr. Finch?"

"Yes, sir," he said aloud. "Bullshit," he thought in silence.

"You would do well, Inspector," Sutler said with finality, "to put it entirely out of your mind."

Finch nodded acquiescence, but the journal, which was obviously going to stay behind when he left, just sat there on the table before him like a bitten apple, refusing to be unbit.

And the only thing that would get the contents out of his mind now was a bullet through the brain.

# THIRTEEN

**M**ay 23rd, the journal had started, as journals do, though it had been quite obvious to Finch that the bare narrative of Delia Surridge's words had only represented the tip of the iceberg, the merest aide-mémoire. The real memories hidden beneath the matter-of-fact record could only be conjectured. But Finch had seen enough, after all the times he'd lived through, all the "government processes" he'd seen, to imagine them easily enough.

And if the world had seemed to forgive Delia Surridge on the night of her death, he had to say that now, after reading the narrative of all the things she'd done and all the other things she'd neglected, he couldn't really understand why.

*My first batch of subjects arrived today, and I have to admit that I'm very excited,* the journal's first entry had begun, and Finch, knowing Delia Surridge personally as he had, was appalled at the ease with which, from the very start, she'd been able to slip into thinking of "subjects" rather than "people." People who would, he knew, have arrived at the camp packed into trucks like cattle, probably without even any room to sit as they rattled along the long-deteriorated roads.

The people you didn't see anymore: Arabs, Africans, Asians, Chinese, Gypsies. People who prayed to different gods. Queers and lesbians. Political agitators. Men, women . . . and children.

But not solid British criminals of Anglo-Saxon origin, of course. Criminals you could always make use of. As concentration camp guards, for example. The kind who would have been laughing as they directed the "detainees" into steel-barred pens, sorting them by type and sex like cattle, tearing families apart, taking children from their mothers. And all with a casual violence quite unrecorded in the journal. If Delia Surridge had ever seen it, of course. Or if she had the eyes to see.

He'd had to rather doubt it. Or at least, he'd hoped she hadn't seen it, because if she had, it opened up a side of this woman to view that he'd rather not know. But then she'd been young back then, and the woman he'd known had had plenty of time to repent. And how easily, after all, we compromise ourselves. Who was he to sit in judgment over her? He always liked to think of himself as an honest copper, but he was still a Party member. And he knew quite well what happened to the people he helped to convict. The country didn't have the financial resources to keep anyone in jail for life, no matter what the official line was. Surprising how many people committed suicide in prison these days . . .

Yes, he'd thought as he read on, and didn't like what the thought said about any of them: she'd known.

*I can't help but wonder if this is how Robert Op-*

*penheimer felt. This could be the dawn of a new age.*
*Nuclear power is meaningless in a world where a virus*
*can kill an entire population and leave its wealth in-*
*tact.*

A misguided optimism that overrode all moral concerns, that saw progress in terms of replacing one horror with another that was only "better" when
evaluated in terms of property and wealth. Science for
science's sake and an appeal to her personal deities,
even if some held them far more morally questionable
than she did. And always that same inhumanity. Or,
no, it wasn't *inhumanity*, it was simply a *lack* of humanity. The same mind-set that was only interested in
test results, and not the people the tests were carried
out on.

And mixed in with the victims, there'd been familiar names; names that, all these years later, had become victims in their turn. And certainly, Finch now
had to think, more deserving victims than those whose
destruction they'd presided over then.

*May 27th. Commander Prothero toured the lab*
*with a priest, the Reverend Lilliman, who I was told is*
*here to monitor for Rules and Rights violations. It*
*made me nervous, but afterwards the Commander as-*
*sured me there wouldn't be a problem.*

I'll bet, Finch had thought. Prothero and Lilliman
would have been thick as thieves, exploiting the situation for all they were worth. The thug-in-uniform and
the sanctimonious snake. "Rules? Rights? Problems?
We make the rules and they're always right—no problem, is there? Fancy the ones in Block Eleven, do you,

Father? Or is it the eleven-year-olds in Block One? Going to help them pray, of course you are . . . 'Down on your knees, my child, and take the sacrament in your mouth.' Oh, yes, did I tell you about the time I was in Aden, with those two girls and the monkey? Real corker, that one!"

Not that Delia would have known anything about that particular evil, being safely immured in the medical research block with her "subjects." Though were the insertions she made with her hypodermic syringes really any less vile than the insertions of the priest?

*June 2nd. I keep wondering whether, if these people knew how they might be helping their country, they would act any differently.*

Except that it quite plainly wasn't their country anymore; and what chance had they had to act any differently anyway? Oh, Delia, what were you thinking?

*They're so weak and pathetic. They never look you in the eye. I find myself hating them.*

Probably, Finch thought, because the only alternative to hating them would have been to hate herself, and then the whole thing would have come apart at the seams. The pretense that this was nothing more than "medical research," that inspecting the wards of dead-eyed men and women with lesions on their bodies and open sores on their faces was a "hospital round," that the "failures" were "properly buried," rather than taken out by men in biohazard suits and hosed with chemicals before being thrown into a hole in the ground, a mass grave where all the bodies of those who'd kept themselves apart in real life—the

Muslims, the Jews, the Hindus, and the Christians—could rot into one another indiscriminately in a vast and fetid heap. After all, the overloaded cremation ovens would have burnt out long before.

*August 18th. Of the original four dozen, over 75 percent are now deceased. No controllable pattern has yet emerged.*

And then there were the last ones. The ones who, amidst the dreadful daily turnover of the general ward, had somehow managed to survive the longest and grown the most interesting "cultures" and had been given their own rooms. The ones with Roman numerals on their heavily locked and bolted doors that, being windowless and tiny, were quite plainly the prison cells she could never quite bring herself to call them. The rooms that, when the occupants died, were locked and given a chalk-mark *X* upon the door and never used again.

*September 18th. There is one case that continues to give me hope. He exhibits none of the immune system pathologies that the other subjects developed. I've discovered several cellular anomalies in his blood that I have been unable to categorize.*

*The mutations seem to have triggered the abnormal development of basic kinesthesia and reflexes. I suspect this may be due to certain preexisting elements initially found in his bloodstream. Upon questioning, the subject said he could no longer remember who he was or where he was from.*

*Whoever he was, he is now the key to our dream and the hope that all of this will not have been in vain.*

Much of the journal had been routine, but it was quite plain that the longer he survived, the more Delia Surridge had become fascinated with this man in Room Five and the magnetic personality he'd seemed to develop as a result of the experiment, quite apart from his speed of movement. She'd obviously been unable to decide whether he was insane, but had noted down the way that, despite saying little, he'd begun to look at her as if she were some sort of insect . . . as if she were the object of an experiment that he was carrying out, rather than the other way round. Eventually his behavior patterns had totally fascinated her, with their semblance of being underscored by some deranged logic that she couldn't quite understand but always seemed to be on the verge of being able to. More and more often, the journal referred to her having spent a whole day studying the man in Room Five to the neglect of her other, more inhuman, duties. Perhaps that was why she'd persuaded Prothero to allow him special privileges; only, of course, after she'd got the tissue samples and cultures she needed from him for the central part of her work, and it had then become a matter of finding out how long he'd survive after what she'd done to him. But once she'd established that he was no longer likely to be infectious, she'd got the Commander's agreement to allow him out of his cell; even to give him a little plot of land for gardening.

The man had turned out to have a genius for gardening, and with the food shortages, Prothero had been delighted, but that was mainly because Prothero was taking all the extra vegetables for himself. Perhaps that was also why Prothero had allowed a corner of the garden to be turned over to him for growing roses. Violet Carson roses.

And to allow Delia to persuade him that the man in Room Five should be allowed to put in an order for some gardening supplies.

And, reading what those supplies were, Finch was absolutely certain that would have been the one fact Prothero had ensured was erased from the official records, even before it was decided to erase the records wholesale anyway. But Delia had been oblivious to all that. She'd merely been watching in fascination as the man arranged certain quantities of his chemicals and fertilizers in piles and lines on the floor of his cell, almost as if he were constructing some sort of model of the world, like a tabletop train set without the tracks and engines, but with all the hills and valleys and houses rendered in different-colored heaps of powder. All kept separate, of course, and in patterns that she was so busy trying to understand that it never occurred to her what might happen when they were mixed together.

*November 6th. It started last night, toward midnight. The first explosions tore open the entire medical section. All that work . . . all my work . . . gone.*

Of course, that was what the journal concentrated on. Not the explosions, the fires, the people running screaming with their clothes and hair in flame, the panicking guards shooting at everyone and everything, the inmates dying shackled where they were because no one thought of their release before smoke inhalation asphyxiated them. How many died that night? No one knew. No one had counted. Civilian casualties hardly mattered. Not those sort of civilians.

But there was the date again. Although the entry was dated the sixth, the events concerned had taken place on the fifth. The fifth of November.

And it was obvious that "all" her work hadn't been lost. The reports had been filed, the knowledge preserved. Whatever it was that Delia Surridge had been working on, and Finch couldn't quite put his finger on that, despite reading the journal with the most careful attention to detail, she'd already succeeded by the time the project, and Larkhill itself, was brought to a sudden, fiery end.

*I was trying to understand how it could have happened when I saw him. The man from Room Five. He'd used the things we'd given him to garden with, the chemicals, fertilizers, and ammonia, to make the bombs.*

*I saw him in the midst of the flames. He looked at me. Not with eyes, there were no eyes. But I know he was looking at me because I felt it and . . .*

*And, oh, God, what have I done . . . ?*

# FOURTEEN

Evey Hammond woke with a sense of déjà vu, or so she thought at first, though she soon realized that Gordon Deitrich's guest bedroom, with its sumptuously silken bedsheets and marquetry-work wardrobes, cloisonné vases and brocade drapes, now parted to let the sunlight stream through in brilliant, golden splendor, was quite outside her experience. Not a sense of "seen before," then . . .

Smelled before.

Uncertain or, more to the point, not quite believing, she began to get an inkling of just what that aroma was and tumbled out of bed, dressing hurriedly in the clothes that Gordon had fetched for her late the previous night, ringing up a friend with some tale of a long-neglected niece arriving from Carlisle with nothing more than the clothes she had on at the time, and then risking the curfew to go and borrow an outfit for her. Such good taste he had too, although now, knowing what she did about him, that wasn't quite such a surprise. Mind you, anything would have been better than the little pink party dress she'd arrived in. And, a night's sleep having soothed away the nerves of the previous day somewhat, she had to say that she couldn't really have hoped to find a better place of sanctuary.

Still, thoughts like that weren't getting that aroma investigated. She slipped on her shoes and headed downstairs. As expected, she found Deitrich in the kitchen, a frying pan in one hand, a spatula in the other.

*"Bonjour, mademoiselle."* He grinned brightly, becoming aware of her standing hesitantly at the door; then pausing as he noticed the confused look on her face.

"What's that you're making?" she asked, taking a tentative pace forward into the kitchen.

"We called it eggs in a basket. My Mum used to make them. Sit down."

She did, still looking a little bewildered, and he served the eggs onto a plate before her. Just the same meal, just the same way . . .

"Is this a dream?" she asked, more to herself than him, though nothing was going to stop her from picking up the knife and fork and making a start.

"What do you mean?" Deitrich asked, a little bewildered himself now.

"The first morning I was with . . . *him,* he made me eggs just like this."

"Really?" he asked, eyebrows rising in genuine surprise.

"I swear," she assured him, not wanting to be laughed at over something that seemed both so minor and somehow so important to her.

"That's a pretty strange coincidence," he said thoughtfully; perhaps with slightly exaggerated thoughtfulness. "Although there is an obvious explanation."

"There is?"

"Yes, Evey," Deitrich said, trying hard to keep a straight face, but not quite succeeding. "I am V. At last you know the truth."

Evey could only stare at him uncertainly, not quite sure if he was joking; not even sure, after all she'd been through, if she *wanted* it to be a joke.

"You're stunned, I know," he continued debonairly, finding the straight face harder to keep by the moment. "You wouldn't think it to look at me, but beneath this wrinkled, well-fed exterior lies a dangerous killing machine with a fetish for Fawkesian masks. *Vive la révolution!*"

"That's not funny, Gordon," she told him flatly, upset enough to forget her eggs for a moment.

"I know," he said deflatedly. "I'm useless without a studio audience."

"I've seen people go to jail for less than that," she added, trying somehow to get him to take the subject seriously. He leaned back against the kitchen counter and sighed.

"That's the problem, isn't it?" he said, suddenly looking world-weary. "V is right. We've been culled into silence."

"V kills people," she said shortly, not certain she liked the direction the conversation was taking.

"Maybe he does, but that doesn't make him any less right."

"So you think that V is doing the right thing?" asked Evey, not quite believing that she was hearing this sort of thing coming from a figure she'd always regarded as a pillar of the establishment. But that, of course, was before he'd shown her what he had last night. Now, having to think about the answer to her question himself, Gordon Deitrich sank into a chair. A few seconds passed during which Evey realized her eggs were getting cold. She hurriedly got back to eating them, wolfing most of them down before he spoke again.

"What I think," he said at length, "is that V is simply giving them the same thing they have been giving us."

"What?" she asked, now genuinely interested in his reply.

"A reason to be afraid."

As time wore on and Eric Finch finally managed to get his thoughts into some sort of order, he began to ask himself questions both awkward and unsettling. Questions that had deprived him of sleep just as thoroughly as the events surrounding the deaths of Bishop Lilliman and Delia Surridge.

Sitting there at his computer, having intentionally arrived before anyone else, including Dominic, he was going through the online archives of *The Times,* and everything he read only made him more afraid of the thoughts that were running round inside his head. Bad thoughts. About bad people. And not necessarily the ones it was his job to catch.

"Terrorists Strike with Biological Weapon," thundered one of the headlines, but that wasn't the only one that interested him, wasn't the only one this particular search had turned up. Bleary-eyed and almost afraid of the way all this was starting to fall into place in his mind, he began to relive the other horrors that had followed that first shocking report from fourteen years ago, through the ensuing series of headlines.

"St. Mary's Virus Kills 178," said another, and he recalled that had included Evey Hammond's brother. "Three Waters Infected." And "Tube Terror." Then, eloquent in its simplicity: "Epidemic!" One he remembered being involved in personally (two of the men under him had been brutally murdered there): "Riot at King's Hospital." And finally, the worst one of all, more of an epitaph than a headline: "8,000 Dead." Even so, he knew, that was just the total for that first outbreak. When you added on the death toll from the other "attacks," like the one in Northern Ireland, the final count was something far, far worse than that.

It was all starting to add up. And the sum total was, quite simply, horrible.

Finch was still reading when Dominic arrived and greeted him with a cheery "Morning, Inspector. You're at it early."

This morning Finch found Dominic's youthful energy and enthusiasm depressing. But right then he found anything and everything depressing.

"Something wrong?" the young man asked, now with genuine concern as he looked at his boss's pasty face. Jesus, the old man wasn't about to have a heart attack, was he? "You don't look so good, sir."

Finch shook his head slightly to dispel any fears Dominic might have about his health. Then he reached down into the lower drawer of his desk and pulled out a small electronic device and flicked it on before he said a single word.

Dominic reacted in obvious surprise as he recognized the jammer, specifically designed, he knew, to knock out the Ear's bugs and listening devices. No one was supposed to have one of them. That was the sort of thing they arrested people for. "I want to ask you a question, Dominic," Finch began when he was sure the machine had had time enough to warm up and function. "I don't care if you answer me or not, but . . ." And now Finch nodded toward the device, making it obvious that this was the reason he'd switched it on. "I just want to say this aloud, but I need to know that the question won't leave this office."

"Yeah, course, Inspector. But . . ."

It wasn't a question of Finch trusting him, yet there still remained the outstanding why? And the "Why?" was contained in Dominic's glance toward the machine.

"Because of the terrorist?" Dominic asked.

"No."

"What is it, Chief?" Dominic felt confused enough now that he wanted to sit down. "What's going on?"

"The question I want to ask is about St. Mary's," Finch told him in a deadly serious and somehow threateningly quiet tone. "And Three Waters."

The names were enough to make Dominic's blood run cold.

"The question that's kept me up for the last twenty-four hours," continued Finch slowly, hesitantly, his own blood flowing sluggish with the enormity of it all, "the question I have to ask is . . . what if the worst, most horrifying biological attack in this country's history was not the work of religious extremists?"

"What?" said Dominic, aghast. "I don't understand. We know it was. They were caught. They confessed."

"And they were executed, I know," Finch concluded for him. "And that may be what really happened." It was certainly the official story, anyway: a band of fundamentalists from the Middle East had got hold of some of the same viral agents that the Americans had been using to win one of their dirty little wars in the same neighborhood . . . the very same biological weapons that so many British agitators had protested so loudly about, until the government had finally been forced to withdraw from the NATO alliance some time before the War. And then, lumping all the Western, Christian countries together under the name of The Great Satan, those extremists had formed a cell over here and carried out revenge attacks in London, in Ireland, and elsewhere. And that was what Finch, like everyone else, had always believed. Until now. It was only reading through the news reports again this morning that he'd realized that the virus they'd been using *wasn't* the same as any of the ones the Americans had been using. Similar, yes, but actually far more powerful. Something the Yanks would probably have given their right arms for, if only they could have used it in the war with China.

"But I see this chain of events, these coincidences," Finch picked up his train of thought again, "and I have to ask: What if that *isn't* what happened? What if someone else unleashed that virus . . . what if someone else killed all those people? Would you want to know who it was?"

"Sure," said Dominic, still trying to get his head round the idea that what he'd taken for certainty, for gospel truth, for so many years, might be a tissue of lies.

"Even if it was someone working for this government?"

"Jesus," gasped Dominic softly, understanding now why Finch had turned on the debugging device.

"That's my question," his boss summed up. "If our own government was responsible for what happened at St. Mary's and Three Waters . . . if our own government was responsible for the death of eighteen thousand people . . . would you really want to know?"

"Honestly?" Dominic asked, trading question for question. Finch nodded.

"I don't know."

# FIFTEEN

The champagne cork popped; the bubbly began to foam. The clink of bottle on glass, once and then twice. Gordon Deitrich handed one of the glasses to Evey and raised it with a smile. A look of real pleasure, and not the rather forced smile, the mask, that she'd grown used to seeing while working with him at Jordan Tower. And in the couple of weeks that she'd been living with him, Evey had discovered that when he took that mask off and became his true self, as he only did in the safety of his own home, there was much to admire about Gordon Deitrich. Even to love, in a platonic sort of way. After all, not only was he gay, he was old enough to be her father. And that was at the heart of it. With him going out to buy her clothes, sharing his meals with her, even reading her favorite stories late at night, she'd begun to feel as if she had a home again, for the first time in more years than she recalled. That was more precious to her than she could possibly express; and he, being part of it, had become precious to her as well. Family.

Father figure or not, he was kind and caring, he made no demands, and, except when the pressures of work left him tired and depressed, he was very good company indeed. And having her around the house seemed to compensate, just a little, for all those lonely years he'd had to pass since he too had been "driven underground." She couldn't help but notice how his spirits had improved since she'd been with him, and at times his sense of humor got so out of hand she wanted less to treat him like a father than to spank him like a little boy. And in the last few days it had got worse. He seemed to be always going round with a secretive smirk on his face, as if he were planning some wonderful practical joke . . . some "wizard wheeze" . . . that he didn't want to tell her about for fear of spoiling the surprise. And that, she had to confess, was starting to get her just a little bit worried.

Now they were sitting on the couch in his living room at two minutes to eight on Wednesday evening, and she still had no idea why he seemed so happy. But the barely suppressed excitement that radiated from him made her rather suspect she was about to find out.

"What's all this about?" Evey asked as he reached for the remote and turned on the television, cranking up the volume with an excited grin.

"I'm celebrating," Deitrich told her, clinking their glasses together and taking a sip. The bubbles burst headily against his palate, matching and then adding to his sense of euphoria.

"Celebrating what?" asked Evey, still uncertain. She'd never seen him quite like this before, either in the old days at the office or since she'd been staying here with him, and she really wasn't sure what to make of his present mood. There was something of the gleeful, mischievous schoolboy who'd just got away with a hilarious prank; something of the wild risk-taking of a man who'd stepped over the line and didn't care who knew it; something that reminded her of her father's revolutionary zeal, and of V's. And something of the innocent, gullible fool.

"This could be the best show we've ever done," he chuckled, as the familiar theme music swelled, the equally familiar night-blue and gold titles for *Deitrich's Half Hour* appearing, with their Futurist-style view of Big Ben, Tower Bridge, and other London landmarks, and in one corner of the screen the BTN logo that made everything official. The hands of Big Ben were set at eight o'clock, and millions of people across the land would eagerly be tuned in.

On the screen, Deitrich appeared from behind the curtains, smiling as he always did, walking out to take the applause of the studio audience. A real studio audience, this one, not like the fake footage and sound track they used to have on Prothero's nightly political farce. After all, this was *genuine* farce, and that was something the authorities considered safe enough to record before a live audience of the "happy British public." That always played well. An audience was something Deitrich always played to well, besides.

"Thank you, thank you and good evening, ladies and gentleman," the on-screen Deitrich began, again as always. The next lines, though, were a little different. "We've got a really special show tonight. You won't believe it. I'm not sure I do. Would you please give a

very warm welcome to our very own Chancellor . . .
*Adam Sutler!*"

The audience gasped, and so did Evey, looking
round toward Deitrich as if she wasn't sure this was
really happening. As if she *hoped* this wasn't really
happening.

"We threw out the censor-approved script and shot
a new one that I wrote this morning," he explained,
eyes sparkling.

"Oh my God!" was all Evey could think to say, turning her attention back toward the set. Surely he
wouldn't do something like that, she hoped desperately; that was breaking the one rule that no one at
BTN ever broke. When she was at Jordan Tower, she
hadn't heard of anyone since before the Reclamation
who'd dared to do that. But if anyone was going to do
it, it had to be Gordon. The only question now was,
how bad was it going to get?

There was a Sutler look-alike stepping out from behind the curtain, just as Deitrich had done a few moments earlier, nodding like Mussolini in appreciation
of the audience response as the crowd went wild.

And then the camera panned away from the
"Chancellor," out across the cheering audience, before lingering on several heavily armed and, for the
most part, heavily overweight and decidedly scruffy-
looking soldiers who were aiming their guns at the
happy-clapping mob, trigger-fingers poised, while
standing beneath a large, lit-up APPLAUSE sign.

"Christ, Gordon!" spluttered Evey, almost spitting
champagne out through her nose. Even so, she knew

that after an opening like that, it was only going to get worse. And it did.

Back on the TV screen, two beautiful showgirls were leading Sutler, who seemed unable to stop himself from saluting and goose-stepping in time to the military march struck up by the studio orchestra, toward a typical chat-show arrangement of comfortable chairs where Deitrich was waiting for him. They shook hands as the music died, Deitrich giving a slightly mocking, overly deferential bow, and sat down. And when they'd made themselves comfortable, the host began.

"I understand, Chancellor"—Deitrich smiled unctuously—"that you've been under tremendous stress since this whole terrorist business began, and so we thought we might help you try to relax."

A glance round then, a beckoning hand raised toward the background. "Girls?"

A gaggle of giggling showgirls materialized at Deitrich's command, all feathers, smiles, and high heels, gushing excitement as they tottered toward the Chancellor. One of them carried a small tray on which was placed a glass of milk.

"Oh, warm milk!" exclaimed the Sutler clone fogyishly, displaying a sort of second-childhood delight. "There's nothing better."

"You enjoy a glass every night, don't you, Chancellor?" Deitrich said knowingly, everything about his tone and body language suggesting he was humoring a senile old fool.

"Since I was a boy," his foil replied with smug delight, taking a sip and smacking his lips before relaxing theatrically as a couple of the more voluptuous showgirls began massaging his shoulders enthusiastically, leaning forward to display their considerable assets to best advantage. And the Chancellor rolled his eyes exaggeratedly to enjoy the view.

"But you're wrong, Mr. Deitrich," he said eventually, apparently making a strenuous effort to get his mind back on the subject at hand. "The terrorist was never a serious concern."

Evey could only watch in growing horror as the camera drew back to show a trapdoor opening in the studio floor next to Sutler's chair. A tall, black Jacobean hat began to appear, then a mask . . . and up popped V, caped as usual, raising a hand toward the mask as if to twiddle his mustache in the style of a vaudeville villain.

Then, crawling between the legs of the showgirls, who looked down at him with expressions of pop-eyed surprise and lips puckered into silent, comical "Ooohs," V sneaked over and, apparently unnoticed by either Deitrich or his victim, began to secretly tie the Chancellor's shoelaces together.

All across the land, Evey knew, the same audience who'd watched V's original broadcast would now be watching these satirical antics that, in many ways, were just as damaging to the powers that be. She couldn't imagine what Deitrich thought he was doing, or where he'd got the idea . . . until she remembered *God Save the Queen* securely hidden down there in the basement.

"So is the terrorist still alive and active?" Deitrich continued blithely, glancing round toward his showgirls, cuing one of them to produce a large cigar. She prepared to light it, only to have it taken away from her by V, who substituted another in its place.

"The terrorist has been neutralized," said Sutler with a smile of absolute confidence, taking the ready-lit cigar and starting to puff.

And Evey knew exactly what was going to happen next. It was going to be one of those Bugs Bunny cartoon moments; and, of course, it was. The cigar exploded with a large bang and a thick puff of smoke, and then, while the audience broke into screaming peals of laughter, some undercostume tubing appeared to send steam shooting out of the raging Chancellor's ears.

As the gale of laughter and applause finally subsided, Deitrich looked round toward the showgirls and seemed to notice for the first time V hiding among them.

"Oh my God, Chancellor!" he exclaimed in surprise, pointing with a finger that shot out just past the Chancellor's nose. "Look!"

"The terrorist!" cried Sutler, leaping to his feet and immediately pratfalling forward on his face as the knotted laces between his feet pulled tight.

"Get him!" the Chancellor commanded next, rolling to a sitting position and starting to untie his shoes. And the soldiers who'd been seen earlier dashed forward and began chasing V round the stage, accompanied by the tittering, tottering showgirls; then the whole crew scampered out into the audience and back to the stage again, while the orchestra played an exaggeratedly speeded-up accompaniment and the audience went wild with laughter. And all through this madcap chase, reminiscent of the closing scenes of an ancient Benny Hill show, Gordon Deitrich sat benignly in his chair, obviously enjoying his finest moment ever on the air, impeccable and impervious to the chaos all around him.

And Evey could only stare in horrified shock, almost unaware that Deitrich was sitting there beside her, enjoying the experience, the glory, all over again.

At last the soldiers, one or two of whom had managed to capture showgirls "by mistake," finally caught V and wrestled him to the ground. And now Sutler, on his feet and all his freedom of movement fully restored, stepped forward and reached toward V's mask.

"At last!" he cried. "And now, for all the world to see—"

But as the mask was ripped away, another surprise was revealed, stunning both soldiers and audience alike. For the "terrorist" turned out to be another Sutler look-alike, and as the soldiers looked on with their mouths hanging open comically, he leapt to his feet, tossed aside the hat, cloak, and wig and revealed himself, wearing exactly the same suit as the first impersonator.

"Unhand me!" he cried. "I'm your Chancellor!"

"What?" the first Sutler exploded. "How dare you? *I'm* the Chancellor!"

"Impostor!" came the pantomime response, and

then they lunged at each other, going down in a tumbling ball of flailing fists and thrashing legs until, wound together like a Möbius strip, it became quite impossible to tell one Chancellor from the other. All it really needed to complete the humiliating farce was for their pants to fall down, revealing red-and-white polka-dot boxer shorts, but it seemed even Gordon hadn't dared to go that far. Or perhaps he just hadn't thought of it.

Finally, they broke apart and leapt to their feet, pointing furiously at each other.

And one cried, "Soldiers! That man is the terrorist!"

And the other screamed, "I order you to shoot that traitor!"

"That liar!"

"That fake!"

"That fraud!"

"Ready!"

"Aim!"

*"Fire!"*

A staccato rattle of automatic weaponry as the soldiers opened fire, and then the two Sutlers slapped concealed blood-capsules against their chests and spun to the ground, the curtain crashing down just after they hit the deck.

And the audience went wild in a way that no one could quite have anticipated.


Certainly not the man who sat watching his TV set with a glass of warm milk gripped rigidly in one hand, staring as Deitrich made a profound, theatrical bow and disappeared behind the curtain.

Was still staring when the masked, smiling face of V appeared through the slit in the curtain a moment later, grin seeming wider than ever, and twisted his mustaches once again.

And the audience cheered.

*Cheered.*

And the glass of milk shattered in the aging man's hand.

Evey was still watching, in a similar shock that was now rapidly turning to stone-cold fear, though not clutching her champagne glass quite so hard, when the phone rang. Deitrich, still chuckling to himself, put down his own glass and went to answer it.

He listened for a while, but seemed quite impervious to the message he was getting from the other end of the line.

"What are they going to do?" he asked, still buoyed up with his triumph. "Fine us? Big deal. We have the most watched show on the air." A pause, and then: "Well, you're a lawyer. That's what I pay you for . . . protect me."

And with that he hung up.

"I should have hired him years ago to be my mother," he said, smiling as he turned back to Evey.

"You're mad," she told him bluntly, still not quite believing what she'd just seen.

"Either that or I wasn't breast-fed," he quipped.

"Is everything a joke to you?"

"Only the things that matter." Though he looked a little more serious as he said that, it was obvious that she just wasn't able to get through to him. Right at that moment, probably no one could.

"Gordon, what if they come after you?" she asked, finally managing to express the dread she felt. Not just for him, but for both of them.

"Look," he said reassuringly, sitting down and taking her hand. "I'll tell you what's going to happen. I'll have to make some kind of apology and do some boring fund-raiser, and in the meantime our ratings will go through the roof. Trust me, it'll be fine."

She tried to nod, tried to smile, but it was quite obvious to both of them that she wasn't convinced.

As the hours passed and the stars wheeled away the time, the gilded moon drew a veil of cloud across her face, almost as if she no longer had the stomach to watch events in the world of men below. And the night became very dark indeed.

The sound of breaking glass woke Evey, that icy tinkle that froze the heart and shattered the silence, her dreams, and her world. It was followed by a loud thump, and movement started once again. The movement of people down in the house below, the thunderous pumping of her heart.

"Gordon?" she queried desperately, sitting up in bed, overwhelmed by the feeling that she'd been through all this before. But it shouldn't be happening

all over again. Surely, it *couldn't* be happening again.
It was.

And the dreadful fear that she'd almost managed to forget since she'd arrived in Bloomsbury . . . *that* was back again too.

A gunshot echoed through the house, and then there was the sound of heavy footsteps on the stairs, stumbling as they reached the landing, pounding toward her. And then Gordon Deitrich burst into her room, slamming the door behind him, wearing only a robe and lathered in sweat, gasping for breath, the whites of his eyes bright in the darkness.

All happening again.

"Hide, Evey!" he managed to choke out quickly, throwing his considerable bulk back against the door. "Quick!"

For a moment Evey just wanted to burst into tears . . . to shut her eyes and make it all go away when she opened them again . . . to be a little girl once more, wrapped up in the love of her Mummy and Daddy, surrounded by the toys that she loved in her turn . . . with Teddy . . . to hug him close and say the magic word that set the world aright . . .

But there was no magic word, and nothing would set this right now.

Panic took over then, and she rolled out of the bed, hit the floor hard, and scrambled into the shadows beneath the bedstead. Lay there quaking with terror, remembering how she'd done exactly the same thing before . . . and all the terrible things that had followed.

Repetitions and coincidences, as if God only had a

limited number of stories to tell per individual person
and just wanted to replay them over and over, making
his cast jump through the same hoops time after time,
until they finally collapsed with exhaustion. Or until,
perhaps, they'd learned the lesson they needed to and
managed to escape the play, into the world of greater
freedom outside the theater.

Only instants later the door exploded from its
hinges, throwing Deitrich aside like a limp sack. As he
staggered, trying to regain his balance, a swarm of
heavily armed, dark-clad paramilitary Fingermen
flooded into the room.

"What do you think—?" he managed to get out,
but a rifle butt smashed into his mouth and cut the
question short.

Beneath the bed, Evey could only see Deitrich's
bare feet, seeming pale and old and venous against the
polished black leather boots, and think how terribly
vulnerable they looked as the Fingermen took their
prisoner in hand.

Then Peter Creedy was there, gloating, his favorite,
well-used truncheon in his hand. It flailed down with a
sick thud, then landed again with much more of a
bony crack.

"Not so funny now, is it, funnyman?" he grunted, as
Deitrich sobbed and gurgled for breath.

Another hit, and then the most famous television
face in the land, now that Lewis Prothero was gone,
hit the floor hard and looked toward the fugitive under
the bed. And both of them knew that that face, now
split open like the skin of a watermelon to reveal the

red pulp within, would never be seen on television again. He tried to say something, to beg them to stop the kicking they were continuing to give him even as they zip-tied his hands behind his back, but his jaw was broken and all he could manage was a gurgling scream. He writhed, looked away, looked back.

His eyes searched for Evey, locked with her own.

All happening again.

She could only stare back helplessly, remembering the way it had happened to her parents and how her mother had looked at her just like that, feeling the panic attack clutching at her throat, starting to hyper-ventilate.

*All happening again.*

Trying not to scream as they yanked the shiny black bag over his head and pulled it tight round his neck like a noose.

*All happening again. Again. Again . . .*

And Evey Hammond, still sick with terror, suddenly found her whole self filling up with a burning, angry hate. For Peter Creedy and his Fingermen, and their arrogant, vicious, and appallingly casual brutality. For Adam Sutler and his Party, who gave the Finger their orders and who had turned this country into a hell in the name of making it a heaven. To a lesser extent, for Gordon Deitrich, for being so wonderfully, stupidly heroic in launching his satirical attack on the evils of the world, and never being wise enough to re-alize the dire consequences that his foolhardy actions would bring. But most of all, for herself, for she felt responsible for all that had happened: for giving him someone to show off his bravery to; for being here in the first place and landing him with someone to protect; for not having the same sort of courage that he'd had, in standing up against them; and still, no matter what she might think of what he was doing, she hated herself for betraying V's trust.

Most of all, she hated the fear she'd always felt, which had never let her live the life she wanted to live and held her paralyzed and quaking beneath the bed even now, despite the self-loathing it provoked.

Then they hauled Gordon Deitrich to his feet—his old, bare feet, now spattered with dripping blood—and dragged him out the door, laughing as they did so. And there was nothing she could do to help him, nothing anyone could do now.

Sound receded from the house then, like the ebbing of the tide. The footsteps going down the stairs, the slamming of the front door, the sound of engines starting outside and driving off down the street.

And when silence finally had the place securely in its grasp, Evey pushed her way out from under the bed, knowing she dare not stay for, after the first raid, others would undoubtedly come to search the place more thoroughly, not for proof against Deitrich—after the evening's television show, no other proof was needed for what was going to happen to him now—but for evidence of accomplices, of fellow conspirators plotting together to satirize and overthrow the state. Perhaps even, if their surveillance was good, for her.

If indeed everyone *had* left the house, she

thought, dressing hurriedly and silently. For all she knew, Fingermen might be lurking there still, just waiting for anyone who, thinking silence meant safety, might now emerge from a hiding place and, seeking to escape, fall into their hands like ripe fruit dropping from a tree.

Not the front door then. Instead she climbed out the open bedroom window and crawled out onto a small roof beyond.

The roof overlooked the back garden behind the house, and she slid down to its edge, grabbing the guttering before she fell right off. Even so, when she peered over, the ground still looked too far away to risk a jump.

She threw one leg over the edge of the roof, then the other, scrabbling for a handhold that would stop her sliding, and managed to ease her body over the edge. She hoped desperately that the gutter would take her weight as she grabbed it hurriedly, feeling herself slipping out of control, going down quickly, catching her jaw a glancing blow on the gutter edge; then falling until she felt her arms snap out straight. She winced with pain at the pull on suddenly stretched joints and shoulders, then felt the gutter pull out of its brackets; and she was falling, trying desperately, in that instant, to remember whether it was better to keep her legs straight or bent, and deciding on the latter. Then hitting the ground with a soft thump, thankful that she'd remembered right, but sprawling heavily on a concrete patio nonetheless.

She stayed low as a flashlight shone out from inside

the house, swung across the garden, and then turned back inside.

Lights and shadows moved around eerily within, all the more threatening for the accompanying silence; obviously they were still searching, waiting for some betraying sound or movement. And as Deitrich had been known to live alone, she realized that meant they were looking for *her.*

Taking a deep breath and trying to calm herself, she began to wriggle away across the patio on her belly, made it to a bed of shrubbery, and began to crawl through it toward the garden gate. No thought of how dirty her clothes must be getting, of how the branches were pulling at her hair; not even of where she might go from here. Escape was the only thing she had on her mind at that moment, and if she had to keep running until she'd left the country entirely, then somehow she would.

A few moments later, she was through the gate and out into the back alley, finally starting to breathe properly for the first time since she'd heard the sound of breaking glass. Now, then . . . away. Anywhere away from here, though she still had no idea of a destination at all. Perhaps the best idea was to try to get out of London, even out of the quarantine "safe zones" the government had established. She'd never been entirely sure what lay beyond them—the TV news kept reporting outbreaks of plague and other horrors, but she no longer believed the media anyway—but if they were beyond the areas where the government writ normally ran, they might be her last, best hope. And right now even the risk of disease seemed better than the prospect of the black bag. Mind made up and starting to feel better simply for having a sense of purpose, she looked up the alley, took a deep breath, and set off.

But no sooner had she started to move than a hand landed on her shoulder, jerking her backward and grabbing her arms with a force that made her sudden, desperate struggles absolutely useless.

"Gotcha!" said a rough, masculine voice behind her, and though she tried to look back over her shoulder as she felt the plastic zip-ties tighten round her wrists, she could only see a dark, faceless figure in the darker darkness of the night. But if she couldn't see who, she certainly knew *what*.

A Fingerman.

"No!" she squealed frantically, shaking helplessly in horrified, bowel-loosening fear. "No! *Please!*"

But plead, shriek, or fight as she might, there was no escape . . . nothing that could be done to stop the black plastic bag from being drawn over her head, being tightened round her neck.

And drowning out her piercing scream of absolute, abject terror.

# SIXTEEN

When they pulled the black bag off, Evey had lost all track of time. She remembered being roughly dragged along, half-fainting, and thrust into a truck, remembered the noise of its engine, the raucous chatter of the guards, and even their very breathing, the smell of them and the odor of her own fear, surprised despite her terror at how swiftly, when the sense of sight was removed, the other senses had become heightened. And the one thing that she did have to be thankful for was that she hadn't been sick inside the bag. Though with the way she thought of herself now, that humiliation would have seemed like a deserved punishment. For it seemed to her it was fear that had brought all this on her, and whatever happened to her from now on, she had only herself to blame.

She was sure she'd passed out at some point, but whether that was before or after they'd buffeted her out of the truck, dragged her down some stairs, and shoved her along a corridor, she couldn't tell. The sound of a shutting door and the grating of its lock was clear enough, and she remembered how they'd merely dumped her on a stone-cold floor, without food, without water, without toilet facilities.

And so she'd had no alternative, eventually, but just to let go on the floor. And somehow that seemed a small revenge in itself.

How long had passed after that before a guard came to collect her, she had no idea. He'd called her a dirty little cow, but he'd finally freed her sore, chafed wrists from the zip-ties and dragged her here . . . somewhere . . . and sat her down roughly in a chair.

And then they did, at last, remove the hood.

She so wanted to look, to see where she was, just to use her eyes again, but the lights that shone in her face were so brilliant, and her pupils were so distended from the long darkness, that she had no alternative but to shut them again. But in that instant she'd managed to see a desk before her, and the dark shape of a man sitting opposite, behind the lights that shone full in her face.

"Do you know why you are here, Evey Hammond?" he said coldly, and blinking and squinting, she tried to open her eyes again, only to see nothing but red shapes that flared upon her retina.

And an unmoving shadow to whom she addressed a simple "Please . . ."

She tried to look round her then, but as she did so, a hand cuffed round the back of her head from behind, making it quite clear that she was to keep her attention on the interrogator before her and nowhere else. But in the instant she'd been able to see, she'd taken in a bare room, windowless and with nothing to break the monotony of the blank walls but a *Strength through Unity, Unity through Faith* poster.

"You are being formally charged with three counts of murder," the interrogator continued matter-of-factly, though not without a hint of malice, "the bombing of government property, and conspiracy to commit acts of terrorism, treason, and sedition, the penalty for which is death by firing squad."

Evey felt as if every word were a punch in the stomach. This was everything she'd dreaded, and every bit as bad as it could get, all laid out in the plainest terms. The only relief was that they hadn't put a bullet through her brain already.

As she rather suspected they would have done with Gordon Deitrich.

That they hadn't must mean that there was some reason for keeping her alive. Something they wanted from her. She opened her mouth then, but nothing came out.

"You have one chance and only one chance to save your life," the interrogator continued, and now she detected a trace of eagerness in his voice. Strange the way her hearing seemed to have become almost supernaturally heightened in the few hours she'd been forced to rely on it most of all; not just sensitive to the slightest whisper, but to nuance and tone beside.

"You must tell us the identity or whereabouts of code-name V," the voice said next. "If the information leads to his capture, you will be immediately released from this facility. Do you understand what I'm telling you?"

There it was. The deal she'd wanted to make when

she'd almost betrayed V to the bishop, the last, best hope she'd clung to all along.

Until . . . when was it . . . last night? Until they'd come along and done what they'd done to Gordon Deitrich.

Poor, old, foolish, brave Gordon Deitrich.

"You can return to your normal life, Miss Hammond," the man emphasized, seeming, to her watering eyes, to lean forward until he was almost but not quite visible in the light. "All you have to do is cooperate."

Cooperate. And go free.

If she could believe them. If they didn't shoot her as soon as she'd told them everything she knew.

"I . . . ," Evey began hesitantly; hesitated some more and sucked in a breath. "I don't know."

"Process her, Rossiter," the man said shortly, disappointment adding venom to the words.

And while she was still looking round, dazzled, to see whom the command had been addressed to, rough hands grabbed her from behind, bagged her head again, and once more dragged her away.


She wept when they shaved her head. She didn't mean to, didn't want to, but her hair was the one thing about her appearance that she'd always been proud of, always thought her best feature. And as the rough hand ran the crude, hurtful electric clippers over her scalp, as the long blond tresses rained down on the floor, she felt that this, more than anything, was stripping away the sense of identity that she'd clung to for years. With this, she was no longer Evey Hammond. She was just a prisoner, without even a number. A cipher. A subject. Nobody.

A nobody who was very, very afraid.

But then they'd known the head-shaving would make her feel like this, which was why they'd done it in the first place. There might be physical torture later, but first there would be humiliation.

They stripped her clothes away next, took her naked into a room and manacled her wrists to a ceiling hook, then left her dangling while they hosed her down with powerful jets of water that buffeted her, left her breathless, bruised her, and eventually became more a form of torture than the washing and delousing it pretended to be. And then, while her skin was still raw and pink and hurting, they pulled a rough hemp dress down over her head, more like a penitent's hair shirt than anything else, refused her any shoes or underwear, and dragged her away to a cell.

A cell with one small window, too high up to see out of, and an electric socket in the ceiling without a lightbulb, so when the day ended, there was only darkness. A grille in the door looked out into a dank corridor with, directly opposite, another of those *Strength through Unity, Unity through Faith* posters, whose message she'd long ago ceased to believe in. She had no faith and fearfully little strength, and she now realized unity for this government meant little more than murdering anyone who disagreed with anything it said. There was a bare shelf to sleep on without any bedding, and a bucket that served as a toilet, which no one bothered to empty until it was full. And a rathole down by the floor, where the only other inhabitant of the cell emerged after dark to run over her body in the night, to eat her dress while she slept. To bite her while she lay there stupefied with terror.

And then they offered her food. One look was enough to make her want to vomit, because vomit was exactly what the "food" they offered looked like. Even the rat wouldn't touch it.

Why didn't they just kill her straightaway? She was sure they were going to regardless of whether she co-operated, so why not do the merciful thing and kill her now? But mercy wasn't on their agenda, of course; and besides, she desperately wanted to live.

Her sense of time began to blur again. The minutes passed somehow, but with only four stone walls to look at and that increasingly stupid poster, there was nothing to divert her attention. At any hour of the day or night they'd drag her away for further questioning, for beatings, torture, and humiliation. They showed her surveillance-camera footage from the alley where first she'd met V, accused her of being a plant, sent in by the terrorist to distract the Fingermen before he moved in to kill and maim them. When she denied it, they questioned her furiously about what he'd said to her afterward, then pointed out how obvious it was that she'd willingly left the scene with him. Showed her more footage taken near the Old Bailey, and at Westminster; demanding to know how she explained her presence there . . . and more than that, how did

she account for her ID being used at Lewis Prothero's
apartment building? Told her too that the young priest
at the Deanery had positively identified her as V's accomplice in the murder of the bishop, and how did
she explain that? And what was the terrorist going to
do next? Endless, endless questions. And when she
couldn't or wouldn't answer and even her interrogator
was becoming exasperated, the man Rossiter would
drench her with buckets of water and take her back,
cold and shivering, to her cell.

She slept whenever she could, unconsciousness
being her only escape, but always it seemed to her that
as soon as she fell asleep, a loudspeaker would boom
into life and a military band would play Sutler's recently written national anthem over and over, sometimes for hours on end, until she couldn't stand it
anymore. And then they'd thrash her with thin bam-
boo canes until her skin was raw, and even if she
wanted to sleep, she couldn't possibly lie down.

That was the part Rossiter seemed to enjoy the most.
The beatings. The cigarette burns. The humiliation. An
evil, sadistic thug, he was everything she'd expected a
Fingerman torturer to be, and the only surprise to her
was that he stopped short of inflicting permanent physical damage. But with everything else added to the random acts of violence—the sleep deprivation, the
interrogation, the miserable state of her cell—the mental damage being caused was quite enough.

Eventually, so disoriented she thought it was night
when the light shone through the window and day
when it was dark, she began to eat the food.

That made her cry in itself: that she'd reached that point of degradation where she'd eat that filth. But crying was what she did most of the time anyway, when they gave her a minute to herself.

And the rat came and went, providing the only entertainment she had, the only companionship. Love-bites in the dark.

And when the rat's attentions were all she had left to look forward to, she realized there really wasn't any lower to go. No better than a rat. Probably worse.

And then the rat didn't come anymore either, and her loneliness was absolutely complete.

And the light shone through the window sometimes; and sometimes it didn't. And the questioning never stopped.


Eventually, in one of those periods of total silence that somehow had become even more difficult to sleep in than the periods of continual noise, she heard a faint scratching sound from the hole down at the foot of the wall. Thinking joyfully that her rat had at last returned, she uncoiled slowly from the fetal ball in which she'd been trying to sleep, painfully eased her emaciated body off the bed-shelf, and crawled across the floor.

There was no rat. But something else was in the hole; something that had been pushed through from the other side. A small roll of toilet paper.

Evey looked at it in astonishment. Toilet paper was something she hadn't seen since she was arrested; something she'd almost forgotten existed.

Even more astonishing was that this little roll of paper had writing on it. Crude, and in pencil, it looked like the sort of script she'd expect to write herself after weeks of torture and starvation.

It could only be, she thought, a message from the prisoner in the cell next door. Unless this was just another malicious fraud on the part of her interrogators.

Either way, it gave her something to do, something to read; a voice from somewhere outside her own personal hell; and if anything could fill up even a minute of the long, lonely hours, she'd gratefully accept it, no matter where it came from. Just so long as it didn't mention V or ask her to explain anything.

Dragging herself over into the light from the window and propping herself up against the wall, she began to unroll the fragile missive.

*I know there is no way I can convince you that this is not one of their tricks. But I don't care. I am me. My name is Valerie. I don't think I will live much longer and I wanted to tell someone about my life. I'm writing this with a pencil that I hid inside of me. This is the only autobiography that I will ever write, and, oh God, I'm writing it on toilet paper.*

Another woman. And that seemed important to Evey; even if it turned out that they had entirely different backgrounds, they still had that basic something in common: the shared gender, the sense of being women together in trouble, of being "sisters under the skin," as the old cliché had it. Avidly, she read on.

*I was born in Nottingham. I don't remember much about my early years, but I do remember the rain.*

*My grandmother owned a farm in Tottlebrook and she used to tell me that God was in the rain. The sound of rain tapping on a window has always felt like home.*

*I passed my 11 Plus and went to girl's grammar.*

Secondary school. Something Evey had never known, having spent most of her teenage years after the arrest of her parents in the Juvenile Reclamation Project, a hellish young offenders' institution over in Wapping. And that had featured an educational curriculum of an entirely different sort: fear, brutality, abuse, and the Bible, followed by the rote slogan-learning they called "political ṛeeducation": "Strength through Unity, Unity through Faith," "England Prevails," "The Different Are the Damned," and on and on and on. And the pointless marching, and "Hold your arm out straighter when you're saluting, girl!" Beatings for the slightest misdemeanor, and as soon as it looked as if you might be making a friend, they maliciously split you apart somehow. Sent your chum to another wing, another prison, another world . . .

Grammar school. School friends. Teenage romance. What on earth could it have been like?

*It was at school that I met my first girlfriend. Her name was Sarah. It was her wrists. They were beautiful. I thought we would love each other forever.*

*I remember our teacher telling us that it was an adolescent phase that people grew out of.*

*Sarah did. I didn't.*

So simply said, but so much pain disguised. Evey began to weep again, knowing that under any normal circumstances she wouldn't, but her nerves were so frayed, her emotions so near the surface, it was just impossible not to. Eventually, sniffing and trying to pull herself together (she had no handkerchief on which to blow her nose, and that thought made her weep again, to think so suddenly of her mother), she read on through her tears.

*Later I fell in love with a girl called Christina. That was when I came out to my parents. I'm not sure I could have done it without Chris holding my hand.*

*My father wouldn't look at me. He told me to go and never come back. My mother said nothing. But I'd only told them the truth. Was that so selfish? Our integrity sells for so little but it is all we really have. It is the very last inch of us.*

*But within that inch we are free.*

Evey heard them coming for her again then. In sudden panic, knowing full well they'd take the message away from her if they found it, she managed to wriggle across the floor and stuff it back into the rathole. She couldn't let them have it; not now, when she'd just discovered a lifeline, a contact with something outside her own personal hell.

A magic word that opened up another world.

Rossiter, the guard, came and black-bagged her head again, as they always seemed to do when moving her round her prison, then manacled her hands behind her and took her into the usual interrogation room and stood her over a table on which, she saw when the hood was removed, was placed a large, full bowl of water. He looked over toward the usual interrogator briefly, asked her yet again about V, and, when she yet again had nothing to say, pushed her face down into the water and held her down for what seemed like hours.

She came up, spluttering and choking, and almost before she'd had time to gasp in another breath, her head was thrust down below the surface again.

"It ends whenever you want it to," the interrogator told her from behind the lights when she was eventually pulled up again. She merely looked at him, dead-eyed.

Down into the water again, this time held under, it seemed, to within an inch of her life.

And Valerie's words came back to her then: "It is the very last inch of us. But within that inch we are free."

"Just tell us where he is," she was asked again.

Integrity, she thought. The very last inch.

"I don't know," she told him.

Eventually, when they were as tired of hearing the same answer as she was of giving it, and when it seemed that just one more semidrowning would make her heart give out, they dragged her limp body back to the filthy, mephitic cell.

It seemed like hours before she felt strong enough to roll across the floor and pluck out the roll that had already become an almost-sacred text to her.

*I moved to London. I'd never been so happy.*

*I'd always known what I wanted to do with my life. A couple of years later I starred in my first film,* The Salt Flats.

*It was the most important role in my life. Not be-*

*cause of my career, but because that was how I met Ruth. The first time we kissed I knew that I never wanted to kiss any other's lips again but hers.*

*We moved into a small flat in London together. She grew Violet Carsons on the balcony for me and our kitchen always smelled of roses. Those were the best years of my life.*

*But America's war grew worse and worse and eventually the same sort of hell came to London. After that there were no roses anymore.*

*Not for anyone.*

Surprisingly quickly, Rossiter came for her again, stuck her head in the black bag she'd used to dread so much but was now past caring about, shackled her hands behind her . . . and simply left her lying on the floor. Total silence fell after he'd left and locked the door, and she could only lie there in sensory deprivation and total uncertainty for an unknown time that seemed to last forever.

Leaving her alone to think, but probably not of the subjects they wanted her to think about.

Of Valerie, and the world's curious parallels and repetitions. An actress, just as Evey had always wanted to be, until the world had gone to hell; the world in general and her personal world. After all, whatever other things one might learn in a Juvenile Reclamation Project—lying, cheating, stealing, and fighting, to name only a few—acting certainly wasn't one. But if Evey could envy Valerie that brief joy, there was nothing to be envied in the way that she too had ended up in this prison hell.

And all, it seemed, for love. For loving too well, too honestly, too bravely.

Eventually the hood was removed, the shackles too. And then the guard was leaning down to shout in her face.

"You won't last much longer! You're going to die here! Why protect someone who doesn't give a shit about you?"

She stared at him blank-eyed, hardly knowing the answer to that question herself. Except that was what they wanted from her . . . and she wasn't going to give it to them.

So when he'd gone, and when she felt strong enough, she began to read once again. To read an unfamiliar person's viewpoint on familiar things. No, that wasn't true. Valerie wasn't unfamiliar to her now. Unless they'd taken her away as soon as she'd forced the message through the hole, Valerie was sitting in the cell next door. Valerie was her companion in adversity, her friend. Her only friend, the last one she had in the world.

Unless she was already dead.

Dead? What did that mean? Weren't they all dead in here?

Weren't they, perhaps with one single exception, all dead in the England of today?

Hadn't they been for years, and wasn't that why they were in the situation they found themselves in today? How long ago had the nation become a corpse? And how had it happened?

*I remember how the meaning of words began to*

*change. How unfamiliar words like "collateral dam-
age" and "extraordinary rendition" became frightening, while things like "Norsefire" and "Articles of
Allegiance" became so powerful.*

*And I remember how "different" became "danger-
ous." I still don't understand it. Why do they hate us
so much?*

*They took Ruth while she was out looking for food.
I've never cried so hard in my life.*

*It wasn't long until they came for me.*

And Evey could only cry again in turn, knowing exactly what must have happened. Ruth must have
cracked under torture, or even just the threat of it. Told
them everything: the relationship, Valerie's name, the
address. All exchanged for a life that, Evey knew,
wouldn't have been worth living afterward. The sort of
life that ends in suicide.

*They called me a criminal and told me my films
would be burned. They shaved my hair. They held my
head down a toilet and molested me. They've injected
me with chemicals. My skin is covered in purple
bruises and I can't feel my tongue anymore.*

*It seems strange that my life should end in such a
terrible place, but for three years I had roses and apol-
ogized to no one.*

*I shall die here. Every inch of me shall perish.
Every inch, but one.*

*An inch. It's small and fragile and it's the only
thing in the world worth having. We must never lose
it or give it away. We must never let them take it
away from us.*

*I hope that, whoever you are, you escape this place. I hope that the world turns and that things get better.*

*But what I hope most of all is that you understand what I mean when I tell you that, even though I do not know you, and even though I may never meet you, laugh with you, cry with you, or kiss you, I love you.*

*With all my heart. I love you.*

*Valerie.*

And, still sobbing, Evey could do nothing else but kiss that signature, that testament on toilet paper.

And doing so, she kissed the world entire.

She knew when they next bagged her and took her away, whether it was from intuition or some subtle difference in Rossiter's attitude, that she was fast approaching the end. And when the hood was removed and she sat there blinking in the interrogation lights, the end was there indeed.

"I have been told to inform you," the man behind the desk began, "that you have been convicted by a special tribunal and that, unless you are ready to offer your cooperation, you are to be executed. Do you understand what I am telling you?"

"Yes," she said softly, staring at the silhouetted head, trying to look the man straight in the eye.

"Are you ready to cooperate?"

"No."

And in the silence that followed, the tiniest hint of a smile passed across her lips.

"Very well," the man said in a voice that mingled

weary exasperation and puzzled incomprehension, and then continued to Rossiter, unseen behind her, "Escort Miss Hammond back to her cell. Arrange a detail of six men, then take her out behind the chemical sheds and shoot her."

If they expected any reaction to that, they didn't get it. The black bag was placed over her head one last time, and just for a moment the thought ran through her head that she wouldn't have to put up with that anymore. But then, she wouldn't actually have to put up with anything, ever again.

Evey was still holding Valerie's letter when Rossiter came for the final time. She had thought to take it with her to her death; one last sentimental gesture, a treasure to take with her to the grave. But why? Ultimately, you couldn't take anything with you. Not anything physical, anyway. Only the one small thing she'd come to treasure most of all.

Integrity.

Instead she placed the letter, reverently, on the bed-shelf, and stood up. And remembered, suddenly, a tale told to her by her father, long ago, that she'd never quite understood at the time.

Of how a Tibetan Buddhist monk, escaping the Chinese soldiers swarming through his country, had almost crossed the Himalayas to safety when he was told that his entire family, left behind after being given assurances of safety, had just been killed. And while his companions could only receive the news with horror, all the monk could do was laugh.

And how, asked about the incident in later years,

he had said that that was the nearest he had ever come to enlightenment. For *everything* was gone then, and there was nothing left but release.

"It's time," said Rossiter, staring at her from the open doorway.

"I'm ready," she said, getting to her feet with an almost-beatific smile.

"All they want is one little piece of information," he said, showing the slightest touch of human warmth; something that he'd never shown before. As if, in the end, he wanted her to survive after all, despite everything . . . as if he couldn't understand why she wouldn't give in, when he most surely would. "Just give them something. Anything."

"Thank you," she said, an almost-mischievous sparkle in her eye. "But I'd rather die behind the chemical sheds."

"Then you have no fear anymore," he said, trying to suppress a smile. "You are completely free."

And he turned and left.

Left the cell door standing open too.

Evey, completely taken aback, could only stand and stare. And eventually, listening to the footsteps receding down the corridor, choke out a single word.

*"What?"*

# SEVENTEEN

S tunned, Evey stepped toward the entrance, all her previous composure evaporating with every pace. She reached out to touch the door nervously, unable to quite believe it hadn't been relocked; then, tentatively, she stuck her head out into the hall beyond.

And saw . . . nobody.

This didn't make sense; but the guard had said she was *free*. And what had she got to lose now, when a few moments earlier she'd been expecting immediate execution? If they captured her again, she'd be no worse off than before.

With that, she stepped out into the corridor and noticed that the plain brick wall with the poster pasted on it seemed to extend for only a few feet to either side . . . to the limits of her vision from the cell-door grille in fact . . . before being replaced by a much more normal plastered wall. That seemed strange in itself, but then of course she'd always made the journey from her cell to the interrogation room with a bag over her head. More puzzling was that there didn't seem to be any other grille-doored cells anywhere in sight . . . as if her own was the only one, especially constructed for her alone. But that meant, of course, that there was no cell next door. No Valerie.

Shaking her head in confusion, she walked—there just seemed no need to even think of running—toward its end, rounded the corner cautiously, and hesitated.

Ahead of her stood a uniformed guard . . . was it Rossiter? But something about his frozen stare, his absolute stillness, kept her from turning back. And the more she looked, the more lifeless he seemed.

A mannequin.

She strode toward him then, noticing a door behind him. A door that also opened as she turned the handle, and pushed her way on through.

The interrogation room next, with all its lights, far closer to her cell than it had ever seemed when she hadn't been able to see her way as they'd led her to it. Another mannequin sitting at the table and, underneath it, a tape player, wires leading up to a small speaker by the mannequin's throat.

And then another room, with a guard's uniform and a flesh mask she recognized as Rossiter's face. A FedCo uniform and another mask. Others still that were completely unfamiliar to her.

And on a table, a small wire cage containing a rat. Her rat.

What on earth did it all mean? Mannequins, disguises, cells that weren't really cells, a prison that wasn't really a prison . . .

There was only one way to find out, and that was to continue until one of these doors opened to the outside world; or at least, to something less confusing.

The next door down the corridor was, finally, the

one she sought. She opened it, tentatively, and cautiously stepped through . . .

And found herself standing once more, to her most intense surprise, in the Shadow Gallery.

*The Shadow Gallery.* At first it just didn't register properly. A place she'd never thought to see again; had no reason to expect that she'd ever be returning here. Was this too another pretense . . . a studio-set imitation of the real Shadow Gallery?

No, somehow, as she ran her eyes over the assembled treasures the place contained, she knew that this was the real thing. Which meant that her prison had always been part of the Shadow Gallery too.

But how could it be? Disbelief almost overwhelmed her, but there was V standing before her, wearing his mask as always, and this was definitely not a mannequin.

"Hello, Evey," he said simply, with a certain warmth that indicated a pride in her accomplishments; though little more than that, as if he was waiting for a chance to judge what her reaction might be: pleasure, shock, disgust . . .

But her first reaction was one of complete incomprehension.

"You . . . ," she began, startled, but then her mouth simply hung open while she stared. At him. At where she was. At a world that was not contained entirely in the concept *prison cell.*

"It was *you*?" she said at last. "That wasn't real? Is Gordon . . . ?"

"I'm sorry, but Mr. Deitrich is dead," he told her,

genuine compassion in his voice. "I thought they'd just arrest him, but when they found the Qur'an in his house, and everything else, they had him executed."

The Qur'an wouldn't have been half of it, she knew; not even a small part. Among all the other stuff, it would have been *God Save the Queen* that got Gordon killed.

"Oh, God," said Evey flatly, hearing everything she'd suspected now finally confirmed.

"Fortunately," V continued gently, "I got to you before they did."

"*You* got to me?" she said, not quite understanding the significance of his words. "*You* did this to me?"

And then it hit her. All that had happened in the last—how long was it? Days? Weeks? Months?—had all been *his* doing. Rossiter, the interrogator . . . *him* in disguise. And that FedCo truck in the street on the Sunday night that she'd arrived in Bloomsbury, that must have been him as well, keeping an eye on her whereabouts in disguise. But mainly . . . *he'd* been Rossiter . . .

She stumbled back against the wall, feeling as if her legs would hardly support her.

"You cut my hair . . . you tortured me? *You tortured me?*"

She began to shake, realizing at last just how thin she'd become, how weak, how sick. And V nodded his head almost sadly, admitting and confirming everything.

"Why?" she asked him disbelievingly. "God, *why?*"

He hesitated then, as if having to explain his actions was almost as painful as having carried them out in the first place. "You said you wished to live without fear. I wish there was an easier way, but there wasn't."

Evey felt her stomach turning over and covered her mouth as she began to retch. But there was nothing in her stomach to bring up.

"I know you may never forgive me," V said, taking a pace toward her as if genuinely concerned. "Nor will you ever understand how hard it was for me to do what I did. Every day, I saw in myself what you see in me now. Every day, I wanted to end it, but each time you refused to give in, I knew I couldn't."

"You're sick!" she cried, looking up at him with a gaze that made him pause. "You're *evil!*"

"You could have ended it, Evey," he said contemplatively. "You could have given in, but you didn't. Why?"

And with that question, he began to move toward her again, seeming to offer comfort and support. Back against the wall, she slid away, looking toward him as if he were some sort of cockroach. Worse by far than her cell companion, the rat. At least she'd been able to understand what the rat did.

"Leave me alone!" she shouted at him. "*I hate you!*"

"That's it," he said, coming to a halt once more, giving her space. "At first I thought it was hate too. Hate was all I knew. Hate had built my world, imprisoned me, taught me how to eat hate, how to drink hate, how to breathe hate. I thought I would die from the hate in my veins. But something happened. It happened to me just as it happened to you."

Evey turned away from him then, snapping her eyes shut and covering both ears with her hands.

"Shut up!" she screeched, shaking now with stress and nervous tension, as well as the sheer physical weakness left over from her ordeal. "I don't want to hear any more of your lies!"

"Your father said that artists use lies to tell the truth," he reminded her. "Yes, I created a lie, and because you believed it, you found out something true about yourself."

"No!" she shouted, hunching over, trying to get away, to make him stop. To make *everything* stop.

"What was true in that cell is just as true now," V told her insistently, adding pointedly, "What you felt in there had nothing to do with me."

"I can't feel *anything* anymore!"

"Don't run from it," he carried on, in that same annoying, unrelenting way that she'd found unnerving about him right from the start; that way he had of forcing her to face unpleasant truths. "You've been running all your life."

"Oh, God," she gasped suddenly, falling to her knees, starting to curl into a fetal ball as the panic attack arrived with unstoppable force. "I can't . . . b-breathe . . ."

Wheezing and moaning, she managed to choke out, "As-asthma . . . when I was . . . little . . ."

But after that the words wouldn't come any more than the breaths. And Evey felt that this collapse of her body was another, final betrayal; and she could do nothing else but cry.

"Listen to me, Evey," he said in a tone of quiet command. "This may be the most important moment of your life. Commit yourself to it."

She didn't want to hear it. Didn't want anything except for all this to just stop. She closed her eyes as tightly as she could, but somehow the tears kept squeezing out, trickling down her cheeks.

"They took your parents from you. They took the man you'd come to love from you. They put you in a cell and took everything they could take except your life."

"P-please . . . ," she managed to gasp, but nothing else would come out. And as V crouched down beside her and placed his hands on her shoulders, she began to bawl like a child.

"You believed that was all there was, didn't you?" he said, more gently now. "That the only thing you had left was your life. But it wasn't, was it?"

Evey shook her head, tears burning her cheeks. But with that simple gesture of acknowledgment, just a little control came back to her.

"You found something else," he told her, and she knew he was right; began to know, at last, that he'd been right about everything, all along. "In that cell you found something that mattered more to you than life itself, because when they threatened to take it, threatened to kill you unless you gave them what they wanted, you told them you would rather die."

And with that her breath began to come back, the panic began to subside, and she sucked in a great lungful of air.

"You faced your death, Evey," he said softly, almost whispering. "You were calm, you were still. Try to feel now what you felt then."

She did . . . and felt that release once more, that sense of putting down all the burdens of the world. And she started to feel a warmth spreading through her entire being. Not just her body, but her mind, her soul . . . every part of her that had been, was now, would be in the future.

"Oh, God, I felt," she began, her eyes clearing now, "like an angel."

V nodded, remembering similar feelings of his own, and offered her his hand. She took it tentatively at first, then squeezed it tightly, a clasp more eloquent than words. She tried to rise to her feet, only to lurch against him helplessly, mental strength being quite unable to combat physical weakness.

"I'm dizzy," she said, raising her free hand to her forehead, grateful for his gloved hand and knowing that, without it, she'd be back down on the floor. "I need air. Please. I need to be outside."

"There's a lift. It'll take us to the roof."

And then he led her, still helping her walk, across the silent Shadow Gallery and to a door she'd always assumed merely led to another room. Instead it opened to reveal the small elevator cage he'd mentioned.

She had no idea how far they had to travel, though the ascent seemed to last forever. Maybe that was because of her distorted sense of time; but she also felt that the Shadow Gallery must be a considerable distance below the ground, this roof some way above it. More to the point, it was lifting her out of the hell that she'd spent an unknown time in, taking her, if not to heaven, at least back into the world she'd left behind . . . the world that she now realized, having overcome the fear that had so narrowed and limited her options, was a world of infinite possibility.

And then the cage door slid back, the outer door was thrown open, and the silence down below was quite forgotten.

The night was rent by a rolling cannonade of thunder that made her think of the night he'd blown up the Old Bailey; made her expect, at any moment, to hear Tchaikovsky struck up upon the wind. And the parallel was given added verisimilitude when jagged, blue, forked lightning split the sky open in a spiderweb of stark electric filaments, before the thunder quaked the low and rolling clouds again.

But it wasn't the celestial pyrotechnics that interested Evey. It was the rain that tumbled down from the clouds, splashing and hissing on the flat rooftop before her, making mirror pools that reflected back the lightning flashes, so many little pieces of sky down here upon the earth below.

"Here," said V, offering his cloak to her, but she simply ignored him. More than that, she wriggled out of the hemp dress she'd worn for far too long and stepped out naked into the pouring rain.

Quietly, peacefully, she raised her head and looked straight up into the sky, felt the heavy raindrops lashing down almost vertically, let them wash over her face, shower over her thin, frail, and battered body. Not washing away her sins, but her sufferings. All gone now, all behind her.

And with them, the tempest finally sluiced away her fear for good.

"God is in the rain," she said slowly, remembering Valerie's words, breathing deeply, filling her lungs as if they'd never been used before. And she knew that Valerie had been right. God, however you thought of Him or Her or It, was undoubtedly in the rain . . . in the clouds, the trees, the buildings, the people . . . in the rat . . . in *everything*. And everything too was God.

And God wasn't just an Englishman, wasn't Sutler's God, wasn't even "Christian." God was everybody's God, or Gods, or Goddesses. And there was only "Godhead" in the same way as there was only "human," and whether you called "God" Jehovah or Allah, Zeus or Odin, Brahma or the Jade Emperor, so in the same way, whether you were Anglo-Saxon, or African, Arab, Jewish, or Chinese, so you were still called a man or a woman or a child. For in the same way that Shylock said, "If you prick us, do we not bleed?" then so the deity, from crucified Christ to idol made of mud, would say besides, "If you worship me, am I not God?" And Evey knew that it was so, and so, for her, it was.

And V, watching her, remembered the night he too had achieved this state. Not through water, but through fire. Not in London, but in Larkhill. Not with celestial fireworks, but with explosives of his own.

The fifth of November, many years ago, when all the sky was fire, all the world was smoke, and he'd been naked too, not to feel the world upon his skin, but because his clothes had burned off and much of his skin was, quite simply, gone.

An inferno. Not just in the sense of a mighty fire, but in the original meaning of the word: a blazing hell. But somehow too, a purifying, alchemical flame that burned away the dross of the world, the slag, and left only the silver and the gold.

And not only his sufferings had been brought to an end that night, but those of many others besides, one way or another, for better or for worse. And if he had been released that night, then to what greater task could he commit himself thereafter than the release of others still, perhaps of all the world?

"Everything's . . . so different," Evey said softly, gently, almost inaudibly through the rain but just loud enough to draw his attention back from that night of his own, when there'd been no such quiet words, but rather screams and roars.

And so it should be, for this was *her* night, a night the like she'd never known before and never would again.

And he would do his best to feel it with her, for all these experiences were as different, always, as they were the same.

Not far away from him, still out there on the roof in a world of tumbling water, Evey began to weep, her tears mingling with the rain; and she, in just the same way, felt her entire being becoming merged with the infinite all.

Overhead, the dancing lightning rent the sky once more with fierce celestial brilliance. Cried, "I am!" as Gods had always done, personified in light.

Illumination.

Enlightenment.

# EIGHTEEN

Days had passed, blurring into weeks, much as they had in her supposed "prison," and again Evey had little conception of the passing of time. Not now because of the continued psychological torture that had slowly scoured away her former fears, but because time itself no longer mattered. Instead there was only the ongoing process of recovery: of feeding and restoring her physical body, of exploring her new mental calm and inner balance, of the previously unappreciated sense, not of well-being, but of simply *being*.

Until one day she noticed she had enough hair to riffle her fingers through again. And by the following morning, she'd come to a decision.

Dressed in street clothes that V had provided—she had to imagine that he had other disguises still, with which to go out and shop for her or, perhaps, remembering how he'd acquired his artworks, to steal for her—and with her bag fully packed, she found V in the main room of the Shadow Gallery, standing contemplatively by the jukebox, seemingly lost in a world of his own. Or was he plotting further moves in his campaign to bring about the anarchy that he saw as the only answer to the repressions of the fascist state?

Even if he didn't wear the expressionless mask, she thought she'd never quite know exactly how his deepest thought processes worked, for despite the little he'd told her of his own history and the insights given to her during her own "imprisonment," she still didn't understand quite what sort of hell he'd gone through at Larkhill. And perhaps, now that the main perpetrators had died at his hand, no one but V ever would.

"V," she began, not knowing any way to say this except shortly; and besides, there was no point in doing anything else but coming straight out with it. "I'm leaving."

It hadn't been an easy decision. Outside, the world was harsh, uncaring, dangerous; full of the things that used to scare her so badly, that she'd been running away from all her life. And she knew her old life was over anyway; she couldn't go back to her job, her friends, her few surviving relatives, even if she wanted to. What had happened to Gordon Deitrich had been a lesson in itself. She couldn't let the same thing happen again to anyone she knew or held dear. And it would, simply because they knew her.

But here in the Shadow Gallery was security, and art, and wonder. The sort of marvelous haven she'd always dreamed of, to be revealed by the magic word she'd always hoped to discover. But now she knew that she no longer needed safe havens like that. She'd found the magic word, and it hadn't turned out to be anything like what she'd expected at all. It was "I'd rather die behind the chemical sheds."

"There are eight hundred and seventy-two songs in

here," V eventually said distractedly, without turning round to look at her. "I've listened to all of them, but I've never danced to any of them."

"Did you hear me?" she asked, a little taken aback.

"Yes."

"I can't stay here," she told him flatly, wondering if, having heard, he still didn't quite understand her.

"I know," he said, finally turning away from the jukebox to face her, the smile on the mask seeming sympathetic now, despite that it never changed. Or perhaps it was just the way he held his head, the language of his body. No, it was more than that. She could read his voice much better now, with all its minor inflections and changes of tone, its subtle shades of meaning. "You won't find any more locked doors here."

She crossed the room toward him, reaching into her bag as she did so, searching for something she'd gone back to her "cell" to retrieve.

"I thought about keeping this," she began, finally pulling out the small roll of toilet paper that was Valerie's letter, "but it didn't feel right, knowing you wrote it."

"I didn't."

It was such a simple statement, so simply delivered, that she had to believe him. Even so, it came as a complete surprise, shattering another illusory item in her mental picture of things that she'd taken as "obviously true."

"Can I show you something before you go?" he asked then.

Rather hesitantly, never knowing quite what to expect when V had "things to show her," she nodded.

He led her away through the Shadow Gallery then, took her to yet another room she hadn't seen before. The place seemed endless, a labyrinthine collection of rooms beyond rooms, connected by passages that wound around each other, seeming to go nowhere but finally ending up somewhere quite amazing, all lit only in the most subdued manner. A maze of mysterious gloom and marvel.

But what he showed her when he opened up this particular door was perhaps the most surprising yet.

The room within was, quite plainly, a shrine. Beneath the same vaulted ceiling found elsewhere in the Shadow Gallery, the cold severity of the stone walls was softened by richly woven tapestries, the floor was strewn with the sort of thick Persian rugs she'd only seen previously in Bishop Lilliman's bedroom. For a moment that gave her pause for thought, about the hypocrisy that could hide behind the mask of "proper" organized religions conducting their ceremonies in the plain light of day, and how it contrasted with the obvious and sincere reverence with which V had established this memorial room, and—she was certain—never shown it to another soul before now. There may have been no deity worshiped here, but it was plain that he kept it holy nonetheless.

To either side of the room, beneath chain-suspended grow-lights, were beds of blooming roses.

Violet Carson roses.

As V led her forward to the inner sanctum, she noticed another bed of Violet Carsons growing on what seemed to be the top of some sort of altar, and just beyond that she saw the inner sanctum.

A portrait stood in the center, but pasted on the walls all around this were photos, movie posters, press cuttings, and reviews featuring the same woman as the painting. For a moment, Evey couldn't quite understand this previously unrevealed and apparently sentimental side to V's nature, for this was obviously something rather more special than the random collection of old horror and gangster movie posters elsewhere in the Shadow Gallery. This was about a single person, and one that he obviously held particularly dear. But then she noticed the name of the actress.

Valerie Page.

And one of the posters was for *The Salt Flats*.

"She was real?" Evey asked softly, wonder in her voice. She began to feel awkward holding the bag and put it on the floor. For just a little while, this woman had seemed so important to her, so real; and then so false, when the nature of the prison was revealed. Now apparently real again, both she and "reality" in general seemed suddenly completely fluid, to the point where reality and falsehood became merged, were transcended.

V nodded in answer to her question, bringing her back to a state where, at least in some circumstances, "real" was important after all. And in doing so, he displayed a real sense of veneration, despite the mask.

"She's beautiful," said Evey, affected by the same feeling herself. "Did you know her?"

"No," said V quietly. "She wrote the letter just before she died. I delivered it to you in the same way it had been delivered to me."

"Then it really happened, didn't it?" said Evey, suddenly overwhelmed. For a while, after she'd discovered that all that had occurred during her "detention" had been no more than a puppet play where V had pulled the strings, she'd thought that Valerie's letter was just a fraud; felt, because of the way it had affected her so deeply, that this was perhaps the greatest betrayal in all the things he'd done to her, necessary though they might have been. But now all the sympathy she'd had for Valerie's suffering came back to her with redoubled force. And with it, a new empathy with V.

"You were in the cell next to her?" she asked, knowing the answer before he nodded an affirmation. So he, then, must have experienced much the same feelings as she had, reading that painful testament of the soon-to-be-dead.

"And that's what this is all about then," she continued, not in any accusatory fashion, but simply stating what had suddenly become plainly obvious to her. "You're getting back at them for what they did to her. And to you."

And to us all, she might have added, thinking of how Sutler's thuggery had extended out far beyond the detention camps and interrogation centers, like an all-encompassing cancer that had turned the whole country rotten, made it hell to live in.

"What they did to me, created me," he told her.

"It's a basic principle of the universe that every action will create an equal and opposing reaction."

"Is that how you see it?" Evey asked, still fascinated, even though she was just about to leave, by the surprises his mental processes threw up, and how they could switch instantly from the apparently sentimental to the almost repellently methodical. "Like an equation?"

"What they did was monstrous," he replied with a sense of simple acceptance. A plain statement of fact that no longer carried any emotional charge.

"And they created a monster," she added equally emotionlessly, equally without moral judgment.

Whatever he might have thought of her summing up, V said nothing, merely watching her as she bent to pick up her bag once more. And for a few moments they stood there in silence looking at each other, perhaps for the last time.

Then she handed him Valerie's letter, watched him as he reverently placed it back on the shrine from which he'd taken it those days or weeks before, and somehow felt the same sense of reverence herself. As if, in leaving the Shadow Gallery, she was now about to say good-bye to two people, rather than just the one she'd expected.

"Do you know where you'll go?" he asked eventually.

"No." She couldn't help breaking out into a smile. "That would have scared me before. I suppose I should thank you for that."

On a sudden impulse, she stepped toward him and

looked up into the frozen smile that served him for a face, almost as if she were about to kiss him. But what was the point of kissing a mask?

"Thank you," Evey said, adding, just as she was about to turn away, "and good-bye."

But before she could leave the shrine . . . just as she felt that she couldn't resist turning back for a last glance at him before she disappeared from his life forever . . . he called her name.

"Evey . . . can I ask you for something?"

She nodded, wondering what he could have in mind. Wondering what she'd do if, at this last minute, he asked her to stay.

"If I had one wish," he said, and a note of urgent sadness in his voice emphasized the importance of his request, "it would be to see you again, if only once, before the fifth."

For a moment she stood there considering. Would it be better just to make a clean break, to put all this behind her, to never see him again? But after all he'd done for her . . . whether she'd wanted him to or not . . . perhaps she could do this one small thing for him in return.

"Alright," she said softly, graciously, with a smile that, somehow, forgave him all his sins.

"Thank you," he said, returning her a smile that was ever the same, ever fixed, eternally unreadable. And with that she turned and left him.

Left, wondering how she'd get on without him.

Wondering how he'd get on without her.

# NINETEEN

High Chancellor Adam Sutler glared down from the large screen in the Cabinet Room, clearly far from happy with the situation being reported to him by his department heads. Were these really the best men available? And were they really making their best efforts to deal with this terrorist imbroglio? Perhaps if he had one of them killed, in full view, *pour encourager les autres* . . .

Etheridge, for example. The useless little toad.

"Based on random audio sweeps," the potential victim was saying now, mumbling nervously as he picked his way through the report he had on the cabinet table before him, doing his best to summarize what he knew the Chancellor could only regard as appallingly bad news, "I've projected that right now eighty percent of the public believe the terrorist is still alive."

Etheridge gulped, took a sip of water from the glass before him, and continued, "We are also showing a twelve percent increase over last month's 'positive mentions' in all four quadrants."

The Chancellor's glare was withering. Did Hitler have to put up with underlings like these? You get rid of all the scum to make way for your purebred Norsefire superman, and you end up with . . . *this?* As if he knew what his master was thinking, Etheridge tried to shrink back into the shadows, to become invisible, to disappear from view. If only they could make the current unrest disappear as well. On the larger scale, apart from the activities of the terrorist himself, it was little more than talk so far and an increase in slogan-painting and poster defacement. But it was a worrying sign. And there were areas in the East End where they were starting to vandalize the security cameras, where petty crime was increasing, where the police thought it best to patrol in pairs . . .

"Mr. Creedy?" Sutler snapped next, and even the normally cool, calm head of the Finger looked a little uncomfortable at the Chancellor's tone.

"We're handling it as best we can, Chancellor." Peter Creedy did his best to sound businesslike and efficient. "Our arrests are as high as they've been since the Reclamation."

That was something to be proud of, surely; or if not that, at least it showed that he and his men were on the ball, doing their job. That there seemed to be more and more people out there who *needed* to be arrested was, perhaps, something not really to be gone into just now. Even so, he wasn't quite prepared for Sutler's reaction.

"I want more than arrests!" he shouted furiously, changing his mind about Etheridge, thinking Creedy would provide a far more effective object lesson. "I want results!"

For a few seconds the very silence seemed to hum

with the violence of the Chancellor's outburst, and the assembled department heads could do nothing but look down at the table before them, averting their gazes, nerves taut, minds racing. Was the old tyrant starting to lose it? Was this damned terrorist situation actually starting to get to him?

And if he was becoming unstable, what about the fallout? Who'd catch the flak? More to the point, who'd eventually come out on top, with his boot on the neck of the others? If there were any others left . . .

Eventually the silence was broken by the rustle of papers being nervously shuffled as they prepared to move on to the next item on the agenda, hoping that by the time they got to it, Sutler's glowering face would have settled back into something more like its normal expression.

Only Eric Finch allowed himself the slightest of smirks at Creedy's discomfort. Serve the bastard right. After all the shit he'd been giving Finch lately, it was about time the evil sod got it in the neck for a change.

Finally, Conrad Heyer cleared his throat nervously.

"I beg your pardon, Chancellor," he began tentatively, not sure why it had fallen on him to bring up the matter of the report that the various department heads had communally been responsible for assembling; or all but one of them, anyway. He'd rather expected Creedy to press forward with the presentation, grabbing all the attention as usual, but after the bollocking the Fingerman had just got, perhaps it wasn't surprising that he didn't. Dascombe didn't give a shit about the Houses of Parliament so long as his news teams were on-site to report events, and Etheridge certainly wasn't the man for the job . . . Finch wouldn't anyway . . . so it was down to him.

"I know no one wants to discuss this," he continued with a rather accusing glance at his silent companions, then started to get into his stride, "but if we're to be prepared for every eventuality, then it can't be ignored any longer. The 'Red Report' before this meeting has been vetted by several demolition specialists. It concludes that the most logical delivery system for the terrorist to use would be an airborne attack."

He paused, having brought the important matters to the Chancellor's attention, and glanced round toward Finch. Well, he supposed one more thing had to be said, ridiculous as everyone else had agreed it was: "However, a separate report has been filed suggesting an Underground train, despite the fact that the tunnels surrounding Parliament have been sealed shut."

"Who filed that report?" Sutler asked, the sneer on his face already suggesting what he thought of the idea.

"Chief Inspector Finch," Heyer told him, passing the buck with considerable alacrity.

"Do you have any evidence to support that conclusion, Inspector?" said the Chancellor from the screen, fixing Finch with a stare.

"No, sir," he replied honestly; after all, he didn't. "Just a feeling."

"If I am sure of anything, Inspector Finch," said Sutler with cold, heavy emphasis, "it is that this government will not survive if it is to be subject to your 'feelings.' "

Across the table, Creedy grinned wolfishly at Finch, returning contempt for contempt, with added interest besides.

Well, thought Finch, they'd see. And he'd far rather trust a copper's instincts than he would the absolute certainties of a jumped-up Nazi throwback like Adam Sutler.

If he trusted anyone or anything at all, any longer.

Finch knew the look on Dominic's face, as the young man entered the office they shared at New Scotland Yard and closed the door behind him, even before he gave the signal they'd arranged. Even so, Finch thought, as he pulled out the debugging device from his desk and switched it on, his assistant was looking particularly harassed this morning.

"My friend inside the Finger came up with something," Dominic said quietly despite the device. Then, with a furtive glance around him even though he knew full well they were quite alone, he reached into his pocket and handed Finch a disc, which the latter immediately began loading into his computer.

"There were three men," Dominic said, joining his boss behind the desk as the file began to open. "Covert intelligence. Original black-baggers. All under Creedy."

"Alan Percy," Finch began to read from the screen. "Robert Keyes and William Rookwood."

"The day after the St. Mary's outbreak," Dominic filled in for him, "Percy gives his Beretta a blow job, Keyes dies in a fire, and—"

"Rookwood goes 'missing,'" Finch concluded for him, looking at the information on the screen.

"Bloody coincidences are making me sick to my stomach," Dominic remarked, no longer believing in coincidence any more than Finch did.

"Rookwood?" Finch asked meditatively, trying to put his finger on something he couldn't quite remember. "Rookwood? Why do I know that name?"

A hunch, an instinct, one of those feelings Sutler despised so much, and Finch opened his mailbox, typed the name into the search facility . . . and found an unopened email from "William Rookwood."

"Holy Christ," exclaimed Dominic softly, looking over his boss's shoulder. Finch opened the message and began to read it.

> *Dear Inspector,*
>     *I understand you are looking for me. I*
> *can only assume this means you are ready*
> *for the truth. If so, return this email and*
> *I will send contact details.*
>                                         *W.R.*

"He must have had a hidden trip on his file at the Finger," Dominic said, though his satisfaction at working out the solution soon gave way to puzzlement again. "But how'd he know it was you?"

Finch shook his head. Sometimes there were questions even copper's instincts couldn't answer.

"So what do we do?" Dominic asked nervously, fearing the answer but guessing it already.

"I'm a cop," Finch told him, clicking on the reply button. "I have to know."

"Shit," breathed Dominic softly, horribly afraid that that was exactly what they were going to get into.

The St. Mary's Mausoleum and Memorial was one of those huge marmoreal buildings that fascist-imperialist regimes seem to do so well; or so badly, depending on one's personal taste. Gigantic, imposing, monumental, the sort of tribute the hapless victims so richly deserved; or overblown, overbearing, and oppressive, the sort of monstrosity an evil government erected to make it feel better about itself. For Finch and Dominic, there wasn't any argument about which.

"I came when they opened it." The younger man shuddered. "Gave me the collywobbles."

He looked around him at the fountains, the lilies, the centerpiece statue of playing children, their angelic faces frozen into cold eternity by the snow-white marble, their running legs never quite going anywhere, the toys and games they held unplayed; at the vast line of slabs engraved and gilded with the names of what seemed the near-infinite dead.

"Still does," Dominic added, and Finch knew exactly what he meant. He'd never been a great fan of mortuary sculpture, beautiful as he knew the Christs and angels in the alcoves round the walls to be. And what was worse about this place was that, for all it looked like a fond and loving tribute to the little ones who'd died, and a fitting replacement for St. Mary's school, now demolished, it was actually built on the site of the playground where they'd excavated the mass grave to dump the bodies into before the infection spread.

A massive tombstone, then, built on a giant grave.

Still, they hadn't come to contemplate the past, but to disinter it. And the man they needed to help them do that was William Rookwood.

The place seemed largely empty at this time of the morning. It was after the still-grieving relatives had paid their respects on their way to work, before the school parties were brought along by their teachers. Round at the back was a museum section, with photos and memorabilia of the victims and the school, most of the latter almost certainly false considering the way the cleanup crews had eradicated everything while disinfecting. The Museum of Dead Children it was commonly known as, and organized visits were a compulsory part of the curriculum of all the schools in London, to learn the lessons of history, and the necessity of vigilance against the threats of the future. A history Finch now suspected was completely false; a future threat he thought less likely to come from without than from those who were actually supposed to protect the citizens of tomorrow.

But the place wasn't entirely empty.

A soft cough brought to their attention a man sitting on a marble bench in a shadowy corner of the memorial, almost hidden by a bed of pure white lilies. Finch and Dominic glanced toward each other, then started toward him.

"That's close enough, Inspector," said the man silently, and they stared at him, remembering the tall, relatively slim, clean-shaven man that Rookwood had appeared to be from the photo in his file. Instead they saw a large, almost fat, and heavily bearded man wearing dark glasses, a wide-brimmed hat pulled down low to shade his face, and a heavy, dark coat. By his side was a small bag, and his gloved hands fiddled with a heavy, silver-headed cane that would obviously double as a weapon even if it didn't contain the blade Finch rather suspected it did.

The beard looked real enough, but Dominic thought the coat covered several layers of padding. Not surprisingly, Rookwood lived in darkness and disguise.

Outside it began to rain again, beating a soft tattoo on the marble paving surrounding the memorial and bringing an added chill to the air. As if Eric Finch didn't already feel cold enough inside when he thought about everything they'd uncovered so far and which, he suspected, was probably going to get far worse by the time they'd finished interviewing their man.

"You're Rookwood?" Finch asked, receiving a nod in reply. And then the man reached into his bag and drew out a debugging device very much like Finch's and turned it on.

"We're not wired," Finch told him, knowing very well Rookwood would be a fool to take him at his word, but feeling he wanted to say it anyway.

"I'm sorry," Rookwood said, "but a man in my position only survives by taking every precaution."

Finch nodded understandingly, gesturing toward a bench not far from the one on which Rookwood sat and, when the latter appeared to give his consent, sitting down on it with Dominic. "You have information for us?" Finch asked.

"No, you already have the information." Rookwood nodded his head forward and seemed to sink even farther down into the shadows. "All the names and dates are inside your head. What you want, what you really need, is a story."

"A story can be true or false," Finch remarked, a touch exasperated. This was supposed to be an investigation, not a game.

"I leave such judgments to you, Inspector." The ghost of a smile played round Rookwood's bearded lips, barely visible in the shadow. And then he tapped his cane on the marble floor, as if calling for his audience's attention.

"Our story begins as these stories often do," said Rookwood, "with a young, up-and-coming politician. He is a deeply religious man and a member of the Conservative Party. He is completely single-minded and, before too long, regardless of the political process."

Finch knew well enough to whom Rookwood was referring. Adam Sutler, swiftly outgrowing his Conservative roots, setting up his own "Norsefire" organization that so many people had initially regarded as a joke. "Adam Sutler, the man who talks to God," they'd called him derisively, in those days when God had long been declared dead, hardly foreseeing the crushing return the Church would make a few years later, reorganized now as an arm of the Party. They'd also said a neo-Nazi outfit like Norsefire would never take root here, not in England, not in the Mother of Democracy—called them Nasties and laughed every time they were mentioned, quite forgetting Oswald Mosley's Blackshirts back before the Second World War, forgetting that had been a movement that had appealed to all classes of society, from the working-class bigot to the aristocratic toff; it was led by *Sir* Oswald Mosley, after all, while most of its supporters came from the East End. But if they did remember Mosley, it was only as an old joke, a minor aberration, certainly not a serious warning. And they also failed to remember Thatcher, Blair, and all the others who'd sent the country lurching dangerously toward the right but had made a better show of disguising their intentions. Good honest Christians too, the lot of them.

History's lessons, still unlearned.

Even when the rallies had started, when the symbols started to appear . . . the double crosses, which, with hindsight, should have tipped *someone* off as to what was going on . . . even when the armbands and the uniforms appeared, the red-and-black motifs . . . when the salutes began . . . surely it should have been obvious by *then*. But, no, fascists the world over have always known how to put on a good show, to play the crowd, to give the people what they want, and, once they've got the fatheads in and listening, to tell them what they want to hear. Or at least, to tell them what the Party propaganda had already *persuaded* them that they wanted to hear, after that same propaganda had subverted the information they received, their moral values, their very humanity. The same old messages of hate: that the country's full of degenerates and idolaters, especially in the schools where they can corrupt the helpless children. That hordes of asylum seekers are taking the jobs, that all the Arab ragheads are nothing but terrorists in disguise, that the Yids have got the money, the Gyppoes are nothing but a bunch of burglars, the Yardie gangs have got the protection rackets sewn up, all the vice is run by Albanian immigrants, the Triads are smuggling in more foreigners every day, and there's no point going into town tonight unless you want to eat curry . . . and then there are the Spicks, the Wops, the Krauts, and, worst of all, the Frogs, quite plainly Communists to a man. Put them all on the boat back home and sink it when they leave. England for the English! Strength through Unity, Unity through Faith! England Prevails . . .

Rookwood's words broke into Finch's memories: "The more power he attains, the more obvious his zealotry, the more aggressive his supporters become." It was true enough, after all. Finch had seen it, lived through it. And, though it seemed more and more shameful to him now, the more of this poisonous filth he was uncovering, he'd joined the Party way back then. All the police were doing it, just as they used to join the Freemasons. In a world where *Law* and *Order* were becoming the paramount watchwords, it was the obvious way to get on. He wasn't alone in selling his soul. None of them were. But he'd sold his soul nonetheless. And he'd had to live with it ever since. All he would say in his own defense was that he hadn't actually attended a rally since the Reclamation; not since his wife and son had died.

"Eventually," said Rookwood, "his Party launches a special project in the name of national security."

And Finch could guess exactly what that project was, and where it was besides. Larkhill.

"At first it is believed to be a search for biological weapons and is pursued without regard to its cost," that all-knowing voice continued, hardly needing to add: and entirely without the knowledge of the public at large. But, Finch thought, there was something wrong here, for Rookwood seemed to be talking about events before the Reclamation, and that would imply that the Larkhill project had started much earlier than he'd suspected, and presumably with the acquiescence of the government of the day, who, with the Americans at war and the world going to hell, were already involved in the detainment-without-trial of "undesirables." He remembered how they'd been more than happy to wash their hands of blame and pass the running of the camps to "private security firms"—and how the worst one, Security Corp., had swiftly become known as Secure-a-Corpse—but now he had to guess that they were nothing more than Norsefire fronts. And the government must have turned a blind eye to whatever went on there too.

"However," Rookwood's story went on, "the true goal of this project is power: complete and total, hegemonic domination. The project, however, ends violently."

Again, Finch could fill in the details, having read

Delia Surridge's journal and knowing how, after all the deaths, the secret mass graves, and the "lost" records, V had brought things to an explosive, fiery conclusion.

"But the efforts of those involved are not in vain, for a new ability to wage war is born from the blood of one of the victims. Imagine a virus, the most terrifying virus you can, and then imagine that you, and you alone, have the cure."

So, thought Finch, that confirmed what it was that Delia had been working on, what she couldn't even bring herself to quite put down in her journal, even though it had obviously been there by implication.

"But if your ultimate goal is power, how best to use such a weapon? It is at this point in our story that along comes a spider. He is a man seemingly without a conscience, for whom the ends always justify the means. His name is not Adam Sutler. It is Peter Creedy. It is he who suggests that their target should not be an enemy of the country but, rather, the country itself. Three targets are chosen to maximize the effect of the attack: a school, a tube station, and a water treatment plant."

There it was then, Finch thought, looking round to see an equally horrified expression on Dominic's face. St. Mary's. Tottenham Court Road tube. Three Waters. And it hadn't been "religious extremists" from the Middle East with stolen American biological weapons at all. It had all been that coldhearted bastard Creedy's idea.

Peter Creedy. Head of the Finger. Government linchpin. Top Party man.

Mass murderer.

"Several hundred die within the first few weeks,"

Rookwood cut across Finch's thoughts, reminding him of the "St. Mary's virus" panic in the days of what he could now see was a completely phony "epidemic" spreading when the situation couldn't be contained. Or, no, the virus was real enough, as were the deaths and the further outbreaks, mainly in Scotland, Ireland, and Wales. Not England, after the first attacks, Finch remembered now, and that made a grisly sort of sense too. Oh, yes, plenty of real deaths. It was the spin put upon them that was a lie.

"Fueled by the media, fear and panic spread quickly, fracturing and dividing the country until at last the true goal comes into view. Before the St. Mary's crisis no one could have predicted the results of the election that year. No one."

Sutler had become Prime Minister in a landslide victory, of course. "Tough on Terror" Sutler, with his promises to reform the laws so that this could never happen again, to bring back detention without trial on a huge scale, to make the country a safe place for decent English people to live and work in; and the electorate had bought it big-time, without realizing that was just the start, the one small part of the much larger plan that was yet to be revealed. So many Norsefire Members had packed the House of Commons that it had taken only a few weeks for them to abolish the House of Lords and rewrite—or rather, write for the first time—a replacement for the unwritten constitution that had served the country well enough for a thousand years. It was only a matter of time before Parliament effectively abolished itself as well, becoming nothing more than the rubber-stamp assembly for Sutler's political machine that it remained to this day. And all the elections since then had shown a 95 percent return for the Norsefire Party, no matter how the electorate actually voted.

The more he thought about it and the more he grappled with the implications, the more Finch realized that the cover-up must have been much more thorough than he'd realized. For everything he'd seen had suggested to him that Larkhill was just another of the many camps set up during the Reclamation, that gross "cleanup" when the immigrants and degenerates had been "persuaded to leave" either the country or the very world itself, which had begun as soon as the Party felt sufficiently confident of its position in power. Now, it seemed, Larkhill's entire operation had run its course *before* then. No wonder files had been "lost," dates altered, details changed. Could any of the records be trusted anymore? Was there any such thing as history now? But then, as they always said, "Truth is the first casualty of war." And the Reclamation had certainly been a war: a cancerous attack when England had turned against itself and destroyed too large a percentage of its own population to comfortably think about.

"And then," Rookwood took up the story again, "not long after the election, lo and behold . . . a miracle. Some believed it was the work of God himself, but it was more the work of a pharmaceutical company, controlled by certain Party members, that made them all obscenely rich. Viadox."

Certain Party members. Undoubtedly Prothero, but probably all the other major players at Larkhill too, though they must have hidden their interests more thoroughly than the late "Voice of London." Maybe Lilliman's apparently high salary was some sort of back-dated cover for the profits he'd siphoned off too.

"A year later, several extremists are tried, found guilty, and executed, while a memorial is built to canonize their victims."

Ah, yes, what about those "extremists" then? Presumably they must all have been stooges . . . well-paid stooges, no doubt . . . who learned their lines and said their piece in court. Who confessed, were found guilty, and then, when the execution date came round, were quietly smuggled out of the country. Easily enough done, when the days of public executions were long since past. Except that, knowing Creedy as he did, Finch couldn't see it working quite like that. Probably they received *promises* that they'd be quietly smuggled out of the country and had, when the time came, been executed anyway. Probably by Creedy in person. Dead men tell no tales.

"But the ultimate result, the true genius of the plan, was the fear. Fear became the ultimate tool of this government, and through it our original politician was ultimately appointed to the newly created position of High Chancellor. The rest, as they say," Rookwood concluded with a knowing smile, "is history."

"History . . . ," thought Finch ruefully, remembering his ruminations of a moment earlier, remembering too the words of Henry Ford: "History is bunk."

"Can you prove any of this?" he asked sharply, still not entirely sure that what Rookwood had told them was 100 percent true.

"Why do you think I'm still alive?" his informant replied, a mischievous twinkle in his eye. But if he expected some response to that, it wasn't forthcoming.

"Every time Creedy needed something done 'below the radar,' " he continued after a few moments, "he'd come to me personally. I never liked him, never trusted him, so when he asked me to deliver the virus to St. Mary's, I secretly recorded the conversation, like I often did."

Finch and Dominic exchanged glances. This was what they'd been waiting to hear. The clincher that would prove their case.

"Alright," Finch said, turning back to the man before them, "we'd like to take you into protective custody, Mr. Rookwood."

"I'm sure you would," Rookwood sniggered. "But if you want that recording, you'll do what I tell you to do."

He stood up then, supporting himself on his cane as if age and obesity made the action difficult for him.

"Put Creedy under twenty-four-hour surveillance," Rookwood demanded next, and that, thought Finch, was something he'd do with great pleasure, knowing how Creedy had been doing exactly the same thing to him. He nodded, waiting to see if the man had anything else to add.

"When I can safely feel that he can't even pick his nose without you knowing, I'll contact you again. Until then, cheerio."

Slowly and with a slight limp, Rookwood began to walk away. But Finch still had one last question.

"Rookwood, why didn't you come forward before? What were you waiting for?"

"For you, Inspector," the man replied, looking back over his shoulder. "I needed you."

And then, like a ghost, he vanished into the pouring rain.

# TWENTY

U naware of the surveillance van a little way down the street, or of the man already prowling on his roof and looking for a way to descend, Peter Creedy concluded his nightly ritual, standing there in the atrium of his luxurious Hampstead home. Beneath the skylight where a shadow flitted briefly in the moonlight, unseen, he was feeding nutrients to his collection of orchids with a syringe. The orchids that were his one pleasure, his one relaxation; his only interest apart from the ruthless pursuit of his career and its ultimate goal. The goal he never discussed with anyone.

The fantastically shaped flowers with their beautiful colors were a major attraction, but more symbolically important to Creedy was the way that, while not exactly parasitic, they naturally grew on other plants. Riding on their backs, the same as he was riding on the back of Sutler, working and waiting for the right day, the right opportunity . . . and then . . .

Besides, he smiled to himself, the name *orchid* derived from the Greek for "testicle," and there was one thing he was absolutely sure of . . . he had far more balls than Sutler ever did.

He didn't get to spend enough time here anymore.

In the past, he'd usually been able to pass an hour or so in the atrium before retiring, listening to Wagner or to Richard Strauss, savoring **a** glass or two of calvados, reading Nietzsche or Hitler and communing with his flowers. Some of those flowers he'd paid the earth for; one he'd even killed its owner to obtain. Now, with all this terrorist shit going down, all he had time to do was feed them before collapsing exhausted into bed. Well, soon, no doubt . . .

Turning away toward the door, he flicked off the light, then turned back for a last, almost-fond look at those vaguely luminescent petals glowing beneath the moon. And saw another pale shape emerge from among the shadows.

The mask of the terrorist.

Before Creedy could react, V was upon him, and one of his long, deadly knives lay glinting by Creedy's throat. And all Creedy's combat training, all those times when he'd had the gun in his hand and the victim had had no other option but to die helplessly before him . . . all that added up to absolutely nothing, when the blade was pressing home with uncomfortable firmness against his suddenly throbbing jugular.

"Shhh," whispered V softly, leading him slowly across to the CD player, knife still poised, and randomly inserting a disc.

As the music began to swell, the two men in the surveillance truck looked at each other in bewilderment. Not Earmen, these, but Finch's ordinary coppers; yet baffled nonetheless. When they'd seen the light go out, they'd expected nothing but silence to follow, and sleep, and a chance to go off watch themselves. Not music. They'd been on this stint for a couple of weeks now, and it had always ended up in silence and sameness before.

"What's he doing in the dark there?" one asked.

" 'Creepy Creedy'?" replied the other. "Not sure I want to know."

In spite of that, they both began to listen all the harder. But the music, as was obviously intended, made it impossible to hear anything else. Well, it would have to go down on the routine report, but it hardly seemed to be anything worth raising the roof about.

And back inside . . .

"Sutler can no longer trust you, can he, Mr. Creedy?" whispered V, barely audible. "And we both know why. Sutler is the kind of leader that survives only as long as he seems invincible. The instant he looks weak, that he seems exposed, he's vulnerable . . . and as soon as he is, they'll be on him like dogs. After I destroy Parliament, his only chance will be to offer them someone else, some other piece of meat. And who will that be?"

The blade forced Creedy's head back then, as if it were about to slice his throat open like carving a joint of beef.

"You, Mr. Creedy."

A pause to let the words sink in. But Creedy only stood there expressionlessly, trying to look round toward the man who held him prisoner; trying to work out if it was worth trying anything, and deciding it was not.

"A man as smart as you has probably considered this," V continued calmly, giving a cool assessment of the situation. "A man as smart as you probably has a plan. That plan is the reason Sutler no longer trusts you. It's the reason why you are being watched right now, why there are eyes and ears in every room of this house, and a tap on every phone."

And now, for the first time, Creedy showed some reaction. One of stunned disbelief.

"Rubbish," he said, though in the instant the word was out of his mouth he began to suspect that it might be true. That was something that would have to be checked out . . . could easily be checked out . . . *if* he got out of this particular encounter alive, of course.

"A man as smart as you, I think, knows otherwise," V told him, almost as if reading his thoughts. Or knowing the thoughts that would logically ensue from what he'd told him. Naturally he'd get it checked out, but quietly. If it turned out to be true, there was no point in letting Sutler know that he knew. That would only precipitate a crisis. Far better to know and leave your enemy unknowing, while still awaiting your opportunity.

"What do you want?" Creedy asked, not wanting to move his lower jaw with so sharp a knife pressed so close against the soft, defenseless tissues of his throat.

"Sutler," V told him, his masked face leaning forward over Creedy's shoulder now, so he could see the way the man's eyes flashed. "Come now, Mr. Creedy, you knew this was coming. You knew that one day it would be you or him. That's why Sutler's been kept underground for security purposes. That's why there are several of your men close to Sutler, men that can be counted on. All you need to do is say the word."

"And what do I get out of this 'deal'?" asked Creedy, mind already racing toward the consequences of launching such a coup.

"I should think that would be obvious," remarked V, confirming exactly what Creedy had been thinking. And then V held up a piece of chalk in his free hand, moving it into Creedy's field of view. "If you accept, leave an X on your front door."

"And why should I trust you?"

"Because it's the only way you'll ever stop me." And then, while one hand held the knife to Creedy's jugular vein, the other pressed on his carotid artery, cutting off the flow of blood. A few seconds later, Peter Creedy lost consciousness, and V lowered him gently and completely silently to the floor.

Equally silently, he left through the skylight, the same way that he'd come in.

The days passed away into weeks, and other cases came and went, and still Finch couldn't let go of the investigation that continued to command his attention. Nor could Dominic, come to that, though each was handling different aspects of the affair.

Not the terrorist case, not V, though that still took up most of their time, with Sutler always on their backs.

The Larkhill story.

And they knew that story was intimately connected with the V case, and that was one of the reasons Finch found it so fascinating, so important. It wasn't just a matter of waiting for V to make some sort of mistake—the man was too good for that—they needed to understand the way his mind worked, what made him tick, where he was coming from. That he'd come from Larkhill was obvious, but beyond that there were all the coincidences, the strange ways that everything seemed to link up. Finch had been reading Arthur Koestler's *The Roots of Coincidence* and become fascinated with the way the world seemed to be constructed like a web, where connections were made that somehow surpassed all normal, everyday understanding. And somehow, plucking the strings of that web like a spider king was V.

Or, at least, it seemed to be V . . . but with all these layers of cover-up and obfuscation, of conspiracy and plot and downright treason, who could say?

Treason and plot. And the fifth of November was drawing ever closer, while they seemed no nearer to V at all.

For Finch, though, it was William Rookwood on whom the focus lay. Something about the man seemed wrong; something about his story didn't add up. One of those feelings again, but it kept sending him back to the man's file over and over, trying to put a finger on what it was. He was at it again when Dominic came over to join him and saw the file open once more on his machine.

"We've had Creepy pinned like a butterfly for

weeks and still no word," Dominic said, frustration
edging his voice. "What's he waiting for?"

Before Finch could think of an explanation for
Rookwood's silence—if there was one—the phone
rang. Dominic picked it up and then passed on the
call: "It's for you, Inspector."

"Yeah?" said Finch distractedly, taking the phone,
still staring at the monitor.

"Is that Chief Inspector Finch?" an unfamiliar
voice asked in an unexcited, routine tone.

"It is," he said shortly.

"This is Inspector Clark at Southend. We've found
him."

"Found who?" Finch asked uncomprehendingly,
though something began to spark his interest. Another
of those feelings.

"William Rookwood," said Clark, a thunderbolt delivered in an offhand voice; another of those damnable
coincidences, when Finch had just been looking at his
file. "The one you've been looking for. I saw your missing person report a couple of weeks back and thought
I'd run it through our John Does. And sure enough, I
hooked him. Perfect dental match. He was a floater; a
couple of fishermen picked him up. No ID. Never
solved. Until now, that is."

"William Rookwood is dead?" asked Finch uncertainly, needing confirmation.

"I'll say so," Clark told him with a small laugh. "For
nearly fifteen years now."

Putting down the phone with a polite thank-you,
Finch leapt to his feet and began to pace around the

room like an angry animal trapped in a cage. And Dominic, who'd heard enough of the conversation to understand his feelings, could only look up at him and wait for the storm to blow itself out.

"Goddamnit!" Finch growled, kicking the wastepaper basket and sending it skittering across the floor. "It *was* him the whole time! That son of a bitch sat there and spoon-fed me that bullshit, and I ate it up! *Goddamnit!*"

Had *any* of "Rookwood's" story been true? Parts of it, certainly, but which? Had the St. Mary's virus really been developed at Larkhill? It certainly looked as if it had, what with the shareholders who'd got rich at Viadox having been, like Prothero and Lilliman, so intimately connected with Larkhill. And even if Delia Surridge's diary remained evasive about the precise nature and result of her work, the amount of guilt she seemed to have been carrying around with her certainly implied that it could have been.

But there remained that contradiction. Everything Finch had discovered before about Larkhill suggested that it was a Norsefire camp, set up during the Reclamation, "processing" the sort of "undesirables" that so many camps dealt with during that enormous, bloodthirsty purge. But if the St. Mary's virus had been developed there, and it was that viral attack that had brought Sutler's Norsefire Party to power, then that implied that Larkhill had been operating at least a couple of years before then.

*Could* they have got away with something so flagrant? And if they could, didn't that imply the wholehearted collaboration of the previous government . . . imply that, actually, Norsefire's fascism wasn't actually much worse than that of any other political party, Conservative or Labour, only more overt? Or was there an even broader conspiracy yet, where Norsefire was only the public face of a plot that had begun with the previous government, the one that Norsefire had apparently overthrown, to abolish the old order and replace it with the new? But that would imply that the whole political system, whether Conservative, Labour, or Liberal, had become unutterably corrupt; had probably been so for years, and that even the prewar elections were as farcical as the ones they had today. That, in the words of an old catchphrase he'd heard in his youth, "whoever you voted for, the government still got in." And was the anarchism espoused by V, then, the only true political answer? A state without leaders . . . that had outgrown the need for leaders because it had realized that the whole concept of "leaders" had become morally and politically bankrupt . . . could that actually work? A *true* democracy, rather than the so-called democracy that the Americans and British had been so eager to spread around the world before the War, which had turned out to be just another shameless euphemism for globalization, and imperialism, and exploitation, an excuse for interference that had finally led to the ultimate folly of the Sino-American War.

Or was even that thought just another bullshit line he'd swallowed down whole from V?

And was Creedy in any way responsible for what

had happened? Or had V just wanted to distract their attention away from himself, perhaps needing them to pressure Creedy with their surveillance, for some nefarious purpose of his own?

Could they even trust those tax records they'd found? Or was the preposterous sum being paid to Lilliman a hidden clue . . . that someone was taking the piss with the entire thing?

Was there any truth left anywhere, or only "versions of the truth"? And were those various "versions" all part of some gigantic web of conspiracies being manipulated for reasons of his own by that devious bastard V?

V . . . V . . . it all came back to V.

"What do we do now, Inspector?" asked Dominic, returning Finch's thoughts, almost, to the situation in hand.

"We do what we should have been doing all along. We find him."

But detective work still had to be combined with the political, and that meant attending the increasingly fraught "Cabinet meetings," where Sutler, obviously feeling the strain of his now vulnerable position, could lambaste both their best efforts and their worst. The only surprise to Finch was that he hadn't grown a little toothbrush mustache by now.

"Every day, gentlemen," he was saying now, his implacable eyes gigantic on the screen as they bore down on his underlings, "every day that brings us closer to

November, every day that man remains free, is one more failure. Two hundred seventy-seven days, gentlemen. Two hundred seventy-seven *failures!*"

Creedy leaned forward into the light from the lamp before him, an action that he knew would immediately focus the primary camera on his face, bringing him to the Chancellor's attention.

"Chancellor, we do not have the adequate force to—"

"We are being buried beneath the avalanche of your inadequacies, Mr. Creedy!" Sutler cut him off, shouting. Definitely losing it, thought Creedy, easing himself back into the shadows. Well, then, watch and wait, and let Sutler dig himself into an ever-deeper hole.

"Mr. Dascombe," Sutler said next, moving on to his next target. "What we need right now is a clear message to the people of this country. This message must be read in every newspaper, heard on every radio, and seen on every television. This message will resound throughout the entire InterLink."

Dascombe nodded, always ready to appear willing, but not prepared to commit himself to anything until he knew exactly what the Chancellor wanted. And now Sutler continued, in his most Churchillian tones, "I want this country to realize that we stand on the edge of oblivion. I want every man, woman, and child to understand how close we are to chaos."

And both Creedy and Finch, enemies as they were, knew what was coming next. "I want everyone to remember why they *need* us!"

Creedy could only nod to himself in the shadows. Exactly as V had predicted, Sutler was starting, if not to look dead in the water, at least to feel the weakness and vulnerability of his position. Well, then, not long now . . .


This was more than a job for Dick and June, Roger Dascombe knew, though naturally they'd have to play their part. But they couldn't be on the television twenty-four hours a day, and round-the-clock broadcasting was obviously what was required here. It was to be a blitz, with a new newsflash every couple of hours, and extended bulletins at breakfast, lunch, and dinner times. As for the newspapers, radio, and InterLink, he'd already delegated that to the appropriate editors and writers: the lesser stuff for the lesser beings. Television was the key, he knew; the same as he knew that he was television's key man.

And, unlike the previous feel-good broadcasting they'd always specialized in, this was definitely going to be a bad news day. Followed by several more.

So all across the country, from tenements to middle-class homes, from bars and restaurants to schools and old people's homes, the population began to find themselves inundated. From the seemingly innocuous but slightly worrying, it got steadily worse, became more and more threatening.

*"Scientists attribute this latest water shortage to the lack of rainfall during the last two years. Ministry officials expect water-coupon prices to rise . . ."*

That was always the first step. Get people worried about the basic necessities and threaten to hit them in the pocket as well; but phrase it carefully so it doesn't sound as if the government has done anything wrong. And if they look out of their windows and see that it's pouring rain, well, so what? Most people have such short attention spans that if you tell them that it's all down to last month, when it hardly rained at all, they'll believe you; especially if you tell them that it's only now raining in *their* part of the country, not anywhere else.

And then, once you've used natural calamities to get them worried about their standard of living, hit them with all the other terrors that are quite obviously other people's fault. That they'll want the government to take strong measures against, before the country collapses into the same sort of chaos that's prevailing everywhere else in the world. The things caused by terrorists and undesirables and the biggest bogey of them all, biological weapons and diseases. The sort of threats that will make people demand that the government take off its velvet glove and smash these people flat with its iron fist, just as it did before, the last time this sort of thing happened. It worked well enough before. It ought to work again.

*"Police arrested nine suspects believed to be responsible for hoarding avian flu vaccines . . ."*

*"In the former United States, civil war continues to devastate the Midwest . . ."*

*"Outside the quarantine safety zone, a new airborne pathogen has killed twenty-seven people . . ."*

*"The authorities have uncovered new evidence*

*linking the terrorist organization called V to the St. Mary's viral attack on London, fourteen years ago . . ."*

In her new apartment, Evey Hammond watched that last item, read to camera this time by June herself, and noted how V had now been inflated into a "terrorist organization" to make the threat seem still more dangerous. And even without the woman's furious blinking, she knew at least that particular news nugget was a downright lie. And suspected that more people than the government expected wouldn't believe a word of it either.

She'd seen what was happening on the streets. The things that didn't get into the news bulletins. The spray-painted Vs that kept appearing on walls overnight; sometimes even on the back of government surveillance vehicles. The defaced *Strength through Unity, Unity through Faith* posters that were being anarchically turned into *Strength through* Disunity, Disunity *through* Fate. The police cars with their unexpectedly flat tires. The knocked-out security cameras and the loudspeakers with their wires cut. They weren't the work of V.

That was the work of ordinary Londoners, starting to wake up at last.

Running a hand through her short and newly dyed black hair, she could only wonder more and more what the approach of November the fifth would bring.

Whatever it was to be, it seemed that FedCo would be delivering it. By train, by truck, by individual deliveryman, the immense number of perfectly uniform boxes, with perfectly uniform and perfectly false return addresses, were sent across the land with the same sort of thoroughness that Roger Dascombe achieved with his broadcasts, to rich and poor, to individuals and institutions.

And to every single member of Sutler's cabinet.

Eric Finch was only half-dressed for work and entirely unshaven when the FedCo man arrived at his door. He merely grunted when the man began to idly chatter about the number of deliveries he was having to make ("Never known anythin' like it, guv, and what the 'ell's goin' on?"), signed for the box, and took it within, having only had one cup of coffee and still too bleary-eyed to even wonder what he'd got. Only way to find out was to open it, anyway.

He ripped the box open roughly and dumped the contents on the table before him.

And a Guy Fawkes mask lay there looking back up at him, a broad grin on its face, and seeming all the broader for the message it conveyed.

The face of V.

"Bloody hell," said Finch, scratching his head. What was the evil bastard up to now?

Making his way to the office, he was given no clearer idea, though from the amount of torn and discarded FedCo boxes that littered the streets, he was getting some notion of the scale of things. This was beginning to look like the biggest mass mailing FedCo had ever had to deliver. How was he doing it when, despite what the government propaganda machine was saying, the "organization called V" consisted of one man? Perhaps two if you included the Hammond girl, but she seemed to have dropped off the radar in the last few months. Maybe if they could find her again, it might be a way to get to him. But they couldn't. She'd gone. Maybe the Finger had got her and the information hadn't been passed back to Finch. Maybe she was dead. . . .

That left just V responsible for the whole thing. Computerization had to be the answer. It was the only way one man could have organized all this, with the ordering of the masks, probably from several different sources to cover his tracks, and the mass mailing through the official delivery system. And if that was it, it meant that V was good enough to hack into the government's own system, putting the trip on the Rookwood file, getting the information on the Larkhill staff who were to become his victims, their whereabouts, their changes of name. No wonder Creedy had been talking about Sutler suspecting an informer within the government; the government's own system had been leaking like a sieve all the time. And no wonder V always seemed to be one step ahead of them.

He should have realized it before, but it had taken something of this scale to actually bring it to his attention. He'd get the tech boys on it, naturally. But it was getting so close to November  he had a nasty feeling that even if they could shut up shop more effectively, it wouldn't make much difference. V probably had all the information he needed already and might not ever hack the system again. So probably no chance to put a trace on him that way, either.

Clever bastard, thought Finch. Trying to catch the man was giving him nightmares, but the way V operated, the way he had everything planned out . . . well, Finch had to admire him. Grudgingly, but . . . but he hadn't had a challenge like this to get his teeth into for years.

It was complete bedlam at New Scotland Yard when he finally arrived. First stop the coffee dispenser, then into the fray. He hadn't seen the place like this in years.

"How many went out?" he shouted to Dominic over the cacophony of ringing phones and shouting staff. Someone had got up a feed to the control room, so they were getting in the radio reports from the ordinary bobbies on the beat as well. And every word was about Guy Fawkes masks and FedCo deliveries and V.

"So far we think it's about eight containers' worth," Dominic yelled back at him. "Several hundred thousand at least."

"Christ," was all Finch could say, though he doubted that even the deity could get them out of this mess.

Making his way to his desk, he'd barely had time to sit down when the phone rang. Not the normal office line, but *that* phone. The direct line. With a sense of weary inevitability, Finch picked it up.

"I want anyone caught with one of those masks arrested!" Sutler immediately screamed in his ear. Finch didn't see any point in trying to explain that in no way did they have enough manpower to arrest what might well total up to be half the inhabitants of London, or anywhere to put them if they did.

"Yes, sir" was all there seemed to say, so he did, adding under his breath that timeless phrasing he'd learned as a bobby on the beat in response to impossible orders from above: "Yes, sir. No, sir. Three bags full, sir." Stupid bastard, Sutler was. Almost as stupid, he was beginning to think, as he'd appeared on that *Deitrich's Half Hour* show, the last one there'd been before they'd had Gordon Deitrich shot. Pity about that. It had been a fairly gross show, but if it had had material to work with like this current situation, it could have given him quite a laugh. And laughs were damnably few and far between these days.

As soon as he put the phone down on the Chancellor, it seemed that every other phone in the place began to ring simultaneously. And they just didn't stop, no matter how many of them were answered.

"We're under siege here," Dominic told him, stating the obvious. "The whole bleedin' city's gone off its nut!"

"That's exactly what he wants," Finch said, a hint of appreciation in his voice for his opponent's skill, for the enormity of his vision. "What his plan needs."

"What?" asked Dominic, not quite grasping the point.

"Chaos. Absolute fucking bloody chaos."

And chaos was indeed breaking out all over; and continued to do so in the succeeding days. Not only all

over London, but all over the country, for the ownership of one of V's Guy Fawkes masks, and the
anonymity it conferred, somehow seemed to liberate
large numbers of the population from their repression,
and to set free all the yearnings they'd so long suppressed in exchange for "law and order" and a society
that seemed to work when all the world around them
was collapsing. And all that in spite of Roger Dascombe's carefully crafted propaganda to the contrary,
which hammered home the message that this was all
part of a terrorist plot and an attempt to overthrow all
the gains that they'd made since the war . . . and the
much more heavily emphasized point that wearing or
possessing one of the aforesaid masks constituted an
act of conspiracy with a terrorist organization that was
grounds for immediate arrest. All responsible citizens,
the message concluded, would immediately destroy
any such masks on sight. And perhaps one in a hundred of them did.

For some of those who didn't, the masks were no
more than opportunities for criminality in the name of
anarchy, and the following days saw an outbreak of
muggings and armed robberies, from minor conve-
nience-store heists to daring bank raids. But for most,
the masks provided cover for far less obnoxious, though
still illegal, acts. For being out after curfew. For fear-
lessly destroying the CCTV surveillance cameras that
stood on every street corner. For slogan-painting, from
"Norsefire out!" through "Hang Sutler!" and "Take
Your Finger and Stick It" and "Bollocks!" Less abusive,
but rather more worrying, were the anarchist cries of

"No government!" and "No leaders!" for they undercut
the very foundations of whatever the political system
might do to try to regain control of the situation.

But most worrying of all to the Norsefire establishment was the simple letter V, spray-painted in a circle.
And of this last piece of "vandalism" (an alphabetical
designation that V himself would certainly have enjoyed), there seemed to be more and more examples,
springing up everywhere, somehow moving ever closer
toward Downing Street itself.

Even, in remote parts of the country where the security clampdown wasn't quite so heavy, the masks
gave opportunities for minor demonstrations.

Perhaps most insidious and spontaneous of all were
the parties being held everywhere. Behind closed
doors for the most part, they were anarchic masked
balls where anything went, from political jokes and
satire to the most riotous drunken orgy.

And anarchism that's started to enjoy itself is the
most difficult movement to suppress of them all.

Well aware of the deteriorating situation, Peter
Creedy sat at home among his orchids, remembering
how Sutler had picked him out at that day's meeting
and holding something in his hand, a small object that
had become talismanic to him now. Remembering:
"Mr. Creedy, I am holding you personally responsible
for this situation!" as if it were somehow his fault, as if
he hadn't shot enough people to fill his quota, as if he
and the Finger weren't the last bulwark between Sutler and a restless population, between order and complete collapse. Remembering too that V had been

quite right: he had been under surveillance, and as the watchers seemed to be ordinary policemen, he had to assume that Finch had arranged this at Sutler's behest. "Who watches the watchmen?" Juvenal had asked, and when this particular watchman found out that it was a battered has-been like Eric Finch . . . well, that was the sort of insult no one should have to put up with. And Creedy's grip grew tighter and tighter around the object in his hand, until it cracked with a tiny noise, bringing his thoughts back to his present situation. And back to the piece of chalk that V had given him, now lying in two pieces in his palm.

While far away in a room at the Shadow Gallery, V began to line up a vast row of dominoes on the floor that wound and curved, came together, and parted once again. Making the pattern of a V contained in a large circle, which would only need one falling tablet to bring all the others down in succession.

The domino effect that would begin when one small event finally tipped the scales, and the whole system lurched over from order to chaos, from rigidity to collapse.

Something, on a cosmic scale, that would be little more than a finger flick, or the flapping of a butterfly's wing, or a dark cloud crossing the face of the moon.

# TWENTY-ONE

"The problem is that he knows us better than we know ourselves," Finch remarked to Dominic, looking over the piles of reports that grew at an accelerating rate as they approached nearer and nearer to November. And this was only the ordinary police work, the actual felonies and minor public-order offenses. Creedy's Fingermen were supposed to be dealing with the political activists, suppressing the minor demonstrations and riots that occurred almost daily now, from protests against food shortages and heavy-handed police tactics to outright antigovernment fervor. The one feel-good factor in the whole situation, Finch thought, was that Creedy was probably even more overworked, more under pressure, than he was. But neither of them could quite get a grip on what V was up to, apart from stirring things up and overloading the system with paperwork.

"That's why I went to Larkhill last night," Finch continued matter-of-factly, knowing full well the impact his words would have.

"You what?" exploded Dominic, only then noticing that Finch had the debugging device switched on. Even so . . .

"That's outside the quarantine zone," Dominic added, even though both of them knew it well enough, knew the risks involved in going there.

"I had to see it," Finch said simply, remembering how, rather than heading directly for home, he'd taken the car and driven, far more slowly and carefully than Dominic ever would, down to Salisbury Plain, arriving there in the twilight glow of a bloodred setting sun. Not that there'd been much left to see. Most of the wire-link perimeter fence had rusted away or been stolen for scrap metal, and the concrete posts from which it had been strung were leaning, sometimes sagging, broken halfway up, like clawing talons emerging from the earth. Or gigantic skeletal fingers of the dead, straining up toward the light from the mass graves beneath.

Quite apart from any medical research, how many thousands had died there? How many more thousands in other camps like it, scattered round the country, in places like Bradford, Liverpool, or Leicester? Far more, he had no doubt, than in the St. Mary's epidemic, but these were the non-English, non-Christian, non-normal—non-humans, as far as the regime was concerned—whose number, whose names, and even whose memories had just totally been erased. Of course, the government said they'd been deported to their countries of origin.

Everyone knew they hadn't.

As for the buildings themselves, most had fallen into ruin, and once the roofs had caved in and the walls begun to crumble, it was hard to tell what was what. Most at least bore evidence of the explosion and fire that had destroyed them, with soot-covered bricks and wooden beams turned now to charcoal. Were these cells or offices? How did one tell the administration block from the medical section? If ever there were signs here, they had long been removed. Even the name Larkhill was no longer to be found anywhere about the site.

A barely remembered Pompeii, he'd thought at first, destroyed not with a volcanic roar and a burying rain of ash, but with homemade bombs, with fertilizers and incendiaries, by a lone man driven by mental and medical torture into a state Finch couldn't even begin to comprehend. But that wasn't quite what it was.

It was more like the shattered remnants of a forgotten necropolis, of fallen mausolea and half-uncovered vaults, of tumbled, lichened gravestones; a remembrance of the dead, more poignant in its ruin than such vast official edifices as the St. Mary's Memorial. And a far more fitting testament to those who'd died, both in the outbreak of the virus and its research and manufacture, for this was not the sanitized, saccharined monument suggesting some happy postextinction survival. This was raw, and decayed, and rotten, just like the whole disgusting business had been from its origins here to its conclusion in London. There was a stench about the place, not of the dead, but of evil and corruption.

If this place had ever had anything to do with the St. Mary's virus, of course. If that wasn't just another of those stories, those illusions made of smoke and mirrors that reduced the entire past to the same sort of chaos that the present seemed to be descending into.

But there had been a row of what seemed to be shattered cells, with the fragmentary remains of a ceramic-tiled floor outside them, their metal doors occasionally still hanging on their hinges, most of them with a chalk-marked X still faintly visible, and numbered with Roman numerals.

And there was one door where he'd paused for many long minutes, deep in contemplation, trying to immerse himself in all that had happened there, all that had led up to it, and all that had followed from it. The door to Room Five.

Room V.

And that was really the thing he'd come to see. The point of origin. Room V. Prisoner V. The terrorist codenamed V. The opponent he'd learned to respect, but whom he still had no idea at all how to deal with. V.

That, at least, seemed to be something real, something he could hang on to. A single iconic fact among the fantasies, on which he could try to build some sort of understanding.

"There wasn't much left," he told Dominic, his mind returning to the present moment and trying to sum up the experience. "But when I was there, it was strange. I suddenly had this feeling that everything was connected. It was like I could see the whole thing as one long chain of events that stretched all the way back before Larkhill. I felt like I could see everything that had happened and everything that was going to happen. Like a perfect pattern laid out in front of me . . . and I realized we were all a part of it . . . and all trapped by it."

He fell silent again then, running it all through his head as he had so many times before. The stories. Delia Surridge's diary. The "Rookwood" tale that he still didn't know to be fact or fiction—or, if a blend of the two, what the proportions were. The tax records, and Lilliman's absurdly high pay at Larkhill . . . unless that too was a red herring? What if there really *had* been some legitimate reason for it? It was as if they had pieces from different jigsaw puzzles, which seemed to fit together somehow, although the picture they made persistently refused to make sense.

And underlying that were what seemed to be the "historical facts." Larkhill had, obviously, been destroyed by fire, whatever had occurred there. The St. Mary's virus was real enough, as were the deaths it caused, no matter who was to blame. Adam Sutler had held all those Norsefire rallies and got himself elected on an antiterrorist vote. And Peter Creedy was a bastard, no matter what he was or wasn't accused of.

And V had blown up the Old Bailey, attacked the Jordan Tower, murdered all the Larkhill staff. Would, undoubtedly, blow up the Houses of Parliament, unless he was somehow stopped beforehand. Had shipped out all those masks and manipulated Finch into watching Creedy, the reasons for both of which he still didn't quite understand.

And mingled in with all of this were those inexplicable, infuriating coincidences.

Another one had occurred last night. Driving back

from Larkhill, where he'd seen the faint-chalked *X* on one of those decaying doors, he'd passed through Hampstead on his way down from the M25 and hadn't been able to stop himself from glancing at the entrance to Peter Creedy's house. And there, on his foe's front door, was another chalk-mark *X*.

What the blue bloody hell could *that* mean?

And yet . . . all part of the pattern. That baffling, infuriating pattern that he knew, somehow, was being ringmastered by the baffling, infuriating V.

Like dominoes, waiting to fall.

The pattern . . .

"So, do you know what's going to happen?" Dominic asked him eventually, when the silence had stretched to an almost-embarrassing length, as if he hoped that Finch would provide some godlike flash of inspiration whereby they could write "case solved" under the whole thing and get back to their normal lives.

"No," said Finch, shaking his head and smiling ruefully. "Like I said, it was just a feeling. But I can guess. With all this chaos, someone will do something stupid. And when they do, things will get nasty."

By another of those coincidences that V seemed to glory in and that Finch had come to expect, someone had done something stupid at the very moment Finch had been standing there lost in his meditations at Larkhill.

For in that same blood-scarlet sunset twilight that tinged the clouds an almost-heavenly, religious pink, a prowling Fingerman had been making his way through a Brixton backstreet when he'd come across a small girl, about eight years old.

A small girl wearing a mask.

If that was all, he'd probably have let it go. After all, the orders to "arrest everyone wearing a Guy Fawkes mask" were plain enough, but surely one could use some discretion regarding little girls.

But the mask wasn't all. She had a can of spray paint in one hand, and was standing before one of the almost-sacred *Strength through Unity, Unity through Faith* posters the Party continued to put up everywhere, despite their ever more frequent, ever more infuriating defacement. And she'd just sprayed one of the goddamned V symbols all over it.

And he was a Party man through and through who'd been on twelve-hour shifts for the last three weeks, without a break, dealing with one sort of protest after another, from sprayers and curfew breakers to stone throwers and young tearaways with Molotov cocktails. And this was just the last straw.

"Hey, *you!*" he shouted, running toward her. Child or not, this little cow was going to jail.

She began to run then, tiny legs pumping, still masked, shrieking in terror. As windows opened and curtains rustled nearby, she threw away the can of spray paint, left it rolling in the road behind her.

Rolling beneath the feet of the oncoming Fingerman, who, eyes only on his prey, trod on it . . . lost his balance and went slamming heavily into a wall. And, as is so often the case, the wall didn't come off worse.

Blood ran into his eye from a gash above the brow.

His head rang from the force of the impact, and all he could do was gasp as the breath was forced out of his lungs. A savage pain shot through his twisted ankle, where he'd trodden on the can . . . and the gun was in his hand before he even knew it, the trigger pulled before he even thought.

One shot was all it needed. One shot to tip an already unstable situation over into a spiraling vortex of ever-increasing uproar.

The girl's body jerked in the air as if pulled by a string, the hole blown straight through her tiny lung quite horrific. She hit the ground in an angular, contorted heap, weltering blood, and never moved again.

The thin papier-mâché mask, however, already loose on her small, childish head, came off and floated briefly in the air before hitting the ground and rolling on its edge, finally coming to rest at the feet of a startled man holding a monkey wrench, who'd been fixing his car when the shot rang out. A man who looked down and saw a mask spattered with a young child's blood.

Someone's daughter.

Not his daughter, but somehow, then, she was *everyone's* daughter, as a crowd began to gather, drawn from their houses by the tragedy that had happened before their eyes. Men and women, teenagers and pensioners. Mostly empty-handed. Some with the knives they'd been using in their kitchens, dinner almost due.

And as the Fingerman limped up to stand over the body of his victim, a horrified realization finally dawning upon him of what exactly he'd done, they began to close in.

They paused when he brandished the gun and showed them his badge, eyeing each other uncertainly as he tried to bluster his way out of the situation. But a low muttering began as the girl's wailing mother forced her way through the crowd and threw herself on her daughter, screaming curses at the murderer.

At that point the car mechanic stepped up behind the Fingerman and hit him over the head with the monkey wrench.

And then the blood really began to flow.

Not just in Brixton. Creedy and his Fingermen thought they'd managed to keep a lid on that one before the riot really got out of hand, even if it did cost them fifteen operatives. Mass arrests and an invasive, brutalizing security presence ought to have done it; and they managed to keep it off the airwaves. Yet somehow word of what had happened got out anyway, not only about the little girl, but about the body count that totaled up in the succeeding hours. Fingermen, after all, didn't let their own go unavenged.

But they could do nothing about the second Brixton riot the following morning. Or the ones in Manchester, in Bristol, in Newcastle, and in Liverpool.

And in New Scotland Yard, where they kept a BTN screen on all the time now for newsflashes to give them the bigger picture of what was going on outside the capital, Eric Finch looked toward Dominic and shrugged despondently. It was no longer a case where "things *will* get nasty."

They already had.

"And so," Finch picked up his former train of

thought, "Sutler will be forced to do the only thing he knows how to do."

Dominic knew very well what that was. Call out the army. Declare martial law. Widespread round-the-clock curfews. Rioters and looters shot on sight.

"At which point all V needs to do is keep his word, and then . . ."

Finch left the sentence hanging there. Neither of them wanted to think about the consequences after that. Although they had to wonder if they could be all that much worse than what was going on right now.

In the Shadow Gallery, V had long been thinking about the consequences, planning for them, working to make them come about.

Now, managing to make the slight flick of a gloved finger into a grandiose gesture of enormous importance, he knocked over the first domino in his grand design, starting at the point of the V, listening in satisfaction to the series of soft, repeated clicking noises, watching as the falling dominoes split into two rows as the motion raced down the arms of the V, reached the circle's edge, and continued back round the circumference, perfectly spaced, perfectly timed, so that the dual lines of falling forms would meet precisely at their starting point with singular inevitability.

Two equal and opposite forces, crashing together simultaneously and with perfect symmetry.

And somehow leaving a single domino still standing.

And V could only stare at it rather as a jeweler would who'd discovered, at the last moment, a tiny, unique, but compelling flaw in an otherwise perfect design.

# TWENTY-TWO

" **I** sometimes still hear this song in my head when I wake up," Evey Hammond remarked thoughtfully, standing in the Shadow Gallery by the jukebox, which she'd just set to start. "I missed it."

She turned away from the machine as the music began to play, looking round at the place she remembered so well, for so many different reasons, some good, some bad. The bad ones seemed so much less important now, and as for the good ones . . . it had been home for a while, and apart from anything else, it was still an Aladdin's Cave, full of wonderful things that she'd come to treasure just as much as he did. She looked fit and strong, confident and at ease, her now-black hair grown to about half the length it had been when he'd first brought her here.

"I wasn't sure you'd come," V said, standing at the edge of the shadows, still masked as always, and in the full outfit of cloak and hat besides. After all, she'd left it until the very evening of the big day.

"I said I would." She smiled. Now a promise was something to be kept, not to be backed out of, as had so often been the case in the fretful, fearful days of the past.

"You look well," he continued, making polite conversation in a way that she hadn't really ever expected from him . . . unless this was the way in which he handled the tension that must be building up before he began the act that, she knew in her heart, would be the grand finale of all he'd ever worked toward.

"Thank you," she said simply. There was no point in returning the compliment to him, when all she could see was a mask.

"You've had no difficulties?" he asked her, although the mere fact that she'd come back made it plain that whatever she had had to face, none of it had been insurmountable.

"For a while." She smiled again, remembering but not wishing to tell him of her early struggles. "Then I was able to buy a new ID. The police were after Evey Hammond. No one cares about Anne Campion."

"Your mask," he said, if not exactly with laughter in his voice, at least with a suggestion that beneath the Guy Fawkes face there might be something of a real smile.

"Of sorts."

"Not uncommon these days," he continued lightly, and both of them knew precisely to what he referred.

"I suppose not." She laughed, not really used to hearing him joke.

And then a silence fell between them, lengthening as each of them waited for the other to speak next. She, because she knew he must have asked her to come back here for some reason of considerable importance, and wanting to give him the opportunity to tell her what it was. He, because he wasn't sure she was ready yet to hear it, or if he was ready to tell her.

At last the song on the jukebox came to an end, and in the quiet that ensued, there seemed no alternative but to go ahead.

"I have a gift for you, Evey. It's the reason I wanted to see you again. But . . ."

Another hesitation. Then, almost shyly: "Before I give it to you, I was hoping you might like to dance."

"Now?" she asked, charmed but taken completely by surprise. "On the eve of your revolution?"

"A revolution without dancing is a revolution not worth having." All his body language showed an eagerness to hear her say exactly what she did.

"I'd love to."

Not far away, aboveground, Dominic was driving Finch back from Chelsea Barracks, where they'd been for a briefing on the military arrangements that had been put into place for protecting Parliament Square that evening. A few minutes more would bring them to the Houses of Parliament, where protocol demanded their presence, but neither of them wanted to be. Not because they feared death or injury if V did actually blow the place up, but because they knew that if he did, the presence of two extra policemen wasn't going to make the slightest difference. And, besides, Chief Inspector Finch was starting to develop one of his feelings again. "Stop here and let me out," he said suddenly, realizing they were passing Victoria Underground Station.

"Come on, Inspector," Dominic protested. "We've got our orders. We've got to do our job."

"That's not my job," Finch told him, as Dominic resignedly brought the car to a halt anyway. "My job is to find him."

"But we've been searching those tunnels for weeks," Dominic said in one last attempt to change Finch's mind. He didn't know where the old man had got this bee in his bonnet from when all the other specialist opinion was that V would attack by air, but he just wouldn't let it go. Apart from the fact that the entire Underground system had been closed down since the Reclamation, "awaiting reconstruction" (or more the point, awaiting enough surplus power to run the thing), everyone knew the Circle, District, and Jubilee lines had deliberately been blocked off for years, and they were the only ones that ran anywhere near the Houses of Parliament. And surely it was far too late, even for last-minute "feelings."

"You're not going to find him now," Dominic called as Finch got out of the car, but nothing was going to get his boss back now. Well, he thought, shrugging as he watched Finch disappear down the stairs into the station, there seemed to be nothing else for him to do except report to his post and hope he could think of some reasonable excuse for the Inspector's absence before anyone actually asked him for one. Maybe he'd tell them the old man was having a nervous breakdown. Or that he'd gone undercover . . . thirty or forty feet undercover.

At the same time, Dominic had to hope that Finch

would be alright, because now he was getting one of those same feelings that his chief seemed to suffer from so often. A feeling that however things turned out tonight, this was one of those pivotal moments when things change forever. For better or worse, he had no idea, but he knew they'd never be the same again. And suddenly he wondered if he'd ever see Eric Finch again too.

The latter, meanwhile, had passed through the station concourse and was already making his way down the now-stationary escalators, with only a flashlight to guide him. Somewhere down beyond the platforms, somewhere down in the tunnels, either on the Victoria line or, more probably, the Circle and District lines . . . that had to be where the answer lay. Maybe even on the other side of the blockades, if he could find some sort of maintenance tunnel they'd overlooked before. There was far more to an Underground station than the train tunnels and the platforms that were all the general public saw. Maintenance shafts, emergency-exit tunnels, underground sidings where trains could be shunted aside to let others pass . . . a maze of passages. An underground labyrinth where you could still hope to find a Minotaur-like monster such as V, bred from some horrible experiment, if only you had the right clue.

And only two London tube stations started with V: Victoria and Vauxhall, and the latter was south of the river, away from the centers of power . . . away from all the scenes of V's exploits.

If it was anywhere, it had to be Victoria.

• • •

Not far away, the target of Finch's search was dancing slowly with a beautiful woman in his arms. A last dance . . . "The Last Waltz" . . . before he brought the world to an end. At least, the world of Sutler's England, long overdue for demolition. "You've been busy," Evey told him, looking up into his mask; that mask that had been all that she'd ever known of him. "They're very scared right now. I heard Sutler is going to make a public statement tonight."

"It's almost over," V said, and one way or the other, she knew that he was right. If not for Sutler's world, for his own.

"The masks were very ingenious," Evey continued, wanting to let him have some idea of her appreciation for the way he'd handled his campaign. In the past, when her fear had made her betray him, or when he'd been torturing that same fear out of her system, there hadn't been much opportunity for that sort of thing. "It was very strange to suddenly see your face everywhere."

He replied with one of those Shakespearean quotes of which he was obviously so very, very fond: " 'Conceal me what I am; and be my aid for such disguise as haply shall become the form of my intent.' "

*Twelfth Night.* She identified the passage easily, never having forgotten the play since she'd acted in it as a child.

"Viola," he added, remembering that had been the part she'd played.

She gave herself up, contentedly, once more to the

dance. Even so, tonight . . . on this last night before everything changed . . . there were still things to say, still questions unanswered. Feminine curiosity, which, in spite of everything, wouldn't quite go away.

"I don't understand it," she said eventually.

"What?"

"How you can be, in some ways, one of the most important things that has ever happened to me . . . and yet I know almost nothing about you. I don't know where you were born, who your parents were, or if you had any brothers or sisters. I don't even know what you really look like."

There was the question then, hanging on the air, not quite asked, not quite demanding an answer.

A bait he could have taken if he'd wanted to . . . but didn't.

"Evey, there is a face beneath this mask, but it isn't me. I'm no more that face than I am the muscles beneath it, or the bones beneath that."

Ambiguous to the end, then. Was she to take that as meaning that the face beneath the mask had been destroyed in the same way as his hands? Or was he saying that a man is not the face he presents to the world, the public persona, but something deeper, more intrinsic, a personality that far transcends personal appearance? That the face itself is nothing but a mask?

Either way, he could still have the face of a devil or an angel hiding behind that of Guy Fawkes, and finally she decided it was better never to know.

"I understand," she said rather awkwardly, continuing with the dance.

"Thank you," he said quietly.

"You know," she said brightly then, changing the subject to something rather safer. "I found a copy of *The Count of Monte Cristo*. I think of you every time I watch it. It's funny, though, now I never feel as sad for Mercédès as I do for the Count."

Finally, the music came to an end and the silence returned, breaking their tenuous moment of intimacy. As he released her from his arms, V seemed to fall back once more into his usual cool, composed self, again as remote from her as he was to the world in general.

"There isn't much time left," he began, turning to usher her out of the room, "and I have something that I must give to you."

Wondering what on earth he could intend, she let him lead her through the labyrinth that was the Shadow Gallery, through a number of doors and then out into a long, tubular tunnel; and so finally, descending some stairs, onto a station platform.

"The Underground?" said Evey wonderingly. "I thought they closed it all down!"

"They did. It took nearly ten years to clear the tracks . . . at least as far as I wanted."

Only then did Evey really notice the old train standing in the platform. Original rolling stock it may have been, but now it was transformed, the outside painted all over not with graffiti as in the old days, but with beautiful art nouveau curlicues and arabesques, with lilies and with roses.

"What a beautiful old train," breathed Evey, eyes

wide with astonishment and recognizing V's hand in the decoration. If trains had always looked like this, she thought, they'd probably never have been vandalized in the first place. And if *everything* had been made and decorated like this . . . if whole cities had been designed by Antoni Gaudí, instead of the architects who gave us dehumanizing concrete blocks to live in and shopping malls that looked like prisons . . . perhaps there would never have been a fascist party, or senseless crimes, or wars. Or fewer of them, anyway.

"Let me show you," he said, taking her hand and leading her toward it. But before showing her the interior of the carriage, he took her to the driver's cab.

"These trains used to work with what was known as a dead man's handle," he explained, "where the power would only reach the motors if the driver was sitting here holding it pressed down. I've disabled that. There isn't any power here anyway. But there is a slight gradient, leading from here down to Westminster, toward where the tunnels are still blocked. All you have to do is release the brake handle here, and the train will run away down the track on its own."

"But why are you telling me this, V?" she asked, confused.

"In case you need to know," he told her mysteriously, then led her back toward the carriage.

As she'd rather expected, it was filled with Violet Carson roses. But there was more than this besides. The front of the train, just behind the driver's cab, was packed with small rectangles of what seemed to be red clay, wrapped in wax paper, all stacked together in the aisle between the seats to make up a sort of platform, almost like a bier. A glance round revealed more of the little red bricks behind them, and she had to conjecture they were packed in throughout the train.

"What are these?" Evey asked, picking one of them up.

"Gelignite," he said offhandedly.

"What?" she exclaimed, taken so much by surprise that she almost dropped it.

"Careful," he said with the faintest of laughs, as she guardedly but hurriedly put it back in the stack before taking a couple of swift paces backward.

"You said the tracks were blocked down at Westminster," she said thoughtfully, then added, "Under the Houses of Parliament?"

He nodded.

"Then it's really going to happen, isn't it?" she said slowly. Somehow, she'd always known that it would, even though she couldn't imagine *how*. But to actually be here, seeing it, being part of it, put the whole thing in a new light. All that planning, all that labor, all those years . . . all leading up to this one night, when everything would explode in flame and fury.

"It will. If you want it to."

"What?" she exclaimed. What on earth did it have to do with her?

"This is my gift to you, Evey." His hand circled in a gesture that at first she thought referred only to the train, although she then realized it was far more all-encompassing than that. "Everything that I have: my home, my books, the Gallery, this train. I'm leaving them to you, to do with what you will."

Evey looked at him with an expression almost of disappointment. This wasn't the sort of gift she'd expected. Indeed, she doubted that "a train full of gelignite" would feature very highly on any girl's wish list. But there was obviously more to it than that; apart from his possessions, he wanted to pass on something more.

"Is this another trick, V?" she asked tentatively.

"No," he said simply. "No more tricks. No more lies. Only truth. The truth is that you made me understand that I was wrong. That the choice to pull that lever is not mine to make."

A few moments to mull things over, and then she thought she understood. After all, if it had been merely his choice, all this would have been reduced to little more than an act of personal vengeance, taken against the people who'd made him what he was. The act, as she'd pointed out to him before she'd left, of a monster paying back the people who'd made him what he was. And the role of monster was obviously one that, in the end, he'd decided to abdicate. Even so, she wanted to hear it from his own lips, wanted to ask the obvious question: "Why?"

"Because this world, the world I'm a part of and that I helped shape, will end tonight. Tomorrow a different world will begin, that different people will shape, and this choice belongs to them."

Or more specifically, to Evey as their representative, which would make it a truly revolutionary act, carried out by the people, for the people, rather than just one of individual malice. And she knew that she believed him. On this last evening, there was no room for anything else but truth. The truth, the whole truth, and nothing but the truth. Like there used to be at the Old Bailey, before the judicial system had become corrupted by the political, and the whole place had to be blown up. A year ago this night.

And now the year had turned, and it was time to destroy the corrupt political system as well.

While she'd been thinking all this, she suddenly realized V had turned and exited from the train, almost as if, in handing it over to her, there was no further business between them. Or at least nothing he could bring himself to mention. She hurried after him, calling him back.

"Where are you going?" she asked, as he turned once more to face her, though she knew he was only pausing briefly before going on his way.

"The time has come for me to meet my maker." She was sure his words implied a double entendre. "And to at last repay him in kind for all that he has done."

"V. Wait . . . please," she called as he began to turn away once more. "You don't have to do it. You could let it go. We could leave here . . . together."

"I can't," he told her. Not brutally, not with any sense of rejection, but just because, in the end, he couldn't.

"I thought about coming back so many times." She understood what he meant completely, but still wished it didn't have to be so. "But I always knew that, no matter what happened, no matter what I said or did, this moment would come . . . and that it didn't need to be any sadder than it already is."

And with that she stepped up to him, and at last, as she'd wanted to before, and as fully as she could, she kissed the frozen lips of his mask. And though he bowed his head to meet her lips, all emotion remained buried behind the mask's façade, behind his over-whelming purpose.

"Good-bye," was all he said; all there really was to say.

Then he turned and rushed away into a lightless tunnel, cloak billowing behind him, and she could only watch as all trace of him was swallowed by the darkness.

Perhaps, she thought, forever.

# TWENTY-THREE

O n television screens across the land, from private
houses to the huge public displays in the city
squares and plazas, as well as on the loudspeakers in
the streets, High Chancellor Adam Sutler was making a
"live" statement to an apparently worried nation, trying
to evoke that same spirit that had carried his countrymen through the Blitz, the Battle of Britain, and so
many other threats, both imminent and potential, real
and imagined.

Assuring them that they, and more important, *he*,
would get through the "battle" of November the Fifth.
Yes, there he was, still at his post where everyone could
see him, a reassuring presence no matter what danger
the insidious terrorist organization called V might represent. England's great protector, the guardian of its
values, its traditions, and its faith. An aging St. George,
England's patron saint, called forth once more to guard
the realm against the revolutionary dragon.

*"My fellow Englishmen,"* he began roundly, addressing the camera with oratorical sincerity, *"tonight
our country, that which we stand for and all that we
hold most dear, faces a grave and terrible threat. This*

*violent and unparalleled assault on our security will
not go undefended or unpunished."*

One of the few places where no television screens
were to be found was on the concourse of the old,
abandoned Victoria tube station, so naturally the
words went unheard by Peter Creedy and two of his
chosen, most trusted Fingermen as they came down
the steps and looked around the place. Mind you,
they'd heard them earlier in the day, when the "live"
broadcast was first recorded, and the ironic contempt
they'd felt for Sutler's words at the time had only increased with the day's subsequent events. But if there
was no broadcast to be heard here, there was plenty of
other activity as a number of the Finger's heavily
armed paramilitary troops, having arrived an hour or
so earlier, continued to sweep the area with metal de-
tectors and electronic scanners.

"The area's clean, sir," one of them reported, quite
unaware that somewhere down below, Finch was continuing his obsessive one-man quest. But Finch was a
long way beyond the range of anyone's detection, far
removed from having any part to play in the drama
that was about to unfold above him.

Creedy looked around at the station, unused as it
had been for years, illuminated now only by a portable
lantern in one corner and the flashlights of his troops.
Old ticket-barriers stood rusting, floor tiles had subsided unevenly, severed piping and cut electric cables
hung dangling from the ceiling. And the more his men
moved around, the more the clouds of musty, odorous
dust rose up to choke what little air there was, making

it look like one of those ridiculous "thick London fogs" that Hollywood movies always showed enshrouding the capital right up to the time when Hollywod had been bombed out of existence, even though fogs like that hadn't been seen for decades.

It wasn't a pleasant place to be, even surrounded by so many of his men, and as their flashlight beams continued to slash through the darkness, Creedy had to admit to feeling far from comfortable. So many potential hiding places here, and all unlit: the old ticket office, the staff restrooms, the station manager's office . . . and though he knew his men would have checked them all, the very shadows still seemed threatening.

"You said eleven o'clock, Mr. Creedy," one of the accompanying Fingermen said, feeling a touch of the same nervousness although the place had been searched from top to bottom and the search continued still. "It's eleven o'clock. Where is he?"

"Penny for the Guy," said a calm voice behind him, with just a hint of irony.

The Fingerman jumped, twisting round and reaching automatically for his gun. By the time it was in his hand, innumerable flashlights had picked out V, making his mask glow in the darkness like a small moon illuminating the night.

*"Our enemy is an insidious one,"* Adam Sutler said in virtually every other place in the land but here, *"seeking to divide us and to destroy the very foundation of our great nation."*

But now the "insidious enemy" stood calmly while

one of the paramilitaries stepped forward with a scanner, sweeping his body swiftly for evidence of explosives.

"Nothing, sir," the man said at last, turning back to Creedy to report, then hurriedly moving away, back to the safety-in-numbers of his fellow soldiers.

"I've kept my side of the bargain," V told Creedy. "But have you kept yours?"

Creedy's smile was not even remotely pleasant.

*"Tonight we must remain steadfast, we must remain determined, and most of all, we must remain united!"*

"Bring him down," said Creedy coldly to his companions, and knowing exactly to whom he referred, they holstered their guns and went, silently and efficiently, back up the stairs.

*"Those caught tonight in violation of the curfew,"* Sutler's voice continued, unaware that, especially throughout the London area, many of the television sets had been turned off and that he was addressing empty rooms, *"will be considered in league with our enemy and will be prosecuted as terrorists, without leniency or exception."*

The implication was obvious. The black bag. The plastic zip-ties. The interrogation, the torture, and, eventually, the execution.

The man the two Fingermen brought down into the station was wearing a black bag himself, his arms fastened behind him. He still struggled weakly, helplessly, pointlessly, as they dropped him to his knees on the uneven floor. Whether through the pain of the impact or because of all he'd been through so far, the man whimpered like a child.

And for once, the smile on V's mask seemed fully alive rather than artificial.

"I want to see his face," he said to Creedy, wanting to make sure at the end that there was no final deception.

*"Tonight I give you my most solemn vow that justice will be swift,"* Sutler concluded forcefully, confidently, and, ultimately, smugly. *"It will be righteous, and it will be without mercy."*

It was Creedy himself who pulled off the black plastic bag, taking a personal, malicious pleasure in his triumph.

And there was Adam Sutler, not as he'd been appearing only seconds ago on national television, the righteous hand of God and protector of the nation, but wide-eyed with terror, with drool dribbling from his lower lip, trying to turn his head away as the flashlights shone fiercely into his face, just as so many interrogation lamps had shone into so many of his citizens' faces during the years since he'd come to power. A battered, defeated, and suddenly very *old* man, sick with fear, who, when his eyes finally adjusted to the mingled pattern of brilliant light and deepest shadow, managed to look round and see the face of the man before him.

Or rather, to see his mask.

"Oh, God," moaned Sutler desperately. "Dear God, no . . ."

"At last we finally meet," V said pleasantly, as if

making a long-wished-for acquaintance, while kneeling down before the terrified man. The former High Chancellor of England had almost totally collapsed, staring uncomprehendingly at the man . . . or was it a monster? . . . who'd tormented him for the last year, who'd turned his last months in office into an ever-worsening nightmare.

"I have something for you, Chancellor," V continued, one hand reaching inside his cape. "A farewell gift for all the things you've done, for the things you might have done, and for the only thing you have left."

With that, like a man making an offering on a tombstone or uselessly propitiating a dead god, he laid a Violet Carson rose before the kneeling captive. And Adam Sutler knew well enough what that signified, remembering the roses found with Prothero, with Lilliman and the others.

"Good-bye, Chancellor," said V almost affectionately, as he rose to his feet.

"Oh, God, don't!" begged Sutler, all control lost now. "Please! *Please!*"

Then no more words would come, and the man who had mere hours earlier been the most powerful man in one of the most powerful nations in the postwar world could only sob uncontrollably, shaking with horror.

"Mr. Creedy?" asked V casually, turning to the head of the Finger, stepping back a pace to give the man room to go about his business.

Creedy pulled out his heavy, large-caliber revolver, the one he'd always used on the Chancellor's behalf,

back in the old days when he'd been the man's "rottweiler," summoned one of his companions forward to
hold his victim still, and placed the gun to Sutler's
temple. He lingered there sadistically while his former
boss wailed helplessly, unable even to speak anymore,
fouling himself in terror.

"Disgusting," said Creedy coldly, and pulled the
trigger.

Bone, brain, and blood exploding from the other
side of his head, High Chancellor Adam Sutler
pitched forward on his face, his head turning to the
side as he hit the ground.

And the Violet Carson rose lay a mere inch before
his sightless eyes, as more blood began to leak copi-
ously from his nose and mouth.

After the echo of the gunshot had died, silence descended on the station for what seemed a considerable
length of time, though in reality it was little more than
seconds. The paramilitary Fingermen could only stare,
stunned, at the suddenness and ruthlessness with
which their former political leader had been so summarily executed, while both V and Creedy seemed to
require a little time to savor the conclusion of one particular and highly important project before moving on
to the next.

Though both of them knew precisely what the next
item on the agenda was likely to be.

"Now that's done with," Creedy said eventually,
raising his gun as he turned toward V, aiming straight
at his heart, "it's time to have a look at your face."

Following their boss's lead, the surrounding Fingermen leveled their guns as well, all concentrating on the same target. But V merely stood there looking straight back at Creedy, arms folded inside his cloak. And with the conical fall of the cloth, the hat and wig and mask, for a moment it almost seemed as if there weren't a man standing there at all. As if this were merely a costume, an image, a shadow.

A symbol.

"Take off your mask," Creedy commanded more firmly, almost as if V hadn't understood him the first time around.

"No," said V flatly.

"Defiant to the end." Creedy smiled, a smile that somehow mingled malice with respect, though containing rather more of the former. "You won't cry like him, will you? You're not afraid of death. You're like me."

"The only thing you and I have in common, Mr. Creedy, is that we are both about to die."

"Is that so?" Creedy laughed, his glance widening to take in the surrounding Fingermen and their weapons. "And how do you imagine that will happen?"

"With my hands round your neck."

Creedy's body tensed then, like a trigger being pulled back.

"Bollocks," he said coldly, confidently, and all round him his men bristled like attack dogs straining at the leash, waiting for the single word that would release them, sending them leaping forward to savage their prey.

"What are you going to do, huh?" Creedy sneered

contemptuously. "We've swept this place and you've got nothing! Nothing but your bloody knives and fancy karate gimmicks! And we've got guns!"

"No," V told him calmly. "What you have is sixty-two bullets. And the hope that, when your guns are empty, I'm no longer standing. Because if I am, you'll all be dead before you've reloaded."

"That's impossible!" Creedy snapped, but now there was an uncertain edge to his voice. What if it *was* possible? What if this was, somehow, something more than a man? Something unkillable?

And that same thought ran like wildfire through the minds of all the assembled Fingermen, made their palms suddenly slick with sweat as they held their guns. For just a moment, they began to look more at each other than their enemy.

*"Kill him!"* Creedy barked then, only just before hesitation turned into something worse.

The words were barely out of his mouth before they were drowned in an explosive cacophony of gunfire; the rattle of automatics mingling with the bark of Creedy's revolver. Time seemed to slow in a repeated thunder of gunpowder booms and whistling lead, mingled with the whine of ricocheting bullets.

But not with the sound of a falling body.

V's body jerked back, the majority of the bullets disappearing into the black folds of his cloak; obviously finding their target, for otherwise he wouldn't have to keep readjusting his footing to cope with the continual impacts. Other bullets sparked off his mask, which, unlike the thousands of papier-mâché copies he'd distributed to the public, was this time made of steel; even so, each impact jerked his head from side to side with the force of a hammer blow.

Yet still he stood, absorbing visible punishment yet resisting the obvious pain. Stood like a monument to human endurance, to the triumph of mind over matter.

To the power of the will.

At last there was only the fading echo of gunfire, followed by silence, as the automatics locked open, the revolver span to click on empty chambers.

And still V remained on his feet. Swaying slightly, but still on his feet.

A moment for silent prayer, that V might suddenly collapse like a house of cards, that they might wake up from this nightmare safe beside their wives or girlfriends, or that the God in which so few of them truly believed might suddenly prove real after all and strike this devil down.

But the cloaked figure still stood there, and the mask continued to smile.

"My turn," said V, his words as chill and final as the words of Death himself.

A soft sound of rattling metal filled the station as the Fingermen, suddenly snapping out of their horrified trance, began trying to reload their guns, before . . .

Before V was among them, moving with the silence of a wind-driven cloud, the swiftness of a darting hawk.

The first Fingerman barely had time to react to the eight inches of cold steel that pierced his heart before the knife was twisted and removed, the exit wound hideous, the long jet of arterial blood rising scarlet before his horrified eyes. A fierce spray of crimson lifeblood that somehow unmanned his companions completely, making fingers seem like rubber, making bullet clips as slippery as soap.

And before the first had hit the floor, a second Fingerman had dropped his bullet clip as the same knife opened up his throat. A swift, silvery blade that moved like greased lightning, and wherever that lightning struck, the blood showered down like rain.

V's cloak billowed behind him then, so swift his movement, like a giant black manta ray gliding from shadow to shadow, from death to death. After that first heart-stab, so demoralizing in its effect, it was always the throat: quickest, surest, deadliest. One or two of the men, realizing there would never be time again for bullets, tried to grapple with him, but V's motions were so supernaturally fast—a long-forgotten by-product of the Larkhill experiments—that powerful kicks drove them away in the same instant that his hands were still about their deadly business elsewhere. And in the end, whatever they did could only slightly delay the inevitable knifework to come.

Circling round the junior Fingermen, carving, slicing, occasionally puncturing, always moving on as the blood began to gush and the body tumble, V was obviously saving Creedy until the last.

And fighting to keep his hands steady, Creedy could only try to keep one eye on V, the other on reloading his revolver. But for every chamber he managed to fill, another of his men died a horrific, gurgling death.

Finally, there were no empty chambers. And none of his men to back him up.

And V was still not yet dead.

He stood there with the bodies of the Fingermen scattered around him, each one every bit as dead as Sutler, and then, as he turned back toward Creedy himself, astonished his opponent by suddenly dropping his knives.

And then V began to walk toward him.

"No!" yelled Creedy, terrified by now, unable to understand what had happened, was happening still . . . raising his reloaded pistol again and firing, his trigger finger jerking compulsively.

*"Die!"* he screamed, emptying the chambers one by one, his aim deliberate, with every single bullet right on target. "Die! Die! *Die!"*

Still V kept coming on, shaken by each individual impact, every step another bullet closer to Creedy's last. And finally, once again the hammer clicked on an empty chamber.

"Why won't you die?" gasped Creedy in disbelief, gun suddenly hanging limply from his hand, staggering now almost as much as V himself.

"Beneath this mask there is more than flesh," V told him, a rough edge to his voice now, but still coming on implacably, unstoppably, a living god of death.

And Creedy could only back away in appalled horror, retreating step by step and matching V's advance . . . until at last his back slammed up sickeningly against a wall, and there was nowhere else to go.

"Beneath this mask there is an idea, Mr. Creedy," V said, looming over him. And now, with the ever-smiling mask pressing closer and closer to his face, terror at last overcame Creedy, robbed him of his ability to move, of his voice, of his very will to live.

"And ideas are bulletproof."

Creedy started to scream then, those final words of explanation still ringing in his ears, and V's gloved hands settled round his throat, as he'd promised, as almost seemed foreordained.

Hands that, as they began to squeeze, choked off the scream, choked off thought. Crushed his windpipe. Made his eyes begin to bulge, eyes that never left that awful grinning mask, the smiling death's-head that would see him to his grave. Eventually his face went dark, his tongue began to protrude . . . and then his eyes rolled up and his breathing stopped forever.

And still V continued to squeeze, now gone far beyond the point of making sure, his hands locked in a spasm that was only, finally, broken when Creedy's inert body began to slide limply down the wall.

Gasping in a deep breath, V turned away then, surveying his night's work: a scatter of dead bodies in a grimy, derelict Underground station that still resonated with the violence of his deeds, awash with blood and reeking with the smell of gunsmoke. A dead dictator, the man who'd thought to replace him gone as well: the totalitarian body politic just about decapitated. Worth all the sacrifices, no doubt, but what of the cost?

V's gloved hands were still held up clawed before him, and he had to wait long seconds further before he finally regained their use. Staggering almost drunkenly, he made his way over to the wall, supporting himself with one hand and reaching beneath the cloak with the other. The hand didn't seem to want to work properly, and he sagged momentarily and had to prop himself up again before, finally, his fingers found the hidden clasp and flipped it open. Then, wearily, painfully, he drew out the thin metal vest that had surrounded his chest.

Virtually the entire surface was pocked and dented where the bullets had smashed into it from short range with horrifying force.

Worse, in several places it was quite plainly punctured; holes formed, he suspected, by the heavier-calibered bullets of Creedy's revolver.

He looked at it briefly, the smile on the mask of the face somehow almost rueful, as he saw the inside of the vest smeared with blood. Then there was nothing else to do but let it slip from his limp fingers.

As it fell, rattling, to the floor, he turned away and staggered off wearily into the darkness, back into the shadows from which he'd first emerged.

And leaving behind a trail of wet, bloody footprints.

# TWENTY-FOUR

S tanding by the armored personnel carrier that was serving as his mobile HQ, General William Byrd felt confident that he had the situation under control, even if the politicians did seem to be running scared. He was positioned in the middle of Parliament Square surrounded by his best men, and the whole area was cordoned off and evacuated. All the streets leading toward the square were blocked, including Whitehall, Millbank, and Victoria Street, and Westminster Bridge was closed as well. There were patrol boats on the Thames, tanks in the side streets, surface-to-air missiles in the square. Farther away, where they wouldn't confuse the issue, helicopters hovered above the streets, ready to give warning of any incoming aerial threat. Westminster Abbey, the great Victorian neo-Gothic pile that was Barry and Pugin's Houses of Parliament, and the Clock-tower containing Big Ben were all illuminated with their usual nighttime flood-lighting, and in the square itself, everything was made almost as bright as day by giant klieg lights brought in specially for the purpose. And there were his men too: handpicked commando units from the Royal Marines, with a tactical unit from the SAS, specially trained in handling terror attacks.

Of course, mingled with them were those blasted upstarts from the Finger, but sometimes one just had to put up with political interference in military matters. He'd rather have had more ordinary police; at least those blighters were used to obeying orders. With Fingermen, you never knew where you were. Could do anything, even if that unpleasant bastard Peter Creedy had given him assurances that the Fingermen would be under his temporary command. Not that the general had much confidence in that; Creedy was well-known for saying one thing and doing another. He'd expected him here tonight, along with that other nobody . . . what was his name? The one who looked as if he got his clothes from a charity shop . . . Eric Finch . . .

Still, Byrd thought, with this sort of firepower assembled here, he'd like to see these goddamned terrorists try anything tonight. Oh, yes, indeed! He'd show them! *Nobody* was going to make this fifth of November a night to remember! Not while William Byrd was in command.

And anyway, what were they going to do to a building the size of Parliament? A thousand rooms or more, he'd been told, and any sort of aerial attack on a place like that would only cause minor damage . . . unless it was nuclear, of course, but this blighter "V" wouldn't have invited anyone here to watch if he was going to use something like that. No, the only way to bring down a place like that would be to attack the foundations, and all the experts had said it was going to come from the air. Had to believe the experts . . . most of them were military men, after all. And anyway, that was what they'd prepared for, so that was the way it would have to be, wouldn't it? A man doesn't keep his job unless he's on the ball, does he?

A slight cough to gain his commander's attention, and then Lieutenant Dowland was there before him, snapping off a crisp military salute and waiting for permission to speak. Byrd nodded slowly.

"Patrols are confirming that people are in the streets, sir," Dowland said promptly, though there seemed to be a hint of unease in his voice.

"Then tell them to arrest them," Byrd told him shortly. Hadn't his orders been plain enough? Dowland was a good man, but surely there was no need to come running and reporting every little detail like this. That was what you had officers for, so you could delegate the authority to them. Let them get on with it. Use their own initiative.

"They say they can't," Dowland told him hesitantly.

"What?" exploded Byrd. Never heard anything so ridiculous in his life. They were soldiers in the British Army, weren't they? Ought to be able to arrest a few civilians without any problems. "Why?"

"They say . . ." His lieutenant didn't really want to say it, but knew he'd have to in the end. "They say there're too many of them."

Evey Hammond was still sitting on a bench in the station, looking at the train that had now become such an important part of her inheritance, uncertain what to do. So beautiful on the outside, so deadly on the inside. Would she actually release that brake lever? Obviously it was what V had intended, had wanted, all along. But what of the consequences? And why, at the last moment, had he suddenly become so uncertain, to pass the decision on to her? She'd been over it time and again and still wasn't exactly certain why, and the longer he was away, and the more time she had to think, the less she was able to make up her mind. Or maybe, considering how plain it had seemed to her when he'd first mentioned passing on the responsibility, it was that she was continuing to think about his motives as a way of putting off having to make the decision herself.

Her train of thought was suddenly broken by a soft sound; then another. She wasn't quite sure what it was at first. After all, she was sure no one else would be down here. And then she recognized the noises as footsteps. But somehow they were uncertain, faltering footsteps.

Leaping to her feet, she called, "V?"

He stepped out of the shadows then, holding himself stiffly upright, an arm wrapped round his chest. And she was so relieved to see him, so delighted at his return, she hardly noticed the difficulty with which he seemed to be walking.

"You came back," she said, smiling radiantly, full of hope and happiness.

"I was hoping you'd still be . . . ," he managed to say weakly. And then, after tottering one more step, he crumpled to the floor, almost as if the man himself were still elsewhere, and only the costume had made it back.

"V!" she cried in alarm, rushing toward him and kneeling by his side. She tried to roll him over to see what was the matter, but as soon as she did, she found her hands covered in blood.

"Oh, no," she moaned, horrified, trying desperately to think what to do.

"We have to stop your bleeding," she said next, though she was uncertain how. Perhaps if his cloak could be bound round his wounds? She could only curse herself for never having taken first aid lessons; but she doubted that even first aid would be able to do anything about the wounds that V was suffering from. What he needed was hospital treatment, and immediate treatment at that. But that would only be followed by execution anyway.

"Please . . . don't," V told her weakly, a hand clutching spasmodically at her arm as she took his head in her hands, moving a knee beneath him to pillow the back of his neck. "I'm finished . . . and glad for it."

"Don't say that," she told him, knowing she didn't want it to be true as much for her own sake as for his.

"I told you . . . only truth," he added, knowing far better than she the extent and seriousness of his wounds.

"V . . ." she said, unable to keep a sob out of her voice. "I don't want you to die."

"That"—his voice lowered almost to a whisper now—"is the most beautiful thing you could've ever given me."

A tremor ran through his body, and he gripped her arm all the more tightly, as if it was the last thing he had to cling to . . . as if by doing so, he clung to life itself. But quite plainly not for long.

"For twenty years I saw only this moment," he gasped, his voice so weak now she had to lean close to hear it. "Nothing else existed until . . . I saw you. Then, everything changed . . . my life . . . my reasons . . . my wishes . . ."

And Evey could only hold him in her arms and weep.

"I fell in love with you, Evey . . . like I no longer believed I could. And every day that drew this day closer made me understand that it wasn't blood I wanted . . . it was another chance . . ."

"Chance for what?" she asked tearfully.

"For roses." No more than the faintest whisper now. "Not for me . . . for all of us."

"Oh, V . . ." A last call of his name. Or at least of the only name by which she'd ever known him. Ever would know him.

An enigma to the very end, his body suddenly grew heavy in her arms, relaxing now into the peace of death.

"V?" she asked softly, realizing but still not wanting to accept what had happened. But at last she had to. Already underground, already deep in the underworld, V had started his final journey to the land of the dead.

And she, left behind, could only wail desolately, as women have always wailed for their men, her mournful cries echoing through the dark emptiness of the deserted station.

In Parliament Square, General Byrd had decided to inspect the perimeter personally, summoning Dowland to accompany him. "People in the streets" didn't sound overly threatening, but they shouldn't be there, and they could always be a cover for something else that was about to happen. Best to check and be prepared for any eventuality. Make sure the men were on their toes as well . . .

They began to circle slowly from Westminster Bridge round to Whitehall, finding everything in the immediate area as quiet as they'd expected, and moved on then to Great George Street, the short road that led through massive, overbearing buildings to St. James's Park. Not enough lights here, Byrd thought to himself, wondering if they could move some equipment from a less-necessary position elsewhere. Maybe over by the Abbey; that had its own lights after all.

He was still thinking of this when he noticed Dowland jerk with sudden surprise. He looked round first toward his lieutenant and then to what the man himself was staring at.

"It's him!" Dowland shouted, pointing off into the shadows toward a white, grinning face.

"What?" choked Byrd, reaching automatically toward the holstered pistol at his waist. He hadn't expected *this* . . . a plane, a missile, perhaps even a salvo of mortar bombs to open the attack . . . but not the terrorist himself, walking quite blatantly toward the assembled troops.

But it was, undoubtedly, **a** man in a Guy Fawkes mask. And as the man stopped, Byrd drew the pistol, started to raise a hand to draw the attention of his men . . . and then froze as he saw another mask appear out of the darkness.

Followed by another. And another.

And then there were too many of them to count. Was this, then, the "terrorist organization known as V"? Surely not, for some of the masks seemed to be worn by women. And some of the masks were so low to the ground that they were obviously covering the faces of children. And rather than weapons, many of them were carrying flowers and lighted candles.

All of them, though, it somehow seemed to the general, had now become if not V himself, at least what he represented. And that didn't seem to be "a terrorist."

All of them had come to watch.

Come to wait.


Overcoming her grief at last, if only for a little while, Evey Hammond had dragged V's body into the train; had laid him out, still masked, at peace upon a pyre of gelignite, surrounded by the roses he'd loved, that Valerie Page had loved as well, that had come to symbolize so much of what he'd already achieved and everything he'd planned. She'd known that this was what she'd do as soon as he'd died there in her arms; knew that this

was the last thing she could do for him, when he'd believed in this project so strongly that he'd actually been
prepared to give his life for it. Now she'd finally bring
his plan to fruition and ensure that he had a personal
part in it, was there right at the very last. When the play
was acted out, the final curtain fallen, and, as that other
tragic hero Hamlet had said, "The rest is silence."

She'd give him a Viking funeral, like those old
chieftains had had when they were set adrift in a blazing boat on a cold northern sea, sailing off through fire
and ice to arrive at last in Valhalla. A notion he would
have enjoyed, she thought, with his passion for the letter V, though actually it was more like the hellbound
train she'd heard about in one of his favorite old blues
songs, on an Underground line with its destination in
an Inferno entirely of his own making.

Just one last touch, folding his gloved hands across
his chest and reaching round to pluck a Violet Carson
rose and place it in his fingers.

A final brief kiss on the mask's lips, and then she
turned away, his face still unseen. And she wouldn't
look, as a last mark of respect.

She stepped out of the carriage, started to make
her way toward the driver's cab. But when she arrived
at the door and looked within, something made her
pause. One last surprise, one last small message from
beyond the grave . . .

For there, standing by the brake lever, unseen before, was a single standing domino, which he'd presumably secreted there on the way out, after showing
her the controls. A double five. Two Vs, Roman style.

Him and her. And when she released the brake lever, the movement would, inevitably, cause that last domino to fall. Make everything, in effect, fall into place right at the last.

She had to smile at that. A small, sad smile, but he'd known all along, had foreseen everything. And now she'd show him he was right.

If she had the time.

"Hold it!" a voice barked out suddenly, echoing along the empty platform. "Stop right there!"

It seemed that, in the end, there was one thing that V hadn't foreseen.

Chief Inspector Eric Finch.

Looking back, she saw him standing there on the platform outside the train, gun in hand, covering her every move. A tired, battered figure who, having found a trail of bloody footprints and followed them to their end, now looked almost as weary of the world as she was feeling just at that moment.

"You're Evey Hammond, aren't you?"

She made no reply, made no sign of acknowledgment. After all, what was the point of admitting anything this late in the day? It was long past the time to "help the police with their inquiries," as the old euphemism for interrogation had it.

Keeping her covered, Finch glanced through the window of the train, saw V lying there among the roses, though he wasn't able quite to see what he was lying upon. But he had a pretty good idea of what the train would be packed with.

Feelings. Copper's instincts. Always trust that more

than "expert opinion." He'd been right all along, and they hadn't believed him. Had laughed at him.

Not anymore.

"Is that . . . ?" he asked, and this time she did nod. No point in denying that, after all.

"Is he dead?" Finch asked next, but now she found she couldn't answer. It wasn't that she wanted to keep him guessing, keep him wrong-footed in case V suddenly sprang to life again and attacked him. It was because to her, somehow, he was certainly dead, while at the same time, he just as certainly wasn't.

For V was both a man and an idea, and while the man was dead, the idea would live forever. She'd known that as soon as she'd decided what she had to do.

"Then it's over?" More of a remark than a query, he was obviously taking her silence for confirmation of V's death.

"Not quite," she said determinedly, reaching into the cab and grabbing the brake lever as he approached.

"Stop!" he yelled, close enough now to see what she was doing, his voice echoing in the tunnel. "Get your hand off that lever!"

He thrust forward the gun then, emphasizing his command. But Evey Hammond had had enough of orders, enough of the police, the government, the society she lived in, of everything. And she'd long ago had enough of fear.

"No," she told him flatly.

"No?" said Finch, baffled. He'd known one or two desperate, hardened criminals who'd disobey a direct order at gunpoint, but only one or two. To have a relatively frail young woman standing there and defying him was an entirely new experience. And yet, such obvious self-belief was radiating through her defiance, her determination to overthrow the society that he'd spent his life protecting, that he could only stop and wonder. *Truth* and *Justice,* they'd always been his watchwords, though justice, he had to admit, had become more than a little compromised in the years since the Reclamation. As had he himself. Could she, then, actually have found another truth . . . a better truth than his, that would somehow restore a real form of justice to the world? And if she had . . . but then he'd always had a third watchword too: *Duty.* And if his ideas of truth and justice were confused, his duty still seemed quite clear.

"I'm sorry, but I've made up my mind," she told him calmly, her own sense of duty clearly a match for his own. "So the only way you're going to stop me is to kill me."

Finch paused then, though the gun remained unwavering. Seeing how determined she was, he realized that another pace forward would undoubtedly have made her release the brake.

Words were the only weapon left to him now, if his duty was still to be carried out.

"Why are you doing this?" he asked, and knew, as he said it, that it was more than just a case of keeping her talking; he really did want to understand. He'd wanted to understand the way V had thought, but now he never would; and he also wanted to know how that

same sort of thinking could spread, infecting someone
else. And how far could it spread? Could it even end
up infecting him?

"Because he was right," Evey told him with the absolute faith of the recently converted.

"About what?"

"That this country needs more than a building right
now," she replied, still with the same superb calm that
he found somehow strangely affecting. "It needs
hope."

Hope. When had he last hoped for anything? Perhaps when he'd joined the Party, hoping it would help
him get on in his career? Well, it had, but had that really been hope, or just desire? And now that he was
confronted with the idea, it seemed to him that hope
and desire weren't the same at all. Desire was little
more than greed, and he'd seen enough of that in the
Norsefire years. Hope was something larger, more all-
encompassing, more abstract. What greed was to hope
was pretty much what passion was to compassion; and
God knew there'd been little enough compassion
under Sutler's fascist government.

But there was still his duty.

Yet here was this woman whom he was looking at
over the barrel of his gun who seemed to personify the
same hope and compassion he'd lost all this time, that
he'd always felt had left a gap that he needed to fill.
And whose invincible sense of duty seemed far greater
than his own. Perhaps, it finally dawned on him, it was
because his duty had always been to the force, and the
principles enshrined in English law; and what had

they done to the English law in the last few decades with their trials without juries, and their detentions without any trial at all? And if he could finally disentangle all those threads of conspiracy he'd found while carrying out his duty, of Larkhill, and St. Mary's, of Creedy and of executed terrorists, could he ever get a verdict in his favor, in the current state of the law? Could he even get the case to court?

No, of course he couldn't. In fact, he realized now, it had been foolish ever to think he could. One mention of it, and the black bag would have been over his head in an instant. Over Dominic's too, and that of anyone else involved. And they wouldn't even bother with interrogation. He must be getting old, even considering the idea.

Was there a greater duty, then, beyond the one he'd always thought he had? And was it embodied here in this girl before him who, he could see quite plainly now, had never been a terrorist? A duty to finally stop saying "I was only obeying orders" and obey a much higher principle . . . to overthrow the entire world order itself?

It was Sutler's Norsefire Party and their goddamned Reclamation that had taken Jane and Peter from him, all those years ago. Not directly, perhaps, but if they hadn't started the trouble that led to the riots, the street fighting . . . and if he hadn't been so busy working on the Party's behalf trying to contain that trouble, she wouldn't have had to go out to the few remaining open shops, taking Peter with her because she didn't want to leave him alone . . . and the car wouldn't have run into . . .

"It's time," Evey said then, and smiled so sweetly at him he really just didn't know what to do.

She did, though. And released the brake lever, stepping away from the cab.

And the last domino fell, its single click an epitaph to a man with no identity, and all the ideas and plans he'd taken with him to his grave. Ideas that lived on, and a plan that would come to fruition as his final memorial.

And Eric Finch had absolutely no idea what to do then, his body almost dead with fatigue, his mind alive with conflict, except to slowly lower his gun and watch the train silently ease forward into the tunnel, so gently at first it seemed there'd still be time to call it back.

But by the time he'd realized what he'd done, the cab had disappeared into the tunnel and there was no way now it would ever be stopped.

And V was going with it, into the darkness. The final darkness.

There seemed no point in doing anything else except putting the gun back in his pocket, forgetting he even had it, and letting the world take its course. No point in arresting the girl before him. No point in trying to raise a warning. No point in trying to save a government he realized that he no longer believed in. Had never really believed in, but had accepted, because it was the only one they had. That would be fallen completely by the morning.

And when he realized he didn't care at all, he felt an overwhelming sense of relief.

Still bewildered as to what he'd done and what, in

the long run, was likely to happen as a consequence, Finch could only stand there as Evey stepped forward. Taking his arm gently and smiling like a daughter that he'd never had, she began to lead him away slowly toward the stairs.

"Tell me," she said almost affectionately, remembering another time when someone else had said much the same to her, "do you like music, Mr. Finch?"

Around Parliament Square, more and more "Vs" were materializing from the shadows, and no longer from just one direction. They came along Millbank, they streamed past the Abbey, they gathered on the other side of the Thames, over Westminster Bridge. They came along Whitehall, which was supposed to have been closed off, along with all its side streets, all the way back to Trafalgar Square; and as they did so, they even passed by Downing Street, in an ultimate show of defiance.

"General?" Dowland asked Byrd uncertainly, desperately needing guidance, but equally desperately hoping the order he dreaded wouldn't come.

It did.

"Ready at arms!" General Byrd yelled, and there was a murmur of quiet voices, a clatter as automatic weapons were checked and raised to shoulders. Even so, it was all done with a certain hesitancy.

For by then there were more of them, and still they came. From hundreds to thousands, and then thousands more. Packing the streets in a vast ocean of humanity.

"What do we do?" Lieutenant Dowland asked again, looking at them with a sense of rising panic.

"Jesus bloody Christ," said Byrd quietly, finally realizing that if they moved forward, as they certainly would at the first outbreak of gunfire, there were far too many of the masked horde for his men to shoot before the human tidal wave broke over them.

And when it came right down to it, the masked figures weren't representing any immediate threat. They were standing and waiting, expectant, hopeful.

And every single one of them was smiling.

And then, softly at first, the music began to play, swelling from the loudspeakers on the street corners just as it had done a year ago, on the Old Bailey's night of pyrotechnic glory.

Music that somehow saved General Byrd from having to issue an order he would have regretted for the rest of his life, that soon grew loud enough that it would have drowned out that order anyway.

Different music this time, though, and even more apt. Chosen especially for the occasion. For the fifth of November.

Handel's *Firework Music*.

Not far away, Evey had led a still rather confused Inspector Finch up from the station and through the Shadow Gallery, hurrying him on gently and hardly giving him time to look at the wonders it contained . . . even so, that brief glance revealed to him so many other worlds beyond the narrow one he'd known, so many things he suddenly remembered with surprise and frank delight, he knew that one day he'd wish to see them all restored . . . and then ushering him into the elevator that would take them up to the roof. That same rooftop where she'd stood naked in the rain on the night that she'd rediscovered her real self, feeling somehow that Finch too was about to arrive at the same sort of revelatory conclusion. Though if she'd asked, he would have had to admit that in the immediate present, he merely felt weary, directionless, and far older than his years. It was time to go, he thought, to leave the work of rebuilding the future to younger hands . . . like those of Dominic Stone and this Hammond girl beside him.

"That music . . ." he said, hearing it now as they emerged into the open air.

"Yes, his music," Evey told him, hardly wanting to imply that it was anyone else's than Handel's, but knowing that V would have arranged this, some automatic switch tripping as soon as the train began its final journey. "It's beautiful, isn't it?"

She stepped away from Finch, moving toward the parapet and raising her hands, just as V had done, a year ago tonight when the tune had been all of heroic resistance, as if now she were conducting Handel's marvelous, celebratory music as its power increased by the second.

Deep below the ground, V's brilliantly painted, rose-filled, hellbound train reached its final destination, hit a mass of concrete blocks . . . and did exactly what a train full of gelignite might be expected to do.

And on the surface, directly above, the Houses of Parliament erupted in flame and fury, in smoke and smashed masonry, as Augustus Pugin's elaborately decorated exterior was blown apart from within, shattered into millions of stone fragments even before the wood and other interior features added fuel to the fire. And then the great Clock-tower tilted and deposited Big Ben into the churning waters of the Thames, throwing up a pillar of water that almost matched the flames in height as the building blossomed into a great orange funeral pyre.

A pyre on which burned the last remains of the government and the Norsefire Party, of England's fascist interlude, of a thousand plots and conspiracies, of histories and fictions that Finch had never quite managed to disentangle. And knew that now he never would, and no longer cared besides.

A funeral pyre on which burned the last remains of V.

"Who was he?" Finch asked then, stepping up to the parapet to join Evey.

"He was Edmond Dantès," she said softly, glancing round to see his slightly puzzled look, and added, "And he was my father, and my mother. My brother and my friend. He was you and me. He was all of us."

All of us, thought Finch . . . and realized that the state had no business oppressing its own people for, ultimately, the state *is* the people. And in the end, he knew, only people are real, and everything else— politics, conspiracies, the state itself—are all fictions, all stories made up by people as a way of organizing their lives. The "truth" about Larkhill? What did it matter in the end? Only the people who'd lived and died there were important, and what they'd done for good or ill. And now the night's events had brought the whole story to an end. . . .

But would they write rhymes about this in the future? And if they went back to burning an effigy each year on this night, whose face would now be hidden by the mask?

Evey stood there contemplatively for a few seconds longer, then turned toward Finch and smiled.

"No one will ever forget this night," she told him, "or what it means to this country."

And then, turning away once more for a last, private thought, she added, "But I will never forget the man, and what he meant to me."

And as the ceremonies were brought to a conclusion by a large eruption of fireworks exploding in the air and forming, once again, the letter V, the assembled crowds began to take off their masks, to lose their anonymity, to become once again the selves they'd been before the long years of repression had imposed quite other masks upon them.

For this time, the letter V quite plainly stood for "victory."

# Not sure
# what to
# read next?

## Visit Pocket Books online at
## www.SimonSays.com

**Reading suggestions for
you and your reading group**

**New release news**
**Author appearances**
**Online chats with your favorite writers**
**Special offers**
**And much, much more!**